ROBBING PETER

By

Kia DuPree

Prism Pages

Robbing Peter

For more information, or to order additional copies, please contact:

Prism Pages
P.O. Box 7189
Hampton, Virginia 23666
757-218-8587
www.prismpages.com
info@prismpages.com

Book production by Prism Pages

Cover Art & Design by Khia Jackson/Blind Spot Design

ISBN-0-9758675-04

Library of Congress Control Number: 2004094086

Printed in the United States of America

First Edition

Dedicated to my Mommy,
Cynthia D. Dawkins,
for carrying both Heaven and Hell on her shoulders for us.
Each day you inspire me more.

ACKNOWLEDGEMENTS

***

There's no adequate way to acknowledge everyone who's helped this dream become a reality and I said I wouldn't do this, but I wouldn't be able to sleep if I didn't at least try. From my Mommy, Cynthia D. Dawkins, my Daddy, John M. Dupree, and my other mother, Darlene Backstrom, my siblings Antwan, Jonathan, Omar, Jamar, Michael, Timothy, DeDe and Jahnae; to my grandparents, the Duprees and the Abrahams, aunts, uncles, cousins …thank you all for supporting and believing in me, even when I didn't believe in myself.

My countless friends, mentors and educators—you've all nurtured me and I am humbly appreciative. Sherry Oden, who's my healthy writing competitor, thank you for motivating me since our eighth grade English class. Thank you Mrs. Nellie Cooke-Jefferson for exposing me to the master works and subliminally encouraging me to grow in that same class. Thank you Ms. Phillips, my ninth grade homeroom teacher, for editing my first manuscript, and making me a believer in my own writing dreams.

Thank you Nikoshia Williams, Wilfrance Lominy, Ivy Carter and I. Shaun Gholston for your undying support and faith in me.

Yuri Rodgers, Towanna Sebrell and Sarita Scott, thank you for letting me experiment with you first and your hours of advice. Thank you Duane Smith and Paul Saunders of Peach Fuzz Entertainment for helping me discover the entrepreneur in me. Thank you The Fuzz Band for inspiring me and helping me reconnect with my inner artist.

Shashana Crichton, of Crichton & Associates, thank you for believing in this project from Day One. Thank you Juliette Harris and Gladys Bell for your counsel.

Many of you believed in me before I had yet to dream. From you all, I've gained so much. Thank you.

"Without struggle, there is no progress."

--Frederick Douglass

CHAPTER 1

Elijah no longer believed there was a God. He stopped believing in Him years earlier. In Elijah's heart, it was the church he was forced to attend all those years that turned the world upside down for him. Most people hated to hear that, he thought. Naysayers refused to believe it was the Pentecostal Holiness church, but rather the brainwashed parishioners and its leaders that led him astray—igniting the vindictive fire that smoldered inside of him. At seventeen, Elijah didn't care whose fault it was that his outlook on life had become as toxic as the gutter he stood in behind his house. The alley—filled with trash, old furniture and rodents—reflected the world as he'd seen it. How could there be a God in a world like this, he wondered while watching a guy not much older than himself, receive the beating of a lifetime on this blustery night. Every fierce blow that landed and every heart-wrenching groan that erupted from the victim's mouth further erased the existence of a God in Elijah's mind.

"What are you just standing there for E?" asked Elgin panting out of breath. The fog his warm breath created left haloed rings floating through the dark December night. "Come on! This nigga owe you money, not me!"

Elijah shook his head, because he knew his brother was right, then turned around and picked up a dirty beer bottle lying in the gutter.

"Who'd you think you were dealing with Dante'?" Elijah yelled infuriated. "This is my block!"

Dante' was lying on the ground holding his side, dazed and in obvious pain. He couldn't respond because his lips were as swollen as over boiled hotdogs—one touch and he was sure they would crack down the center. In a desperate attempt not to choke to death, he coughed up blood that bubbled and spewed down the crevices of his mouth.

"Man, what are you waiting for? Fuck this nigga up!" Elgin yelled. "I'm tired of this! He thinks he's going to get away with that shit. Stop bull-shitting!"

Elijah threw the clear bottle forcefully to the ground and it shattered about a quarter-of-an-inch from Dante's head. He gasped and rolled slightly to his left, looking around for passers-by to help. But being in a dark alley just off of a fierce city street was useless. Fights came a dime a dozen in Washington, D.C., and people were too busy to care and too heartless to help.

Elijah grabbed Dante' by the collar of his coat and lifted his head a couple of inches off the frigid pavement.

"You will pay muthafucka. And tonight...it's going to be with your life," Elijah whispered words colder than the night's howling wind. Dante' rolled his eyes upward, sensing what was next as Elijah began to pound his head into the pavement. He pounded and pounded until he heard Dante's skull crack like the sound of a brick hitting a frozen lake.

Elijah would never forget the glazed eyes that stared at him—they appeared to see through his soul. Blood trickled out forming a putrid dark puddle around Dante's head.

"Aiight. Now leave 'em there," Elgin said panting heavily. "Turn around and let's walk away slowly."

Elijah looked at his knuckles and noticed they were bleeding. It was so cold that he stuffed his hands into his front jacket pockets despite the velvet red stain it would leave. He walked toward Elgin with his head hung low, trying to regain his cool.

"You did good E," Elgin said regaining his breath and sending more halloed circles evaporating into the night's cold air. Elgin wrapped his arm around his twin brother's shoulders like a warm blanket comforting him against the haunting chill that held his soul hostage. Elijah knew if there was a God, he wouldn't have just done what he did.

"Fuck that nigga! You owed him that...you did right," Elgin reassured him. His confident posture resembled a general in the midst of war encouraging a doubtful soldier to press on.

Even though Elgin was convinced that what they did was right, Elijah didn't know how to feel. He had become numb to everything around him. And at seventeen, Elijah began to feel like this was all life could ever offer him.

"You wanna go blaze one?" Elgin asked with a proud smile spreading across his face.

Elijah took a deep breath, blew out the air of anxiety and nodded his head in concurrence. He pushed his hands deeper in the warmth of his pockets and followed his twin brother towards the twinkling lights of the hardened streets.

***

"Ma, he's trying to hit me!" yelled Evan as he ran down the stairs from Elgin. The combination of their footsteps sounded like a thunderous hailstorm hitting a roof.

"Look, I don't have time for that right now," Vivica yelled at her sons while she stood in the kitchen washing dishes. "And stop running in my house. Y'all need to get up there and clean up those filthy rooms. Did anybody wash any clothes today?"

"Man, see that's what I'm talking about. Every time one of 'em trying to do something to me, you don't say nothing," said Evan shaking his head. The fifteen-year-old was one of Vivica's quietest children—the middle child, but Vivica knew that being quiet didn't always make Evan the innocent one.

"Evan Ricardo Jeffries, go do what I said do, right now! And don't give me any lip!" Vivica stood with one soapy hand on her hip as she watched him.

"Man..." he sang, sucking his teeth again and stomping up the stairs.

"And stop calling me man!"

His older brother, Elgin, smirked and edged back toward the stairs in a threatening manner.

"Elgin, you leave your little brother alone. I don't know why I always have to tell you that," said Vivica irritated, throwing the sudsy dishtowel in the sink.

"I didn't even do anything," Elgin complained. "You always listening to everybody else. I can't do anything around here. That's why I can't wait 'til I move out! I'm sick of this place."

"You know I can't wait either. You think you are so grown. I'm sick and tired of your disrespectful attitude," Vivica said frustrated. "I hope you are making plans because when you turn eighteen, you know where you are going right?"

"Whatever...I'll leave when I want to leave."

Vivica placed both hands on her hips, rolled her eyes toward the ceiling and began counting to ten. "One, two, three..."

Elgin mocked her while stomping up the stairs, further testing her patience.

Vivica's blood boiled like a cauldron as she listened to Elgin's feet hitting the floor. Thump. Thump. Thump. The sounds mocked a bass drum. She wiped her forehead with the back of her hand and closed her eyes. The smell of fried chicken still saturated the room from the night's dinner.

"Why me?" she asked.

3

Vivica's five children drove her up the wall, especially the twins. They plucked her nerves so much she knew hell had frozen over and no one bothered to tell her about it. She hated knowing that she'd lost complete control over them. It was like admitting defeat especially after all of the sacrifices she'd made for them. Why couldn't they understand all of that, she wondered.

Vivica lost complete control several years earlier, though. Their behavior and attitudes switched over so fast that Vivica felt like she had been sleepwalking in the Twilight Zone when they transformed. In the past year alone, small things like staying out after curfew had become huge things like stealing cars. She never managed to regain control of them as they approached adulthood.

But it was back in the early 1990s, after Vivica put their father, Eddie, out of their three-bedroom Section 8 apartment for the final time that she noticed Elijah and Elgin's attitudes had grown as bitter as olive stuffed lemons. Eddie's drug addiction and his abusive and volatile behavior was no longer tolerable. The twins were almost eight years old and Vivica knew she could no longer shield their innocent eyes from the things happening around them.

One of Eddie's tirades landed her in an emergency room at the District General Hospital and it was then that Vivica knew cutting Eddie out of their family picture was necessary to survive. She could still remember as the twins cried the day she put all of Eddie's things in the garbage. Though it was a moment of reclamation for Vivica, the twins couldn't understand how the man who had made them paper airplanes, showed them magic tricks and taught them how to find salamanders in the wooded area near their apartment building, was gone for good.

They began to despise their mother, but Vivica knew that there were no words that would best explain her decision. Besides, Vivica reasoned she was the one who'd brought them that far—her and God. In her heart, she'd made the right decision for her family by deciding to redirect their future.

The Jeffries had come a long way from Justin's Terrace—the first apartment complex they lived in just off of Livingston Road in Ward 8. It was in one of the poorest sections of Southeast D.C. Those days of living in the roach infested, poverty-stricken, half boarded-up projects were long gone. But she could still remember them like yesterday and often wondered how much that environment added to the negative outlook her sons now held.

Vivica and Eddie moved into Justin's Terrace soon after they were married in 1985. The four-story apartment building overlooked a man-made creek, which was more like a gutter since it was filled with garbage including shopping carts and dirty pampers. It ran a couple miles down the street and led to the Potomac River. The low-income housing complex was designed in a maze-like formation, with interlocking apartment buildings that made it easy for chaos and crime to fester.

The off-white colored concrete buildings were an eye sore. Rats and roaches shared their living space. Toilets remained backed up while drains stayed clogged. Trash littered the hallways and the bulk garbage was rarely hauled away on time. Justin's Terrace was a blight in the community and the city government offered little interest in any renewal efforts.

Many of Vivica's neighbors struggled, just as her family did. But it was all Vivica and Eddie could afford. Justin's Terrace was their paradise amongst ruins even if crime, drugs and violence tormented everyone in some shape of form there. Vivica despised raising her family amongst the street fights, random shootings, police raids and everything else. Her destitute neighbors just wanted to survive poverty and hopelessness. And for most young men in Justin's Terrace, that meant gambling, stealing or selling drugs—all things Vivica prayed her children would avoid.

However, it wasn't the children she ended up having to worrying about in the end. Eddie became caught in the perilous web as soon as he realized a lot of his dreams weren't panning out the way he envisioned. Eddie was becoming as despondent as many of their neighbors. But by the time Vivica realized Eddie's disposition negatively changed, it was far too late.

Crack destroyed him—layer by fragile layer.

The handsome looks that once attracted Vivica had begun to perish. Before the drugs, Eddie's skin had been the color of maple syrup; his jet-black hair was soft and had curls scattered like a Samoan's. Vivica fell in love with Eddie easily. Neither his looks or his charisma lured her, but it was Eddie's illuminating smile that brought rainbows out on rainy days and won her heart.

She was a sophomore in high school when they met—she, fifteen, and he, twenty. Eddie took an interest in Vivica despite her age, and the attention he gave her made Vivica feel exceptional. Somehow, he made her feel like an essential part of his life, and she couldn't believe someone his age could feel that way about her. Vivica's relationship with Eddie made her popular amongst her naïve group of friends. And she liked the feeling of that, too.

Vivica managed to hide the relationship from her mother, whom she knew would read Eddie like a book and immediately disapprove of him. She never gave her mother a chance to judge him and kept him a secret as long as she could. She met Eddie over friends' houses and began missing school to keep their relationship concealed.

A few months with Eddie taught Vivica a lot. She learned things faster than her mind could process at her age. And it wasn't long before she also learned that Eddie and his brother robbed liquor stores as a side hustle to working at the auto body shop on Martin Luther King Avenue. At first, the idea of him being involved in the streets frightened her. But his carefree, do-or-die lifestyle only intrigued her more.

A year into their relationship, Eddie was convicted of robbery for holding up a crowded corner store on South Capitol Street. Vivica wrote him just about every other day while he served an eighteen-month sentence in Lorton. The prison was about twenty miles across the Virginia state line. Vivica never imagined herself catching a bus to visit a prisoner, but when it came to Eddie, a lot of things changed.

Vivica became pregnant soon after his release and Eddie asked her to be his wife. He promised he'd get a job to take care of her and their child and she believed him. Besides, Vivica never believed in abortions and she could never imagine herself as a single parent. The mere thought of having to carry the burden of bringing life in the world alone terrified her.

But she loved Eddie, even though she had reservations with his proposal. His fascination with trouble waved before her like a red warning flag, but a future without him was unimaginable. So without further hesitation, she dropped out of high school to start a family. Vivica's mother cut her off, offering no support. She was faced with coping with her pregnancy without her mother's guidance and began receiving prenatal care only after her stomach began poking from her over-stretched shirts and when she began feeling abdominal pains.

Vivica had never heard of prenatal care until one of her friends told her about a free clinic on Good Hope Road. On her very first visit, she learned she was carrying twins. Once she learned they were boys, she named them Elijah Marques and Elgin Maurice before they were even born.

In the beginning things ran smooth. Eddie had gotten a job through a friend as a mechanic at a shop on Southern Avenue. But that didn't last long, because the boss discovered that Eddie was using work supplies for side jobs and was fired. Once Eddie found other jobs, he had difficulty keeping them longer than a few weeks because of his criminal record. No one wanted to give him a chance to prove himself, and often he felt like banging his head on the wall.

Vivica tried to hide her frustration and be supportive. She knew her husband was feeling low, but Eddie saw through it and disregarded her concern. He'd begun staying out later with his friends to avoid her penetrating stares. And it wasn't long before Eddie began holding up liquor stores again to make ends meet. The mounting setbacks he faced left him feeling defeated and insignificant. With each door of rejection slamming in his face, a new jeopardous window opened. Feelings of meaninglessness catapulted Eddie towards the drug scene. It was there that he found a temporary escape from his dismal reality.

Vivica knew Eddie smoked marijuana, in fact, she'd asked him not to do it in front of the babies. But she had no idea that his habit had escalated to smoking embalming fluid-saturated marijuana—a concoction that elevated his high to limits gravely close to heroine.

After awhile the buzz no longer provided the same euphoric state that he craved. Eddie began lacing his weed with heroine only because he knew it would help alleviate the pressure he was feeling. He thought lacing it wouldn't lead to an addiction, since it wasn't that much. But that type of high fell flat quick, it wasn't enough. He needed something to send him straight to nirvana.

The day Eddie was introduced to crack was the day Eddie's role as father and husband withered like a rotting fruit.

Vivica noticed Eddie turning to the streets more. He hung out later and the sun often beat him home. Vivica turned to the Bible for guidance, believing Eddie would find what he was looking for from his family and not in the streets.

One Sunday afternoon while checking her mailbox in the hallway of her apartment building, Vivica overheard some of her neighbors chatting about a sermon they'd heard at church that morning. She asked them about the church they attended and was immediately invited to join them at their Wednesday night Bible Study. Vivica knew she'd find the answers she needed there. She agreed to join her neighbors at the small Pentecostal Holiness Church in Oxon Hills, Maryland. Although Eddie had no interest in going, she brought the twins along so they could have the same strong Christian upbringing she'd had.

Rightway Pentecostal didn't approve of two things: divorce or birth control. The Lord wanted his followers to "Be fruitful and multiply," she was told. So Vivica, who wanted to do right by God, got rid of her contraceptives, despite the mounting problems she was having with her husband.

Elder Roy, Rightway's pastor, told her to be patient and supportive of Eddie during his times of trouble. And Vivica did. But it wasn't because of

Elder Roy's urgencies, but because she felt God would want her to do that. She knew God spoke through her pastor. But despite rich words from the Lord, Vivica saw that there was more to Elder Roy than what met the eye.

He was a smooth, older round-shaped man. Elder Roy always seemed a little more laid back than the average preacher should be. The shine from his clean-shaven head could illuminate a dark cave. His chubby face wore a graying goatee that maintained a razor sharp trim. The expensive tailored suits hugged his frame perfectly and they were amongst the finest she'd ever seen a man wear. They were always hard pressed, and he looked sharp like the Fruit of Islam brothers. He wore diamond cufflinks, a gaudy platinum watch and a diamond-studded cross around his pudgy neck. Vivica thought Elder Roy was too flashy to be all about Christ.

She noticed that he tried to deflect attention from his attire, by handing out ounces of the Lord's wisdom at every given opportunity. But a year after attending the church, Vivica grew tired of listening to Elder Roy's half-hearted rhetorical spills. Nothing he told her to do worked for her or her family, she realized. Even though Eddie became a full-time groundskeeper with St. Elizabeth's Hospital, during his off-hours, his lips were wrapped snugly around a glass pipe.

One day, Vivica wrapped the twins up and caught the bus to Rightway to speak with Elder Roy about Eddie. He was hitting rock bottom and she needed Elder Roy's guidance. He was surprised to see her, but welcomed her into his office. The room was filled with the spicy smell of after-shave lotion. The smell was so thick and strong, she became nauseated.

"How can I help you Sister Jeffries?" he asked with a sneer spreading across his face. The expression made Vivica slightly uncomfortable. She tried to ignore it as she sat down.

"You know I love being of service to those in need," he added with what Vivica thought was a wink.

She frowned slightly and pondered for a moment, but then she brushed it off just as quickly as the thought arose. Vivica began to tell him about Eddie smoking his weekly checks up faster than he could cash them and she told Elder Roy that Eddie had begun showing up high at work, and became disrespectful to his supervisors.

"I just don't know what to do," she confided. "I think I've done all a woman can do for her husband at this point."

"Well, are you doing enough praying, Sister? You know the Lord answers those who seek him."

"I do Pastor. But do you have *any* idea how it feels to have your hus-

8

band sneak in and out of the house at night, on a quest to seek satisfaction in the streets. He's turning his back on us every time he decides to put that pipe up to his mouth. Apparently, we are no longer a priority in his life. How am I supposed to care for these two," Vivica looked at the twins, "if he's not bringing any money home?"

"Sister Jeffries, need I remind you that the Lord is with you," Elder Roy said with a thick voice that vibrated her soul. "He's with your husband, too. The Lord will not see you suffer long. The church will certainly not see you suffer. You must continue to trust in Him."

Vivica nodded listening intently and then said, "Pastor, I'm three months pregnant. If this continues I just don't know if I'll be able to make it. I might just have to leave him."

Elder Roy stood up from behind his huge desk and walked toward her. He placed his chubby warm hand on her shoulder and said, "Sister, you can't give up. Just trust in the Lord. You've got to praise Him in the morning, praise Him in the noon time and praise Him late at night." His voice rose with excitement from the sound of each word. "Praise him when you just can't praise Him no more, and He'll be there. Remember that it is your faith that makes you stronger. You can't let go of faith. Just pray on it."

Elder Roy took a bottle of olive oil from the edge of his desk and poured a dab in his palm. The smell added slightly to Vivica's nauseousness. He delicately drew a cross in the center of Vivica's forehead and said a prayer so low that she could barely make out the words. She said Amen, as soon as he did and decided to pray again when she got home.

And Vivica continued to pray often. But the prayers she and Elder Roy summoned up were huge misfires and Vivica grew more and more pent-up. But her heart told her to continue trusting in God.

Once Eddie realized the control he thought he had, wasn't there, he gave in, promising Vivica he'd go to counseling. He said he wanted to become a better man, and she believed him. But that vow became a faded memory once Vivica noticed things were disappearing from their sparsely decorated apartment piece by piece. Because of the inconsistent income, they only managed to have the bare necessities: a few furnishings from thrift stores or collected from evicted neighbors. Even though their family didn't have much, Eddie found things to sell.

In fact, he sold just about everything with an electrical pulse. When he was done, he stole the babies' diapers and sold them to people right outside of their apartment. The saddest thing about it was the neighbors knew where the Pampers came from, and they continued to buy them from him. From cookware to clothes, he stole and sold everything.

One day when Vivica was returning home from the grocery store, her stomach the size of a watermelon pushing the twins in their double-seated stroller, she stared at her husband from afar. Eddie stood on the corner, near their apartment building, heckling their neighbors; trying to sell their hand-me-down, 13-inch, color television.

"Eddie, what are you doing?" Vivica asked out of breath, demanding to know. The soft hum of laughter, chatter and deep-throated sighs from neighbors sitting on the steps and leaning against the fence in front of the building, filled the air.

"What it look like I'm doing?" he asked nervously. He looked like he hadn't bathed in weeks, and an odor similar to spoiled chicken stifled the air. She hadn't seen him in days and knew he hadn't bothered to do anything for himself in that time. Her face read like a billboard advertising a horror movie. Her spirit became clouded with feelings of confusion and disgust. It was as if she had just noticed for the first time just how bad his addiction had gotten.

"Is that our TV set?" Vivica asked. Eddie grimaced and pushed passed her.

"Move out of my way. Unless you got some money to give me," he barked.

She stood there stunned. But at eight months pregnant, Vivica began to wrestle the TV from her husband. She could care less about who was paying attention to them. Vivica knew he was much stronger and quicker, but she just couldn't deal with the fact that he would steal from his own family and then try to sell it right in front of their home. She felt the need to salvage what was theirs—their property and her dignity.

Eddie knocked her to the ground like she was an annoying dog. She dropped like a sack of potatoes tossed to the floor. Lying on her side, feeling defeated, Vivica rolled her eyes and stared up at his back as he sauntered down the street. After a few seconds, some of her neighbors helped her back to her feet, giving her a pitied look. She felt humiliated. Some of the guys, who sold drugs in the neighborhood, came to her defense, snatching the TV back from him. "They must feel guilty," she thought to herself. The women wiped Vivica's dress off and told her to forget about Eddie. But the screeching wails from the twins sitting in the stroller erased any thought of that.

Eddie needed help and even though he was not the same man she remembered marrying, he was the father of her children. What Eddie did to himself and their family left Vivica mystified and appalled. She felt alone and abandoned. She felt rage and pain. Fighting the battle alone wasn't an option, she was certain. She found herself reaching for the yellow and green plaid prayer pillow she used for kneeling, more and more these days. Vivica continued to turn to Elder Roy and God for help, sure that they both would lead her to refuge.

When Vivica found a four-inch glass tube with a fake rose, a spoon, a syringe, aluminum foil and a rubber band in Eddie's military fatigue jacket pocket, she snapped. That was one thing Elder Roy hadn't taught her how to cope with—Eddie bringing the drugs into her home. Again she went to her pastor seeking counseling to nurse the wound that would not heal in their family. Surely, he would be the light out of her dark tunnel, Vivica thought.

But still, Elder Roy discouraged her from leaving Eddie.

"It's your duty to be there to support your husband. He is the head of the household and will always be," Elder Roy told her. "Bring him to the church. We'll pray over him. We'll bathe his body in a spiritual elixir that will heal his soul."

Vivica rolled her eyes as soon as his broad back was turned. She could not whole-heartedly accept the message he was giving her. How much more could she take of being Eddie's wet nurse—supporting, ignoring and tolerating everything he brought before her? The solution Elder Roy proposed had not proved to be the answer. Her husband was out of control, he was an addict and she was trying to cope with it the best way she knew how. Her world was falling apart, brick by brick, and all her pastor could suggest was to be supportive. Why not to leave him, she wondered. Vivica didn't understand his logic, but saw no other resolution than to continue praying.

She tried to talk to Eddie about what she was going through. She begged him to change his ways and to leave the drugs alone. "Look at what you're doing to us," she argued. But she knew she couldn't get through to him, not on that level. So she simply encouraged him to come to church with her.

"Can't no preacher tell me what to do! He's a man just like me—flesh and blood. You better get the hell of out of my face," Eddie yelled. "Are you going to tell me that nigga don't have any problems?"

She felt even more defeated when he spoke to her in such an inferior tone. But what was she thinking? She knew he would never consider going to church. He didn't go before he became addicted. Why did she think he would go now? Vivica wanted to surrender all of her will, because she was losing in the battle to save her husband, her marriage and their family. The white flag she had been waving over the years was now raggedy, gray and shredding at the seams.

For three agonizing years, Vivica did exactly what Elder Roy requested. During Eddie's addiction, she stood by him even though she was miserable and depressed. She continued to pray and push forward. Her prayer pillow had a permanent indentation in the middle from all the many nights of her falling to her knees. Things that she regarded as valuable went missing. And Eddie's health deteriorated like an old quilt discarded in a moth filled attic. Vivica had become accustomed to the destitute life she was living with Eddie—it was full of challenges and sadness. Every now and then, she would find an inner-strength that would flash signs of hope like a lighthouse begging her to come in from the turbulent storm that Eddie created. On those rare occasions she ignored Elder Roy and put Eddie out—changing the locks on the apartment door almost as soon as the door slammed shut.

But on other days, when Eddie showed up with the humility of a shunned dog, she unlocked the door and opened her arms to him. Sometimes Vivica refused to answer the door, even though she empathized for him. She was torn between the man who stood before her, and the man she remembered from yesterday. While clean and sober, Eddie brought bags of groceries and new clothes for the children. Vivica agreed to let him in then, hopeful that the man she married was home for good.

During this seesaw-like period, Eddie committed himself to a drug rehabilitation program. It was hard for Eddie in the beginning. He refused to accept any visitors for a few weeks. Vivica gave him time, because she knew he needed to cleanse himself mentally and physically. The constant supervision and daily counseling seemed somewhat helpful on the days Vivica visited him in the clinic months later. The rural Talbot County Maryland setting along with the care of the staff seemed to help ease his suffering. Eddie appeared tranquil to her.

But although he looked a lot healthier and peaceful, something in his eyes managed to disturb Vivica. Nonetheless, just seeing Eddie look healthy was enough to know her prayers were being answered. She had begun to smile more often. She smiled so often at church, that Elder Roy stopped her one day to comment on it.

"Sister Jeffries, you're smiling an awful lot these days. Things going well at home?" he inquired.

"Yes Pastor, they are. Things are just fine." Vivica couldn't hide her smile.

"Well that's wonderful. I can see you smiling all the way from the pulpit. And it's such a wonderful glow, I just can't stop looking your way."

Vivica didn't know what to say to that, and looked down to check on Elijah, Elgin and Evan. "The Lord is blessing us right now."

"He sure is. You're looking a whole lot better these days and I'm glad me and the Lord took a part in that."

"Uh, yes," she stammered. "Well me and my husband are expecting another child soon, so it's best that things are finally on the upswing. Lord knows we've been in the devil's pit for far too long. The Lord truly does answer prayers."

"Yes, he does. Well if you ever need any special attention, feel free to come by my office. You know my doors are always open."

Vivica smiled, but she didn't like the dual-meaning of his words. She gathered her three children and walked toward the door.

She wasn't going to let her suspicions ruin her joy. It seemed that the Lord's word for the day was exactly what she needed to hear. And she was feeling good.

Eddie made promises of things he planned to do when he was released. He had a lot of plans for changes to make in his life. He promised to get a stable job and promised to spend more time with her and the children. Vivica only smiled when he said such things. She wanted to be encouraging, but it was the prayer that kept her encouraged. She prayed that the streets' beckoning calls of crack would never tempt Eddie again.

Vivica wanted so badly to believe Eddie was a changed man when he returned home. She prayed he would stay clean so her family could live the normal life she'd always dreamed she would have as a child.

Even though Eddie spent a lot of time repairing things around the apartment and taking the children to the park, she couldn't ignore the haunting look of despair in his eyes. It was the cautious look of a man having an affair, except it wasn't with a woman. It was the look of someone who wasn't satisfied with the cards they had been dealt. But Vivica looked passed the look and continued to love Eddie anyway. She only wanted to love him up enough that he wouldn't return to the streets. They were expecting another child soon. And they all needed him.

But the discontented look in Eddie's eyes never went away. Not long after finding solace at home, he was back on a mission to find comfort in the streets. It had only been three weeks since he'd left the program. Once Vivica realized he had turned back to crack and had given up on their family, Vivica wanted out—regardless of what her church thought about her. God would never turn his back on her, she thought.

But Vivica never imagined just how hard it would be for her to let go of

Eddie or to turn her back on the messages of the church. The word defeat wasn't in Vivica's vocabulary, so she tried whatever she could to prevail. No longer could she watch as the man she loved, tortured himself. Vivica ended each night on her prayer pillow.

Ignoring her husband and not seeking help for him wasn't easy for Vivica. Pain filled her soul as she watched Eddie fall victim to the vice that ate him up from the inside out. There were many times when she woke up in the middle of the night, feeling an empty spot in the bed beside her. She always knew Eddie was out in the streets, spending money that he'd just stolen from her pocketbook.

His addiction plagued more than his body, which had become frail over the years, and it was really the least of Vivica's worries. The corrosion of his mind and spirit scared her most. Eddie stayed with her and the children a couple of nights each week. On the days he was there, he scarcely spoke to her and when he did speak, he never made much sense. Usually he spoke so fast and was so agitated that a conversation was impossible. When Vivica managed to break down some of what he saying, it never turned out to be anything logical. He rambled on and blamed her for everything that was going wrong in his life.

She loved a man who flocked to drugs like a bee to fresh flowers. When did he lose his strength, she wondered. The way he hovered around alleys looking for someone to split a hit with or for his supplier, was disgraceful. She watched in amazement and disgust as Eddie examined any white thing he could find—from crumbs in the living room carpet to trash in the streets. Vivica imagined him feeling lucky on those days, since he obviously believed in happenstance. But how did the man she abandoned her mother for as a teenager, come to be this way?

"How long Lord?" she cried many nights while on her knees praying. "You told me to be patient and I am Lord. You told me to believe in your word, and I do Lord, but how much longer must my family and I suffer?"

Vivica waited for an answer from God. And when it didn't come she continued to pray and fast. Then Eddie began beating her.

The first time he hit her, Vivica knew it should have been the last time. But she found herself making excuses for him. "He was high and he didn't mean it. He'd never beaten me before," she told herself as she applied a bag of ice to her throbbing cheekbone. But it wasn't the last time because there were more days like that ahead.

Twice, in a six-month period, Eddie had beaten her to within an inch of her life—in the presence of their young children, no less. She had two more children since the last time he'd received rehabilitation treatment—Eric and Eve. Eddie beat her because she wouldn't turn over welfare checks she had been receiving to take care of the family.

He'd showed up at their apartment on the first of the month, three months in a row, demanding money and each time, she gave him a few dollars just so he'd leave them alone.

The straw that broke Vivica's back happened just after she agreed to let him visit the children on one humid summer afternoon. But she knew he was high and wouldn't let him in. Eddie stood on the other side of the steel door, begging her to let him see them. When she told him no and to go away, Eddie began calling the children's names one by one, telling them he had ice cream that was melting. Irritated, she urged him again to leave them alone. The cries of her five children only grew more intense and the looks in their faces made her heart weak. The moment she opened the door she knew she'd made a colossal mistake. Eddie looked horrid and she knew he had only one mission: to get the check she'd cashed earlier that morning. She just hoped that whatever was going to happen wouldn't be that bad this time.

Eddie asked her for the check no sooner than she opened the door.

"The mail didn't get here yet," she said as she saw the frustration spread across his face like the early morning sunrays spreading across a dark sky.

"Don't lie to me Viv," he said. "I know you got that muthafucking check this morning. Give it here!"

Vivica knew he was growing impatient, because he couldn't keep still, shifting his weight from one leg to the other. His eyes bulged out of his head like a frog's and white foam formed in the corners of his mouth. Eddie had been scratching himself, and she could see where his fingernails had left thin red lines across his arms near the old drug needle marks.

She wanted to appear in control, even though she was growing more nervous by the second. In a soft, calm voice, she asked him to leave again. But Eddie ignored her and began to scurry around the apartment looking through drawers and in kitchen cabinets yelling and cursing.

Vivica followed him into the kitchen and around the living room, begging for him to leave. But this time he pushed her down on the pleather sofa as he ransacked the apartment looking for her purse.

"Where the fuck is the check Viv?" he demanded while going through mail on the dining room table.

"Get out Eddie!" she yelled.

Vivica jumped on his back to stop him from getting to the bedroom, where her purse hung on the back of the doorknob. But Eddie turned around and swung her into the wall, pressing his weight up against her until Vivica released his neck. She yelled and screamed for him to leave.

The children—all under age seven at the time, were clueless to what was going on and looked on in confusion as their father tore up the apartment.

When Eddie finally found the purse, he laughed, grabbed the money and stuffed it in his pocket. Again, Vivica tried to stop him as she ran behind him. But Eddie, in a rage and full of excitement for the treasure he'd found, balled up his fist and punched Vivica in her jaw. The back of Eddie's hand felt like a sledgehammer slamming down on her cheek. She heard a crack that sounded like ice popping out of an ice tray. The force, so powerful that it slammed her against the living room wall, left a dent the outline of her body in the plywood.

She felt dizzy, but managed to keep standing on her feet. Before Vivica could reach her hand up to touch the sore spot on her face, she felt another punch come down on her, ringing like thunder through her ears. Her small frame could be knocked to the floor with just a small push, let alone a thunderous blow. Smacking the bare floor, Vivica's crushed nose spewed blood drops on the linoleum. Eddie ignored the blood running from her nose and pulled Vivica back up to her feet by the back of her jeans. She felt like a lifeless puppet as she tried to place her feet on the floor below her.

"Not in front of the kids, Eddie," she managed to whisper through aching lips.

"Shut the fuck up! The next time I tell you to open the muthafucking door, you do it!" he yelled as he threw her body across the room. "I am still your husband, damn it!"

She laid on the floor in agony and could barely open her eyes because of the swelling that was beginning to weigh her eyelids down.

"Get out," she mumbled. "Please get out!"

Eddie kicked her in her chest and in her side until he no longer heard sounds coming from her. He looked around at his children that were bawling at his feet, wiped the sweat from his brow, and the foam from the corners of his mouth. Then he checked to make sure the money was still stuffed in his pockets before he ran out the door.

It took Vivica eight long minutes to crawl towards her telephone. Her children stood stunned watching her, but Evan, who was six, handed her the telephone. Her body ached with her every move and the operator could barely hear her when she cried out for help. She needed to be rushed to the emergency room.

Moments later, the sound of ambulance sirens pierced her thoughts as she lay on the gurney in pain. Her neighbor volunteered to watch her children until Vivica's mother could reach them.

A week of rest in the hospital helped her body to heal, but she needed healing for her mind and her spirit. Vivica was amazed she lived. She knew she would never survive another beating like that and now was the time for her to change things, with or without the support of her church.

CHAPTER 2

Elder Roy visited Vivica in the hospital a few days after she arrived. Her bruised face and body—the color of avocados and ripe plums—did little to discourage his prayers for her husband. She could barely see through swollen eyes, or speak with a jaw that had been dislocated and wired shut. She couldn't even respond to Elder Roy when he told her to "trust in the Lord with all thine heart" and to pray that things would get better. After a while, all she saw was his mouth moving, but she heard no words coming forth. She didn't want to hear them. The sound of his voice made her skin crawl.

Inside she replayed thoughts of telling him what he could do with his prayer. But instead, she prayed. Even though her body was numb, and she could barely swallow her own saliva, she prayed. After all she was going through, Elder Roy's decision to remind her how the church felt about divorce was the straw that smashed the camel flat for her.

"God put certain people in your life for a reason," he told her with his plump hands lightly placed on her cheeks. "Even Jesus was persecuted." The words seeped from his lips like poison. A solitary tear glided down Vivica's face. Unable to wipe it away, Elder Roy softly ran the back of his hand across her cheek. In that very moment, Vivica vowed not to return to Rightway ever again. It wasn't only what the pastor was saying to her, it was how he made her feel when he said it and the stroke across her cheek that revolted her. His touch felt like the cool underbelly of a snake slithering across moist dirt. Vivica felt like he was getting some vile rush from her suffering. The feeling of knowing that was unbearable.

Soon after Elder Roy left the District General hospital, she asked her doctor to tie her fallopian tubes. Shocked, the doctor asked her if she was sure.

Vivica nodded and said, "Just give me the paper work, so I can sign it."

"You must be sure you never want children or will never want more children before you agree to do this procedure," the doctor said in his rich Indian accent. "There is an operation to reverse sterilization, but it is very,

very complicated. It is also very expensive and may not work," he warned.

"I said do it, damn it!" Vivica whispered harshly.

The doctor shook his head and grimaced.

A change was eminent and a new mission for Vivica was just over the horizon. She pressed charges and Eddie was convicted for the abuse he put her through on that traumatic afternoon. Though he only received a three-month sentence and a restraining order upon his release, the time was plenty for Vivica to make needed changes to her life.

When Vivica regained some of her strength while lying in the hospital, she jotted down a plan which would help better herself and the lives of her children. She wrote it on the back of a Get Well card and decided to stick it on her refrigerator door as a daily reminder. The top three things on her slate were making amends with her mother, getting her General Equivalency Diploma, and getting off of welfare.

Her mother promised to help her in any way she could on the day she brought the children to see Vivica in the hospital. Vivica cried because she was glad her mother was in her corner again. As soon as she was released from the hospital, Vivica began working on her second goal—returning to school. She never wanted to feel so dependent on the decisions of men again. Vivica looked beyond getting her GED; she wanted a college degree in nursing. Fortunately, a program through the welfare system would help her pay for just that if she attended the District of Columbia University.

Although Vivica thanked God for welfare, because it provided when no one else would, she despised the system. The system's restrictions made her feel like a wingless bird. It promoted single-parent homes and it wanted complete control of people's entire lives. If Vivica were to acknowledge that a man lived with her—including her husband, the government would cut her assistance in half. But when Vivica first applied for the assistance years earlier, in her mind, her husband wasn't there because she was doing everything by herself.

She had no qualms in acknowledging that it was because of the system she had prevailed without her husband. It provided a roof over her family and food in their stomachs, and that was something her husband ceased doing long before he was convicted of assault and battery.

Yet there was a high price for receiving the government's help. Vivica lost small personal freedoms in exchange for the funds she received. Her right to make decisions about her life and her kids' lives was all but taken away. Many of the decisions had to be made by social workers or brought to the attention of the social workers. Basic things like how she should better budget her $550 monthly check were among the services the social workers offered. But if she saved too much money, they would cut her monthly checks in half.

Vivica knew she would do whatever she could to make life better for her family, including being deceitful. There was no lie too white for her to tell for the survival of her family.

Having a personal savings bank account—something most working people took for granted—was not even an option for Vivica under the government's severe guidelines. In order to have an account the government needed her banking information including her account number so her finances could be monitored. That way, if she ever saved a lot of money, the government would deduct a percentage from her monthly checks, making it impossible for her to become independent of their help.

But Vivica was no dummy.

She asked her mother to set up a side account in her own name, which Vivica secretly deposited money into, even if it was merely $50 a month. Typically, that's exactly what she deposited, because the $550 monthly check she received, broke down to $110 per child and that was not enough to stand on one foot back in the 1990s. In addition to the monthly check, Vivica also received $200 in food stamps.

But that wasn't the only major hindrance the system perpetuated. Vivica also was not allowed to own any assets including something as simple as a vehicle. Objects that the government considered luxury items were prohibited and a car—no matter how broke down or unreliable, was not allowed. Vivica had to be creative with different ways of getting to and from the grocery store and doctors appointments. She begged neighbors for rides or caught the bus. A couple of times, when money was thin, she got cab drivers to drop her off at neighboring apartment buildings and then bolted to avoid paying for the rides.

Going clothes shopping or taking the children to the doctor on the bus in the winter or the summer or any season—was not an easy feat for her. Vivica decided to save up enough money to purchase a $300 station wagon, which she had also put in her mother's name to make life a little easier for them.

The old gray station wagon barely ran and had never passed city inspection. The little red temporary failure stickers she bought from crackheads were permanent fixtures in the front window. If the car started, she had to pray that she would make it back home. She hated taking her children around in it, because it was so unreliable. The defroster didn't work in the winter and the air conditioner didn't work in the summer. But Vivica never complained when she lifted up the hood just to open the gas tank or when she rolled down the window just to open the driver's door.

Though she stressed a lot, Vivica did what she had to do in order to improve the life of her family. If any of her children wanted to go on school trips, even as far as to Disney World, she scraped up the money some how. Selling old clothes at consignment shops, helping her neighbor sew dresses for proms or weddings; and other times she sold bake goods to neighborhood children or braided some of the young boys' hair for extra money.

If things got tighter than usual, Vivica would sell or buy food stamps, which ever she needed at the time to make ends meet. She even bought large portions of candy from Sam's Wholefood using a friend's card, and sold them to neighborhood kids for extra, tax-free money, which she saved in the account her mother set up for her.

But for some reason, her children had the nerve to question her about where the money went during times they couldn't get what they wanted. The twins were ten-years-old when they got up the courage to ask her about it.

"You always claim to be so broke," Elgin had said under his breath one day.

"Sweetheart, I do the best I can. If it's not good enough for you, feel free to get a part-time job—a paper route or something," Vivica told him. "It's plenty of doors around here that you can knock on to take the garbage out for pocket money."

"You are supposed to take care of me, not me take care of you," he said. "What I look like begging for money?"

"Little boy, go to your room 'til you learn how to talk to me with some respect," Vivica said.

Elgin stormed off to his room and slammed the door.

Ever since she divorced Eddie, Vivica noticed the twins had become more and more disrespectful to her. They often complained about the way she raised them. Vivica believed it was to her children's benefit to know the truth about their father, so she never withheld any information. She knew sharing gross details was pointless, but she wanted them to know about Eddie's addiction, his abusive behavior and financial neglect. They never believed her and yearned to be with their father—who in their eyes was a different man to them.

But this time, when Elgin was disrespectful to her, Vivica let his temper cool down for a couple of hours before she walked in the room he shared with his twin. When she told him to sit at his desk, Elgin rolled his eyes and slowly moved to the chair.

"Take out a sheet of paper," Vivica said. "Here, I want you to see this."

"What?"

"Just be quiet and listen. This is a check stub. Do you see how much I make a month?"

"Yes, and that's a lot of money."

Vivica sucked her teeth and said, "OK, write that number down."

Elgin did just that.

"OK, now, see this," Vivica said holding up an envelope. "This is what is called an electric bill. Do you know what that's for?"

"Yes, Ma," Elgin said perturbed.

"What?"

"It's for the lights and the TV," he said with his tone bordering on rude.

"How much is it?"

"Ninety-three dollars."

"OK, now subtract that."

Elgin wrote a minus sign and counted on his fingers the difference.

"It's $457.00."

"Right. OK, now here's the rent, the gas bill, the car insurance, the cable—that you all love so much, the phone bill that your sister loves so much and take out $25 for the McDonald's that you all just have to have every now and then."

"I thought you could use your food stamps for that."

"Oh, now you are worried about the food stamps. You mean those things that you and your brothers hate using when I send you to the corner store to buy some food for me to cook for you all?" Vivica mocked.

"Yeah, those," he said rolling his eyes.

"Well, you can't spend food stamps on cooked foods, sweetheart."

"Oh," Elgin said shocked. "I didn't know that."

"There are a lot of things that you don't know. If you learn to listen to me, you will learn a lot. Now finish calculating those bills for me and tell me how much I have left."

Elgin, with a look of determination, on his face was set to prove to his mother that she had extra money to give to them each month. When he was done, he was surprised to see that she only had $37 to spare.

"Are you satisfied now?" Vivica asked. "Now when you all need or want clothes or new shoes or change for the candy store, do you see what I'm dealing with?"

Elgin balled up the paper, grabbed his jacket and ran outside. Vivica shook her head, because she knew that she was having a hard time reaching Elgin. He was stubborn and hot-headed just like his father. Unlike his twin brother, he was also very aggressive, and sometimes, she realized he only thought about himself. Vivica knew she let him see a side that he needed to know—that they were poor.

But with hard work, Vivica graduated from the District of Columbia University with a nursing degree. It took her six years going part-time, but it was worth it. Once she got her first job at the same hospital where she had a rude awakening years earlier, she bought a three-story row house on Florida Avenue—a big difference from the projects they were all too familiar with. The house was on a busy thoroughfare in the Northwest area of D.C. and things started to get better, rather quickly, or so she thought.

CHAPTER 3

Mrs. Jeffries, your boys have not been to school for three days," said a grouchy voice over the answering machine that announced herself as the middle school assistant principal. "Therefore, we have placed Elijah, Elgin and Evan on suspension until you can provide reasonable excuses for their absences."

"What?" Vivica gasped. Her neck jerked back because she couldn't believe what she heard. "Three days! What in the world is going on around here? I want all of you to come here right now!"

It was midnight and Vivica had just gotten home from working a late night shift at the hospital. It was a shift that the newest employees had to work. And she hated it because she had to leave her kids home alone, and even though fourteen was old enough in D.C. for older kids to be left home to baby-sit, she was not happy about leaving them alone that late with Eric and Eve, no less. But Vivica knew there were sacrifices and risks she had to take to continue improving their lives. She could not afford an overnight sitter, yet. Being a single parent was not a cakewalk and sometimes she had to make compromises.

Sleepy-eyed and frazzled they all filed into her room one by one.

"Yes mom?" Eric, the baby boy, asked with a groggy sounding voice.

"Eric and Eve, sit down on my bed. It's these three I really want to talk to," Vivica said pointing to the older children.

"Yes?" Evan asked.

"Why have you three been absent from school all week?"

Silence filled the room. The only sound was the clock ticking above Vivica's dresser.

"No one has anything to say?" Vivica asked with her hand on her hip.

Blank, sleepy faces stared back at her.

"Mommy, I was in school," Eve said innocently.

"I know baby," Vivica said rubbing her hair. "You two go back to sleep," she said to Eve and Eric. "I didn't mean to wake you, but you three—we got a lot to talk about."

"Who said we wasn't in school?" Elgin snapped.

"I know you weren't, so that's neither here, nor there!" Vivica yelled. "But that's OK, because none of you are too old for a beating. Where's my belt? All three of you are going to get it!"

Vivica searched her room for the thick brown leather belt. She found it hanging on the back of her bedroom door—her trusty disciplinarian over the years. The children called it a Santa Claus belt, because it reminded them of a belt he would wear. Before Vivica could swing back to whip Elijah, Elgin ran out of the room and straight out the back door—leaving the screen door swinging behind him. Vivica ran after him. Once she realized she wasn't going to find him in the darkness of the alley behind the house, she went back in and thrashed the behinds of the other two kids.

She sent them to bed, turned on the back porch light and went to her room for the night. It wasn't the first time Elgin had run away from her, and she knew just how to fix him.

The very next morning, an hour before they were expected to wake up for school, she poured a cup of ice cold water on his face. Elgin jumped out of his bed startled. As soon as he realized he wasn't drowning, Vivica began whipping his behind with her big brown belt. Elgin couldn't get away fast enough to escape the whelps she left on his legs.

Vivica drove them all to school that morning, but before she dropped the middle-schoolers off, she went in to see the assistant principal. She wanted to make sure they would not be suspended for their absences. The assistant principal agreed to only give the boys in-school suspension during their lunch hours for the next three weeks. Vivica also punished them for two months—no going outside after school and no television.

***

Vivica could count on one hand how many times Eddie had called since their divorce and after being incarcerated for a drug charge where he served 24 months again at Lorton. One day out of the blue, he showed up at the house missing two teeth from that infamous smile and showing a head full of prematurely gray hair. Vivica was appalled by his appearance, but knew that the kids wanted to see him. She told Eddie, that she didn't want the kids to see him like that. One look at him and she knew he was still using drugs. She didn't know what he was liable to say to her children while he was like that. Vivica was certainly not going to give him an invitation into the house that she had worked so hard to get.

25

Vivica saw one of her sons ride by the house on his bike. She knew Evan noticed his father standing on his porch, but was surprised when he didn't stop and come up.

"Hey son!" Eddie yelled in a contrived excitement.

But Evan kept riding by with an embarrassed-look on his young face.

"Do you even know which one of your sons he is?" Vivica asked in a sarcastic manner.

"Look, I did not come here to argue with you Viv. I just want to see my kids, OK?"

"Why?" Vivica said confused. "Why now?"

"Are you going to let me see them or not?"

"I shouldn't. What have you done for them? Not a thing. Why should I burden them with your pathetic presence? Showing up here, empty-handed, filthy and smelling like sour milk. Why? So you can feel like some sort of hero or something?"

"Look Viv, they are my kids even though that Evan one, don't look a thing like me."

Vivica's mouth fell open in disbelief. His comment felt like a blow to her stomach.

"How dare you? Who in the world do you think you are? Get off my porch. Get! You trifling lazy bum!" Vivica hollered. "All of this you see— look around—I've done by myself. That boy—the one who don't look like you—that bike he's riding, I bought it. Those clothes he's wearing, I paid for them. And, my, doesn't he look healthy. That's because I feed him. All of it is because of my doing, my hard work.

"What have you done? Look at you. Just get! Crawl back in that parasite infested hole you crawled from out of and the next time you show up here, show some respect and I might let you get to know your kids," Vivica asserted. "But right now, you don't deserve to know how precious and important they are."

Eddie shrugged his shoulders and turned his back to leave. He didn't look back for a whole year. Surprisingly enough, he called the house to wish Elijah and Elgin a happy birthday when they turned fifteen—something he hadn't done in years. When he called, Vivica didn't have much to say, she just called the twins and told them to pick up the phone. While waiting for one of them to pick up, she heard Elgin answer, and before she hung up the phone she decided to listen to their conversation. She still didn't quite trust Eddie and wanted to see what state of mind he was in.

"Hey Dad!" Elgin exclaimed when he realized it was his father on the phone.

"Hey son! Happy Birthday!"

"Thanks Dad. When are you going to come get us?"

"El, your mom won't let you come. She doesn't think I'm a good father."

"Huh? How does that make any sense? How can you be a good father if she won't let you come by to see us? Can we come live with you?"

Vivica smirked while listening because she was dying to hear Eddie's answer. She knew he didn't want them. Even if Eddie wasn't addicted to drugs or if he had his own place, he had never been the type to want responsibility. He wiped his hands of his responsibilities years ago. Eddie was immature and always looked for a good time and a short cut. It was a quality she noticed moments after they were married, but didn't want to accept. That's exactly why he was where he was in his life, she thought.

"El, your mom won't let that happen. Plus there ain't no room over here for y'all. Maybe y'all can come spend a weekend or something with me, but I doubt it. Do you know how many times I asked her to let y'all visit me?"

Elgin gasped. So did Vivica, who had her finger on the telephone's mute button.

"I've tried time and time again, to send you all money, to call, to come by—ask Evan. He saw me once."

Vivica couldn't believe how Eddie was lying and was biting her tongue trying not to reveal the fact that she was on the phone. The urge to give Eddie a piece of her mind was rising like the mercury on a thermometer in August. But she didn't.

"Put Elijah on the phone so I can tell him happy birthday, too."

"OK, hold on," Elgin said as he passed the phone to his brother.

"Hello?"

"Hey E, happy birthday son!"

"Hey Dad. What's up?" Elijah said it in a way that Vivica couldn't tell if he was happy to hear from him or not.

"I got something for you and your brother."

"Oh yeah," Elijah said perking up. "What?"

"Well, I'm going to see if I can pick y'all up and bring y'all over here for the day. If your mom let's me."

Vivica smirked.

"Why wouldn't she? It's our birthday. We should be able to do whatever we want."

"Yeah, I know, but you know your mom, she doesn't want me to be

27

with you boys."

"Yeah," Elijah said distantly. "What did you have for us?"

"I got something special since ya'll are getting older."

"What?"

"Well, don't tell your mother, but I got you each a dime bag, and I can teach you how to make a couple of different drinks for this girl I got waiting for you at the house."

"What?!?!" Vivica yelled hysterically into the phone. "What the hell is wrong with you—you sick asshole. You are determined to destroy us aren't you?"

"Viv?" Eddie asked confused.

"You need help bad Edward. I wish I could jump in this phone and break your neck. I want you to stay the heck away from them. Do you hear me? Don't call here anymore! If you do I will call the police and get another restraining order put against you. Do you hear me? I am five seconds from calling them right now—you are Satan. They are fifteen Eddie, fifteen. You want to corrupt them like you? You want to see them dying like you? You want to see them in and out of jail like you? Don't you?"

"Viv, I'm just trying to teach them about the real world..."

Vivica slammed the phone down. She paced back and forth in her room, trying to fight back the tears that were welling up in the corners of her eyes.

"Why?" she yelled, walking with her fists balled up so tightly that they were turning reddish purple from stopping the once easy flow of blood. Vivica waited a few minutes before she went to talk to the twins. By the time she went in their room, they had already left the house. Vivica prayed that they didn't sneak out to go be with their father. She knew in her heart that she was losing them slowly to the curiosity of the streets.

***

Thinking about prayer frightened her sometimes. She wanted to pray that the Lord would watch over them, but didn't have the strength or the true desire to. She didn't know if He would heed her call. After all those years of trying to better herself she had stopped going to church, but she never stopped believing in God. She just no longer wanted to be a part of a congregation. What Elder Roy preached distorted her belief and her views. And though she hated to admit it, she felt like he was a hypocrite.

The Pentecostal Holiness faith was a strict interpretation of Christianity and the Bible that Vivica knew all too well. The denomination focused on perfection and purity of the heart. Besides the beliefs about contraceptives and divorce, there were other rules that different sects of Christianity didn't adhere to. The majority of the rules applied to the women—which she had come to view as an obvious bias.

Vivica had a hard time understanding why women were not allowed to beautify their exterior. Wearing makeup, jewelry, skirts above the knee and sleeves above the elbow was prohibited. Women also could not wear pants—something that Eve dreaded for awhile, because she had to wear thick tights or legwarmers and a thick layer of Vaseline in the winter to cover her tiny legs in below-freezing temperatures. Women also were not aloud to chemically process their hair.

While at Rightway Pentecostal, her life was so unlike everyone else's she knew. She used to spend four to five nights a week in church, if it wasn't Bible Study, it was missionary service or some other sort of service. Eddie had never been a part of the church. He didn't agree with the teachings and he never wanted to be in an environment like that anyway. Vivica realized that, too, was a sign that they were not supposed to be together—even if she eventually did break away from the church.

There was something else strange about Rightway that had bothered her. Although she always felt like she was a part of a huge family while being a member, the relationship Elder Roy had with many of the parishioners baffled her. He was an older man, in his mid-sixties, and he had a wife and two grown children. But there were rumors that he had multiple relationships with some of the single women in the congregation. Vivica hated to listen to any of it, but the rumor about him fathering two children with one of the single mothers at the church, seemed to have some truth to it.

Sister Gayle Milton's sons favored Elder Roy with their round faces and cocoa skin color. But Vivica didn't want to pay attention to any of that gossip, because it was un-Christian to participate in such hearsay. Her distrust for the pastor mounted one evening, when she watched as Elder Roy and Sister Gayle, demurely chatted with one another at the end of a Tuesday night Bible Study. It was something about the way they looked at each other and the way that she smiled that let her know there was something much more than just the Lord that joined them together.

Seeing them chat in that manner may have been the first time Vivica began to doubt her presence in the sanctuary. It wasn't the expansion plan to add-on to the church that never seemed to materialize after a lot of time devoted to prayer and calls of offerings for the building fund. And it wasn't even seeing the pastor buy one Mercedes after another or the many Armani suits, car phones and other technological gadgets he purchased for himself. It was seeing him standing there at sixty-plus-years old, wooing a woman who was half his age that made her skin crawl.

Vivica tried to ignore the feeling tugging at her heart, but knew there was something that just wasn't quite so wholesome about Elder Roy. Why preach about perfection and purity of the heart when your own behavior is soiled? On the day Elder Roy came to see her in the hospital to give her encouragement after Eddie had beaten her like butchered meat, Vivica had finally seen her pastor in another light. The light helped her see that he abused his authority, by misleading the members of his church and twisting interpretations for his personal benefit. If she had to see him at the pulpit again, he might as well have been saying "do as I say, and not as I do," because that's what he represented at that moment.

Vivica's faith would never be the same because of him. Though, she occasionally pulled out her Bible, and her prayer pillow, Vivica had decided to stay away from churches. And she wondered if not being there had an affect on how her children had come to disrespect her.

CHAPTER 4

Iralaun stared at the ceiling watching the reflection from the annoying Christmas lights blinking from the 7-Eleven across the street. The lights were beginning to make her dizzy—so were the constant huffing sounds of her roommate's boyfriend. Although her legs were wrapped around his back, the feeling of Craig's warm sweat dripping across her upper body only annoyed her more. She was bored with their secret relationship. Craig was a good lover, but he was no longer satisfying her; not in the special way people in love felt satisfied. For in love they were not.

At 5 feet 11 inches tall and the complexion of honey, Craig was not hard to look at; Iralaun had always been attracted to guys that looked like Craig. He was bow-legged, and resembled Allen Iverson, especially when he wore his vintage sports jerseys and baseball caps cocked on top of his head. Craig was her exact type. Her roommate, Brea, knew the day she introduced Iralaun to Craig that he was her type. But it never crossed Brea's mind that Iralaun would consider going there.

Iralaun smiled to herself thinking of just how clever she had been veiling she and Craig's secret. But the excitement of sneaking around had evaporated nearly a month to the date that their innocent flirting had turned into spontaneous casual sex. She began to realize that she and Craig weren't on the same page about their romance. It was clear that he wanted more, and Iralaun could see him wrestling with the idea of ending his six month relationship with Brea for her.

Understanding why it was so easy for Iralaun to spread her legs as wide as the wings of a bald eagle taking flight was beyond her own comprehension. There were a lot of things she could care less about, and building and maintaining relationships, be it romantic, business-related or friend-driven, was not on her priority list.

"Hurry up, I think I hear Brea coming?" she said pushing on Craig's chest.

"Wait, I'm almost..." said Craig while thrusting inside of her deeper.

"Hurry," Iralaun said trying harder to push him up. She wasn't really sure if she heard her roommate coming or not, but relief was all she was seeking at the moment.

After the session was over, Craig grabbed his white T-shirt, which laid across the back of a chair in her room and slide into it. The colorless shirt, hanging limp, was the surrender towel she wanted to throw in, to end their affair.

"You are a trip. Brea won't be here for at least another hour." Craig put on his sweatpants and then added, "I don't know why you are trippin'—trying to act brand new. What's up?"

"Nothing," Iralaun said reaching for her clove-flavored cigarette. After dragging on it for a second, she said, "We just need to chill out. I'm starting to feel uncomfortable."

Craig shook his head and headed toward the bedroom door.

"Craig, I'm serious," she said flicking ashes in a glass that sat on her nightstand.

"Right," he said in a sarcastic tone.

"No. We need to cut all this out. I don't feel right about it anymore," Iralaun said shaking her head.

"Of course you don't. The thrill is gone, huh?" Craig asked. "I know your type."

She rolled her eyes, stood up and grabbed her silk robe, which was hanging on a hook on the back of her bedroom door.

"Excuse me," she said tying the robe's belt tighter. She started squeezing past him to go to the bathroom, because he wouldn't move. She had had enough of the game they were playing. It was too risky and wasn't worth it, she thought.

***

Iralaun was dog tired after staying up all night studying for her final exam. She needed a break. Her head was throbbing like a pulsating heartbeat from all of the reading. She knew she needed glasses, but was too lazy to get them. She was a sophomore at Maryland University, studying communications. But at the moment, memorizing the Freedom of Information Act was the last thing on her mind. She wanted to get out of the house for a change of scenery and some fresh air.

Iralaun laced up her Timberlands, threw on her cream wool coat and her matching cream hat and grabbed her purse. She got in her two-door candy apple red Honda Accord and drove up the street toward the mall.

Lately, Iralaun found herself with less and less money to shop.

Although the majority of her tuition and living expenses were paid for from an academic scholarship and some of the money her mother left her, she received most of her spending money from the many men she dated. But ever since she and Craig had become intimate, it was getting harder and harder for her to date other people. Craig always seemed to be around, she thought. "Him and that cocky smirk," she mumbled. She felt like he was blackmailing her in a sense.

Since Iralaun had started to lose interest in their affair, the little trinkets that he offered were becoming harder to accept. Craig was the spoiled younger son of a congressman who lived in D.C. He thought he deserved to have anything he wanted in exchange for helping Iralaun get anything she wanted. At first she loved taking advantage of him, but it was becoming too much for her to handle.

Sometimes he would leave money on her dresser after he left her to slide back in the bed with Brea in the early morning hours. It was on those nights, that Iralaun felt like a whore the most. Over the years, she had become accustomed to accepting gifts from the men she dated, whether they were monetary or material. Before her mother's death, the credo she instilled was that money was the only thing men were good for providing. How could she tell Craig no, when she could always use the money, she reasoned. He even paid her last car note.

Although Iralaun was low on cash, she needed to escape so her mind could begin processing information again. She couldn't wait until her exams were over.

The wind fiercely blew dry leaves toward the car window as she drove down the street. Her defroster wasn't working fast enough so she cracked her rear windows while waiting at a traffic light. She noticed that the driver of the car next to her was trying to get her attention. Iralaun smiled at the handsome hazelnut-colored guy who smiled back at her. With her quick glance, she could see he was clean cut and that he wore thin-framed glasses and had a goatee. She turned back to focus on the street in front of her, but she could see the guy motioning for her to roll down her window in her peripheral. Iralaun loved to flirt, so without hesitation, she did.

"Yes?" she said with emphasis on the letter S.

"How are you doing?"

"I'm OK. But it's cold so, I'm going to roll the window back up."

"Wait, a sec...do you have a cell phone?" The guy asked.

"Yeah, why?" Iralaun asked batting her eyelids. Oh how she loved flirting; it was her favorite sport.

"If you give me your number, I'll call you right now so you won't freeze to death."

Iralaun smiled and began rattling the seven numbers that would put his call through to her phone. And in a moment's time, her phone rang.

"Yeah?" She said answering the phone.

"Is that how you answer the phone?"

"Mmhmm," Iralaun said while looking to her left watching the guy in his silver Maxima. His tires looked wet they were gleaming so much. They happened to be decorated with rims that sparkled and spinned even when his car was stationary. They were hypnotizing her like the scales of a male fish reflecting the light of the sun in the midst of a mating dance.

"Oh, OK. I guess I can get used to that," he responded.

"Oh really? What makes you think we're going to be talking again?"

"You can cut out that tough girl role, because you wouldn't have given a complete stranger your number if you weren't interested in me."

Iralaun was taken aback by his brashness and asked, "What's your name?"

"You sure you want to know?"

"I asked didn't I?"

"My name is Allen and yours?"

"It's Iralaun."

"Nice to meet you Iralaun."

"Nice to meet you, too."

"Where are you on your way to?"

Iralaun frowned, but decided to tell him. "The mall and you?"

"I'm about to go pickup my wife. It's our anniversary and I'm taking her to dinner."

Iralaun's mouth dropped and her butter scotched-colored face became flushed.

"Hello? Are you still there? Iralaun don't hang up I'm just playing," Allen said laughing.

She disconnected the call and made an immediate right down a street she didn't need to get to the mall. Iralaun didn't have time to deal with someone with such a young mind, she thought while rolling her eyes and pursing her lips.

"Playing with me like that," she mumbled. Iralaun began to take a back route to P.G. Plaza mall. When she was within two blocks, she noticed that the guy was in her rearview mirror. "What in the world?" she said startled. She couldn't believe he was still following her.

When she pulled up in the mall's parking lot, she started to park and then realized that he was right beside her. She started the car back up and decided to leave. Then her phone started ringing. She noticed it was the same number Allen had called from, so she didn't answer. She drove back to the main intersection and made a quick left, before she noticed he was still in her rearview mirror.

She was scared and started beating herself up for the dumb thing she had did. What was she thinking giving him her name and phone number, she thought? She continued to drive until she saw, exactly what she was looking for, the police precinct. She started laughing to herself because she could see the expression on Allen's face when he realized what she was up to.

"Guess that will show him," she murmured to herself. She pulled up in a spot and waited to see what he would do. He pulled right up beside her. "This guy is freaking crazy!" she exclaimed.

He rolled down his lightly tinted window and motioned for her to do the same. She shook her head no. Then he motioned for her to answer her phone.

"No!" she yelled.

Then he showed her both of his hands and wiggled his fingers. Then he mouthed, "I'm not married."

Iralaun rolled down her passenger window and yelled, "I don't care!"

"Come on Iralaun, I was just playing. Let's start over."

"Why would you follow me? Are you crazy or something, don't make me lean up against this horn, because I will," Iralaun threatened putting both of her hands in the center of her steering wheel.

Allen started laughing. "Girl, you can do that all you want, but I haven't committed a crime. They're going to think you are crazy."

Iralaun shook her head because she knew he was right, and that she was overreacting. But she couldn't help it; she always overreacted when it came to certain things—especially when it came to trust.

"Let's start over, for real, OK? I'm Allen Richardson and here's my license," he said stretching his arm as far out of the window as he could for Iralaun to read it.

"That picture doesn't look like you," Iralaun said shaking her head.

Then she smiled and said, "Not anymore."

He snatched his arm back in the car to examine the picture. "Do I look better then or now?" Allen said embarrassed. He tugged his face as he looked in the rearview mirror.

Iralaun smiled, but this time her mouth spread so easily that she showed her teeth—something her mother had always warned her about doing when she was growing up. She could hear her mother's voice in her head.

"Letting a man see your teeth when you smile is just like letting him see your panties. You hear me?"

Her mother died of breast cancer when she was fifteen.

"Just don't do it! They think they did something special when they make you smile, like they've won a prize or something. You need to protect your heart child. And the worst thing is to have your heart unprotected. You do that by getting close to a man. You see how your father left me, didn't you."

Iralaun would never forget the stories her mother would tell her about her father. That's all she had were tons and tons of stories of the "trifling man" he was to her. When he left, Iralaun was too young to remember him. She couldn't even remember what he looked like. She only knew a portion of his name and that's because she still had it attached to her own. Fugere.

That's all she knew about him. Her mother never mentioned his first name again after he left her. She only referred to him as "Your Father." Isabella never got over him and she reminded Iralaun every other day about how no good he was and that he left her for a woman who lived on the same block that they lived on. She told Iralaun stories about how her father would drive by while she was struggling up a hill carrying her in one hand and bags of groceries in the other.

Isabella also used to tell Iralaun that one day she might run into a sister or brother while in school because of the multiple relationships her father had with women all over Washington. The real sad thing, her mother said was that he didn't take care of any of them, the women or the children. That disheartened Iralaun and a callous quickly formed around her heart. She didn't understand how a man could produce so many children out of wedlock, and turn his back on them. The thought disgusted her.

"Even animals take care of their own" Iralaun's mother often said. There were more than enough words of wisdom her mother had left with her before she passed. But among the ones that made Iralaun cringe the most was when her mother talked about her having relatives that she probably didn't know about. "Be careful about who you hook up with, because you never even know they might be related to you. And you can't have kids with your relatives, sweetie. That ain't right," she'd say.

"Hello? Are you still there?" Allen was waving his hands back and forth. "I'm starting to think that you really are crazy."

Iralaun blinked and smiled again, but this time with her mouth closed.

"I don't know if we should get involved."

"What? You act like I'm asking you for your hand in marriage. I just want to be able to call you to ask you if you saw that funny thing that just happened on MTV or if it's too cold for you outside or if you heard what happened on the news."

"That's the second time you've said something about marriage," Iralaun said joking.

Allen took a breath and shook his head. "Are you always this analytical?"

"I should be, shouldn't I?"

"I guess. Sometimes people aren't analytical enough so..."
Iralaun nodded.

"Well, you have my number on your phone. I'll let you have your space now. Call me if you want to talk to me. I really would like to get to know you, but if you don't want to, believe me, I'll understand."

Iralaun nodded and proceeded to roll her car window back up.

"Damn. Just like that?" Allen asked. "No bye, no 'I might', no nothing, huh?"

Iralaun smiled again, because he was funny to her.

"OK," he said smiling back. "Drive safely."

"I will." Iralaun backed her car out of the precinct's parking lot and drove down the street in the direction of the mall. She checked her mirror to make sure he wasn't following her. When she saw that he wasn't, it wasn't relief that she felt. It was longing-ness. While she waited at the next light, she immediately saved Allen's number in her cell phone. She knew that she would call him.

While she was driving, her thoughts returned to her mother. Her mother really made her think twice before dealing with men. Isabella told her to check the last names of the guys she dated, because her father was adamant about his children having his last name. "He acted like he was making an army or something," her mother had said.

The only time Iralaun could remember ever getting into an argument with her mother, it was over her father. One day, she exploded, because she was tired of hearing about a ghost that her mother wouldn't let go of. She was a chain cigarette smoker—something Iralaun had become over the years. And even though her mother remarried years before she died, she didn't love her second husband. During her alcoholic binges, she would tell him that he would never amount to anything either. She told him over and over that she didn't love him and never had. She even told him, that she married him for his military health benefits.

It really was no wonder why her second husband didn't show up at her funeral. But her stepfather's absence only infuriated Iralaun more, and her feelings toward men only deepened. It was hard for her to shake those emotions. Iralaun knew that was why none of her relationships with men, ever panned out. As soon as she could sense an emotional attachment brewing, Iralaun disappeared. She concocted excuses for why she didn't want to keep seeing them or she did something that would make them want to stop seeing her. She wanted to avoid the hurt that she felt was eminent.

***

When Iralaun returned home from the mall, she saw Brea and Craig curled up on the sofa as soon as she opened the door. The sight made her sick. She knew first-hand how trifling he was—and to see him affectionate with Brea made her want to throw up. She put the Hecht's bag, full of Christmas holiday specials, on the floor while she took off her coat.

"Hey y'all," said Iralaun before making a beeline toward her bedroom.

"Hey Iralaun, what's up? Come watch the movie with us," said Brea in her usual energetic, former cheerleader tone. "You don't hang out much with us anymore."

"She doesn't, does she?" Craig concurred. "Come on. Chill with us."

"I've been so busy. I got all these end-of-the-semester projects and a final I have to take tomorrow."

"But you just went to the mall?" Brea asked sarcastically.

"OK, OK," Iralaun relented. "What are y'all watching?"

"The Matrix," said Craig, making space for her on the couch. "Here, here's a spot for you."

Iralaun rolled her eyes and plopped down in the seat on the couch next to him. She folded her arms across her chest and didn't even notice that she had begun to tap her right foot. Brea had her feet in Craig's lap and a throw-blanket over her while she watched the movie. The movie-watching activity was going pretty smooth until she felt the warmth of Craig's hand radiate her thigh. He laid it there not long after she sat down. She began to blush, but didn't want to move it—hoping to avoid making the situation a big deal.

Craig smiled as he noticed her discomfort. He could feel the muscles in her thigh flex. The arrogant smile spreading across Craig's face made her want to claw his eyes out. But at the same time her body couldn't ignore the sensations his touch induced and she relaxed. Iralaun hated herself for putting herself in such an awkward position. All it would take was for Brea to look her way, and she would notice Iralaun's light cheeks turning red.

She tried to focus her attention on Keanu Reeves' character, Neo, but Iralaun could feel Craig's gentle hand crawling toward her inner thigh—gently massaging it. His touch sent small shimmers throughout her body. She tried, in vain, to shake her leg enough to get Craig's hand off of her without drawing concern from Brea. But Craig was relentless. His fingers inched closer and closer to her crotch, sending a penetrating heat through her soul. She was starting to tremble and a thin layer of sweat began to form sprinkles on the bridge of her nose.

She pulled the collar of her cowl-neck sweater to conjure up a small draft of wind to cool her off. How could she get up without making a big deal of anything?

"Are you getting hot?" Craig asked her slyly.

Iralaun rolled her eyes, but said "No, this sweater is making my neck itch. I need to take it off." She wanted him to stop touching her, but then again she didn't. What if Brea found out what was going on? Before Iralaun could decide whether she should knock his hand away or leave, Craig succeeded in reaching what he was so determined to touch. As his fingers caressed her, Iralaun exhaled. She was torn between pleasure and guilt.

Although his hand was feeling pleasurable, she couldn't do it. She couldn't just sit there and let that happen, even as callous as she was; she couldn't do that. But Craig continued massaging her until he knew that Iralaun was aroused beyond return. He watched as she bit her lip to hide her arousal. He knew her body, and he could feel her relaxing even more as the pressure of his touch increased. She could feel herself pulsating.

"Ooh," Brea said jumping and lifting the cover up. "Did y'all see that? That was amazing. The special effects in this movie are like that; I can't believe that!"

Craig snatched his hand back, in one swift motion and began rubbing Brea's feet. Iralaun felt disgusted—not only at him, but at herself as well. How could she just sit there and allow her body to be touched like that by him, especially at that moment?

"That was tight! I love this movie," Brea said smiling. "I'm about to get something to drink? Y'all want something?"

Brea started rising to her feet and stretched.

"No, but I'm about to go finish reading," Iralaun said standing up, too.

"You are a party pooper," Brea said nudging her. "Well, OK. Baby, push the pause button until I get back."

Iralaun grabbed her bag and went to her room. She couldn't believe what had just happened. Once again she felt like a whore. How come she couldn't control her body's responses, she thought. She began peeling off her clothes as if she had done something dirty. She went to the shower to get rid of the nasty feeling she had. Iralaun let the hot, thick drops of water pulsating from the showerhead massage her body. Her mind began to drift as she thought about the guy she met earlier. "Allen and his lips," she said while the water covered her body. Then she began thinking about Craig and his hand and the warmth it created between her legs. Before she knew it, she was touching herself.

Later, when she got out of the shower, she noticed that the television glow was gone in the living room. She assumed that the movie had ended while she was in the shower and started walking to her room. It wasn't long before Brea's occasional shrieks and the soft, yet audible thuds from the room behind her began to plague her mind. Iralaun's stomach began to bubble like a frenzied volcano, as the gases in her stomach erupted. She covered her mouth to keep herself from throwing up.

CHAPTER 5

Is the head of the house available?" asked a tall, muscular man in a starched police officer's uniform. He stood in the doorway of Belinda Maxwell's two-story condominium. He wore a stern look on his exhausted face and rested his hand on his gun holster. His shoulders were as broad as the doorway.

"This is my home," Belinda said curiously, her eyebrows arched. "How can I help you?"

The police officer glanced over her shoulder and studied the living room before, speaking. "Is anyone here with you?" he asked.

"What is this all about officer?"

"Is anyone else here with you?" he repeated in a stern voice.

"Officer, can you please tell me what this is all about?" Belinda said placing her left hand on her hip.

"We've received a number of complaints about disturbances and frequent domestic disputes coming from this residence."

"Really?" Belinda tried to sound shocked.

"Yes. Can you tell me what that is about?"

"No, because I would like to know what it is about my self. Frankly, I have no clue as to what you are referring."

The officer frowned before asking if she would mind letting him come in to take a look around.

"Yes, I do mind," Belinda said in a coarse tone.

"What is your name Ma'am?"

"Officer I know my rights, OK. What did you say your name was?" Belinda responded. "And what's your badge number?"

The officer smirked, looked over Belinda's shoulders again, and said, "You have a nice day."

"Yeah, you do the same," she said as she sneered at him.

The officer turned to leave and before Belinda could close the door, the officer scarcely saw the shadow of a tall dark figure in the far corner of a hallway in her unit.

Belinda sighed as she closed the door. It was a sound of relief. She leaned up against the door and exhaled, but when she saw James reaching for his jacket, Belinda panicked.

"You're leaving already?" she asked concerned.

"Yeah, I need to make a run real quick."

"But you look a mess," Belinda said referring to the evidence of the plate of food she threw at him moments earlier. "Are you coming back?" Belinda asked.

James shrugged and looked through the peephole of the door to see if he could see the officer still waiting.

"You're coming back, right?"

The sound of the door closing sounded like a gavel slamming—giving her the unwanted answer to her question.

***

James had not called Belinda in days. She hadn't heard from him since the night he rushed out of her lavish home like a freed hostage. Belinda called him on his cell phone enough to know that it was no accident that he hadn't responded to any of the messages she'd left him. It was becoming quite obvious that he was ignoring her and inside, Belinda knew she couldn't blame him because of the last argument that they had.

When she noticed that James was speaking to her in a sarcastic tone— something he had begun to do quite often—she threw a plate full of pasta Alfredo at him. She knew she'd crossed the line, but Belinda wanted him to explain why he had cancelled a number of their recent dates. She wasn't buying the excuse that he had emergency meetings with his clients. There was much more to his absurd stories and his cynical responses that particular night had pissed her off for the final time.

Weeks earlier, Belinda had begun to worry that James, an attorney she had been dating for several months, was no longer happy with her. He was ten years her junior and at first, she didn't feel that age would ever create a problem. But time and again, she was starting to have trouble holding his attention. James was getting bored with her—even though Belinda did every-thing in her power to keep him interested. She had bought him countless gifts, taken him out to eat, and treated him to Wizards' and Redskins' games within the last few months. She did it all just to please him. She could afford it, she reasoned.

The Honorable Belinda Maxwell made a hefty chunk of change with her position as an associate judge for the D.C. Superior Family Court system. She'd been appointed only the year before after having spent the majority of her young adult life focusing on her career. The whole time she had her eyes on the prize, she never once stopped to notice that she had not married or had bared any children. She wanted success, so she devoted lots of energy toward earning it. She'd dated along the way, but nothing could ever fully come between her and the success she craved.

***

After Belinda spent the entire weekend alone she admitted that the relationship was over between the two of them. They'd dated for only four months, and she knew that he had already lost interest in her. Although initially James found her status as a judge and her wit to be impressive, he never felt like he was adding to her happiness.

Instead, he told her that he felt like a trophy boyfriend—someone who she loved to look at and show off. He was a lawyer that lots of women found attractive, but he didn't feel Belinda respected him because he was much younger. He often told Belinda that their relationship would never progress if she continued to treat him like a child. To add to his frustration, Belinda argued more and more lately over tiny things. And although James was a defense attorney, he never won arguments with her.

Just as Belinda loved picking fights, she loved making up even more; that was one of her favorite parts of being in a relationship. She loved to know that her man knew he didn't want to be without her. It was almost a power trip for her. She knew that their arguing would eventually lead to domestic disturbance calls from neighbors, but she didn't care. For all she had invested in him, that when she wanted James by her side, that he was supposed to rush to her.

And when James said that he was with a client on a night that she'd planned to take him to see a concert at the Kennedy Center, Belinda became heated. Belinda met James while overseeing a case several months earlier. It wasn't that he was overly handsome, but he was attractive in his own little way to her. She loved the way he headed his cases. His confidence exuded him and he demanded attention when he walked in a room—that's what initially attracted her to him. His sex appeal overshadowed his cocky attitude and she was instantly fascinated with the young man.

But she had given up on James and was hurt because the Christmas gift she'd purchased for him a day earlier was certain to win him over.

On the Monday morning before court was to be in session, Belinda checked her mail and her e-mail. She was excited when she noticed that

James had sent her an e-mail invitation that requested her presence at lunch Tuesday. She was so excited and replied that she would be honored to meet with him. Monday couldn't have gone by any slower, for every single hearing seemed to drag on. Belinda tried not to stare at the white clock on the wall in the back of the courtroom during the hearings.

But immediately after she wrapped up for the day, she high-tailed it to Neiman Marcus on Wisconsin Avenue to pick out a new suit that would be perfect for a lunch date. She chose a heather gray two-piece that she thought fit her body perfectly, and a gray and white Picasso-design scarf to accentuate the outfit. She couldn't wait to see James. Thoughts of his smile alone, made her body tingle. She wondered what was on his mind and why it had taken him so long to contact her. The fact that he'd chosen to send her an e-mail, rather than pick up the phone to invite her, didn't bother her. She was just thrilled that he'd reached out at all, and Belinda couldn't wait to apologize for her behavior.

Before she left the store, Belinda called her hair stylist to see if she could be squeezed in for a quick wash and roller wrap. Her stylist couldn't resist the double compensation Belinda offered for the last minute request. And Belinda was thrilled to hop in her chair—she wanted to make sure James was reminded of what he'd missed.

Before rushing to the restaurant a few blocks from the courthouse on Tuesday afternoon, she freshened up and checked her makeup. The swanky restaurant on Pennsylvania Avenue was one of their favorites; she always took James there and it had become one of his favorite mid-day spots, too.

When she walked in, she anxiously told the maitre'd that she was waiting for someone.

"Were reservations made?" he asked.

"I'm not sure, but his last name is Lomax." She clutched her purse and marveled at her freshly painted fingernails as she waited.

"Oh yes, he's here," he responded.

"OK, where?" she said toying with her diamond earrings. She was nervous, yet eager to see James' face.

"He only reserved a table for two," the maitre'd said confused while glancing over his shoulder and back down at the list.

"I know," Belinda said, "Please take me to him."

"You don't understand he's already here with someone. But I'm sure we could pull up a..."

Belinda walked past the maitre'd and began to scan the restaurant.

When she spotted James sitting at a table with a woman, and a bouquet of white tulips lying on the table, her mouth fell to the floor.

"James?" Belinda asked confused.

He turned around surprised to hear the voice that called his name. His face looked like a deer frozen with fear as it stared down the gun-like barrel of a car's headlights. The sound of James' fork dropping must have jerked him back to reality, because he said, "Belinda? Ahhh…"

"Hello, I'm Belinda Maxwell, a friend of James," Belinda said extending her hand to the woman seated.

"Hi, I'm Cassandra Middleton," she said smiling and taking Belinda's hand.

"Nice to meet you," Belinda said perplexed and looking at James for clarity. She looked at Cassandra and noticed her staring at the diamond ring on her engagement finger.

"James, who is this?" asked Belinda as she stood before them confused. She tried to maintain her wavering dignity by lowering her voice.

James stared back at her and then slowly shook his head.

"Why did you invite me to lunch? What is going on?" Belinda asked flustered and desperate for answers.

"What are you talking about?" James said hunching his shoulders. "I haven't talked to you in over a week!"

Belinda jerked her head back, in shock. Then she relaxed her jaw so she could suck in some air. It became difficult for her to breathe. Through stiff lips Belinda said, "That still doesn't explain any of this! Who is she? Are you two dating?"

Cassandra smiled to herself as she watched the scene unfold. She and James had been dating off and on for years and a few months earlier he'd finally proposed to her and confessed that he was ready for only her. They were at the restaurant celebrating her recent promotion at the bank. Cassandra had learned of James and Belinda's relationship through a close friend who saw them at the Baltimore Harbor a couple of months earlier. But Cassandra was no fool, she'd been working on James for years. He was "in training" as she liked to put it and she wasn't going to let him go that easily.

Cassandra's plan was to let him know she knew about their affair without ruining the relationship she had been working so hard to maintain. James was a good catch, despite his measureless affinity for women. When James accidentally left his e-mail account open the last time he'd visited her, she learned even more about the man she loved.

E-mailing Belinda was her clever way of letting James know that what he did in the dark, would come out in the light. She hoped that his chance run-in with the two of them would make him want to straighten up his act. Cassandra didn't like to argue over minor issues. She had a ring now and was ready to get married.

As Belinda stood waiting for an answer, Cassandra pitied her. Meanwhile, Belinda began to feel embarrassed and horrified. She began to feel sick. Her face turned into a sordid scowl that showed James exactly how she felt. Then she turned on her heels and sauntered toward the restaurant's exit. James stood up, with his chair scraping the floor, and reached for Belinda.

"Belinda?" he started. But when she turned towards him, with tears forming in her eyes, all she could see was Cassandra laughing in the background. The crackling sound of her voice felt like pins pricking her heart.

"Do you *know* me?" Belinda asked, her face growing ablaze and the sign of tears rapidly evaporating.

Cassandra took a sip from her champagne glass and winked at Belinda—a smile slowly slinked across her face. Sweat beads began forming on James' brow; for a moment he looked nervous and the confidence that Belinda found so attractive about him had disappeared.

"Yes, I know you," Cassandra said with her neck dancing to the tune her words created.

"How the hell do you know me?"

"I know enough to know that he'll never be yours, because he's already mine. Ain't that right, baby?" Cassandra said laughing and looking at James. "You're looking at four years, right here sister."

James shook his head in disbelief. The moment had no where to go but downhill.

"I knew he was cheating on me—months ago. But never did I realize you would be that old," Cassandra said with a twisted expression. "Baby, what were you thinking?"

James looked sheepishly at Cassandra and then stared at Belinda whose face had formed into a grimace.

"Anywhoo... I thought it was only fitting that you had lunch with us. Thanks to you, he finally realized what he had in me," she said waving her engagement finger at her. Cassandra loved making the two of them feel uncomfortable. She didn't raise her voice because she really didn't enjoy scenes, but how could she resist—Belinda looked vulnerable.

More than that, Belinda was taken aback. She was appalled at what was transpiring and was speechless. She didn't know if she was sleepwalking or hallucinating. She stared at James, then back at Cassandra and exploded with anger.

"You know what? I don't know what you are talking about, but this whole thing is ridiculous!" Belinda yelled while putting her hand up to separate herself from them. "And you..." she said turning to James infuriated. Belinda shook her head in disgust. She paused to gain control of her temper. "Neither of you are even worth my breath! You can have his ass."

Belinda turned hastily and stormed out of the restaurant, with her scarf blowing in the wind her quick exit created. That was the end of her fascination with James.

***

She sat in her car crying before she started her engine. Belinda couldn't believe any of what had just happened. Why did she always have so many problems with men? Why didn't she acknowledge the signs with James? She stared at herself in the mirror recalling the many times she debated getting counseling. But the idea of lying on someone's couch, revealing secrets didn't seem realistic to her.

The drive back to work seemed much longer than usual. She had a lot on her mind. Belinda went through the last two hearings of her day in a daze, eager to get home to curl up under her fluffy goose-feathered blanket. But before she did that Belinda decided to stop at a bar near the courthouse. She was itching to order a shot of tequila—her favorite drink. Drinking during the week was a huge no-no, but the desire to wet her palette with the intoxicating liquid beckoned her.

"Hey judge, you aren't planning to drink and drive are you?" asked Larry, the bartender, when she sat on one of his bar stools. He had a smile on his face but she knew he was truly concerned.

Belinda swirled around, her knees slightly brushing the bar. She put her index finger to her lips. "Shhh," she said. "I just want one shot, Larry."

"Mmhhmm, you know how many times I've heard that tonight?" he said nodding towards the other patrons.

"Really, just one. If I have more than that, I promise I'll get a cab, OK? I promise."

Larry nodded and put the little glass in front of her with a wedge of lemon.

"Can you pass me some salt, Larry?"Belinda sat staring at the glass for a few seconds before she sprinkled some salt on her wrist, sucked the lemon and licked the salt before letting the warm Jose Cuervo fill her throat.

47

There she was again contemplating her decisions. It had to be something about her that made all of her relationships end in such irrational ways, she thought while staring at her glass. She couldn't understand it for the life of her how James could've possibly been seeing someone else the entire time they were dating. It just didn't add up. Belinda glanced up at the clock behind the bartender, and her eyes fell upon the mirror below it. She rolled her eyes at her own reflection, and stared back at the glass.

Belinda first noticed that she had a problem maintaining relationships back when she was a law student at Yale. She didn't know how to be herself when she was with them. She found it easier for to be who they needed her to be. It they needed a friend, she was there. If they needed companionship, she was there. If they needed just about anything under the sun, she was there for the cause. It was a trait she saw in her mother Ingrid. And it was a characteristic Ingrid acquired after years of caring for her father, Frank, who lost his legs in a work-related accident when Belinda was a sophomore in high school.

The sound of the barstool next to her scraping the wooden floor interrupted Belinda's thoughts for a moment. She glanced towards her new neighbor, an older white man with salt and pepper colored hair, and smiled.

"OK, Larry...I might need a cab, because I'm definitely going to need another shot," Belinda said smiling.

Larry winked at her, then fixed her another glass. Belinda toyed with it as thoughts of her parents drifted back into her mind.

While Belinda lived with them in undergraduate school, she watched day after day as her mother struggled to rebuild her father's pride. Frank let everyone around him know that he didn't feel like a man anymore. At first Belinda blamed her father's construction company since it didn't cover his care expenses, even though it happened at work. But later Belinda realized, she couldn't hold the company completely responsible, because her father wanted to wallow in self-pity. And his metamorphosis into a self-destructive and miserable man began to sicken her.

She watched as her mother became her father's nurse—feeding him and caring for him as if he was an invalid. Ingrid even did simple things like reading the paper for him, shaving his beard, and taking him for occasional walks around the block—all things her father could do if he tried. Although he lost his legs, he was still capable of caring for himself. But Frank never tried to do anything; it was as if progress was the enemy. Eventually, all of his friends stopped visiting and even his family members stopped calling as often. Her father's spirit was like that of a caged bird.

And she resented him. Her mother often chastised Belinda's own lack of visiting, but she didn't enjoy watching her parents interact. Belinda thought about Christmas approaching as she sucked the last few drops of tequila from the glass. She didn't want to go, but it was one of the few visits she made during the year.

She signaled Larry for another shot.

"I'll buy her next one," a thick voice from Belinda's left offered.

"No, thank you," Belinda said without looking up. "I only want one more."

"Let me pay for it," the voice said again.

Belinda turned and looked at the person who was speaking to her. The voice was coming from the police officer that had knocked on her door several days earlier.

She smiled. He was in plain clothes, but she recognized his face and his broad shoulders. She shook her head again and turned back to the empty glass in front of her.

"Do you remember me?" he asked.

"I hope you don't remember me," she said slightly embarrassed. "Can I have your badge number now?"

The man smiled and asked, "Can I finally have your name?"

She smiled easily. "It's Belinda. But you still aren't going to get my last name," she said while raising her eyebrows.

The man smiled, extended his hand and said, "Officer St. James. But call me Kevin."

She rolled her eyes at the mention of the name James.

"What's wrong?" he asked.

"Nothing," Belinda said shaking her head. "Are you still going to pay for my drink?"

"Sure. Larry, get her another shot will you, and get me a Hennessey on the rocks?"

"You come in here often?" Belinda asked recognizing his use of the bartender's name.

"Only when I've had a hard day." The peanut butter-colored man took a deep breath and reached for a cigar case in his coat pocket. "I spent all afternoon over at the courthouse for one of my cases."

"Hennessey, huh?"

"Yeah. It's a hard drink for a tough man," he said smiling.

"I guess. That's what my father's addicted to."

Silence fell between them and Belinda took her time with her glass. For two turbulent years her father drank like a sailor after his accident. Frank developed self-esteem problems and turned to Hennessey, rather than his family, for comfort. Her parents became distant then—as if something had formed in between the two of them. The distance hung in the air like a stale odor for years. Her father no longer surprised her mother with calla lilies, her favorite flower, and she cooked fewer carrot cakes, his favorite dessert.

Ingrid went beyond the call of duty trying to please Frank because she yearned to make him feel loved, wanted and needed. And the only thing that soothed his soul was Hennessey.

Kevin nursed his drink awhile before he said, "So what brings you here?"

"A long hard day."

"Really? You, too? Couldn't be no worse than whatever it was you were arguing about the other night," he joked.

She smiled. But then her smile saddened.

"You want to talk about something?" he asked in a sincere manner.

Belinda shrugged her shoulders and shook her head. "I don't know. I think I'd rather just forget the whole day. Maybe even forget the whole past week. Hell, why not even the past few months."

Kevin smiled, "It must be something really wrong for you to want to forget that much time. I almost hate to ask what happened. And it better not have anything to do with a relationship. Please don't tell me that. It would be so trite."

Belinda leaned back and inhaled deeply, trying to control her instant resentment. "Well, excuse me Officer St. James, but...yes, it's over a relationship. I guess your life is perfect."

He sucked his teeth and took a swig of the final swallow in his glass. He asked for another drink before responding."You are too gorgeous to be having any sort of problems in that arena. What wise person would let someone like you fall out of their good graces?"

She was pleased with his response, but still rolled her eyes. "You are saying that because you don't know me. Believe me if you did, you might feel the exact same way the last person felt."

"All I know is, if someone was with you for a few months, there had to be something about you he couldn't resist. Now why you two aren't together anymore is really none of my business," Kevin asserted. "But all I can say is you don't look happy."

Kevin was right, she wasn't. Belinda felt the sudden need to glance at his left hand to see if he was married and was surprised to feel disappointment wash over her when she saw that he was indeed wearing a wedding band.

"Are you happy?" she asked.

"I'm comfortable, I guess," Kevin said. Then he took a long pause before saying, "Things could stand to be better, but hey...I make the best out of it. I get what I put in."

Belinda nodded, and then she leaned forward to ask Larry to call her a cab.

"I'm about to go on home now. I think I've had enough. Thank you for the drink," Belinda said sliding a few dollars on the table to cover her tab.

"I don't mind taking you home," Kevin said.

"Now what sense does that make? You've been sitting here drinking right along with me, Mr. Officer."

He smiled and said, "I've only had a drink and a half. I'm sure my tolerance level is a lot better than yours."

"Mmhhmm."

"Let me take you home. I mean, it's not like I don't already know where you live."

Belinda smiled and then told Larry not to worry about the cab. Kevin smiled and put some money on the bar, and then helped Belinda into her coat.

"Does this mean I get to ride in a police car?"

"No not this time. I'm off duty."

"Dag," Belinda said and burped.

"Ahhh—no you didn't just do that?"

Belinda laughed and covered her mouth, "Oops." She took a few steps and noticed that she was leaning on Kevin for support. Maybe she had had too much to drink she thought before letting another burp leave her mouth.

"You are nasty," he said opening the door of his sports utility vehicle to help her into the front seat.

"Not as nasty as I can be," Belinda said with a slight hint of seduction.

Kevin shook his head and closed her door. While he walked around to the other side, Belinda noticed that she was a little woozier than she thought she was. Having Kevin take her home was a wise decision, because she knew she wouldn't have made it safely on her own.

He got into the truck and started the engine. It was so cold outside, he waited awhile to let the car warm up before turning the heat on.

"So are you going to tell me about this man?"

"I'd rather not talk about him anymore."

"OK, well...let's talk about what you do. What do you do for a living? You are sure dressed to the hilt."

"I'd rather not talk about that either."

"Hmm...why is that?"

"Let's talk about you."

"OK? What about me?"

"How long have you been married?"

"Ahh...about five years."

"Really?"

"Yep."

"Any kids?"

"No, not yet."

"How old are you?"

"33."

"Oh, I didn't know you were that young."

"That young? How old did you think I was?" Kevin asked shocked.

"I was going to say about 37, 38."

"Damn. You weren't even going to lie to me, huh? Thirty-seven or 38 — good gracious," Kevin smiled. "I guess it's all these years on the street, chasing bad people into gutters and what not. I guess it catches up to you over the years."

Belinda nodded. "You still are nice looking. You just have a 'Been there, Done that' kind of look."

"Well, Geez. I don't know if that makes me feel any better Belinda."

"I didn't mean it that way. I guess I mean, a mature look," Belinda said laughing.

"That could mean two things. Usually the only people who want to look mature for their age are teenagers, and I know that's not what you meant."

They both laughed effortlessly.

"How old are you, if you don't mind?"

"Oh I don't," Belinda smiled and rolled her eyes at the same time. "Because I look damn good for my age. I'm 38, thank you very much."

"You work out, huh?" he teased.

Belinda rolled her eyes and laughed. "So tell me about your wife?"

"Well," Kevin paused. "To be honest...she and I are separated right now. We haven't been together for about nine months."

"Really?" Belinda could feel her soul smiling. She quickly considered the possibility of his availability. "Why is that, if it's OK for me to ask?"

Kevin took a long deep breath before sharing. "It's this job."

Belinda nodded.

"And I don't know what to say, because we met while I was working. She knew what I did," Kevin said finally pulling his Explorer out of the parking space. "But she's not comfortable with it, never really has been."

"Right."

"She's scared for me. D.C. isn't the easiest place to be a cop, you know?"

"Yeah, I know."

"And to be honest, that's why we still don't have any kids."

"Why is that? I don't understand."

"She said she doesn't want to end up being a single parent."

"Wow. That's hurtful."

"Hell yeah it is."

"But...at the same time, I understand where she's coming from."

Kevin turned and looked at Belinda puzzled.

"Well, just hear me out a second. I know I'm a little drunk but...my reasons are valid."

"OK, I'll give you fifteen seconds to explain yourself," he teased.

"Well...two things. I didn't grow up in a single-parent home. In fact, both of my parents still live together. But just before I moved out of their house, it changed from having two people who was there for me, to there being only one parent there. Remember earlier, when I commented about my father being addicted to Hennessey?"

Kevin nodded.

"Well, that's part of what I mean. He was there, but he wasn't...so it was just like having one parent. And that's a totally different feeling than the warmth of having two parents constantly showering you with love; encouraging you and taking care of your needs. Just the things you learned from two different sides of the fence."

"I understand the importance of having two parents raise a child. What does that have to do with what my wife said?"

"Kevin, I'm a judge down at the same courthouse you were at all day today."

He looked surprisingly at Belinda, but turned back to watch the street.

"You would be surprised at the different cases I see on a day-to-day basis. It's heartbreaking. I've had to work on cases involving not only single-parent families, but cases where police officers have lost their lives during a crime due to something an adolescent did, who probably came from a single-parent household. It's a cycle. I have seen first hand the affects of it, to both the families and the children. I have had to tear families a part because of the lack of nurturing and time spent toward raising their kids."

Kevin nodded. The car instantly filled with silence. Belinda was tipsy, but she knew what she was talking about Kevin reasoned. They rode in silence toward her neighborhood. Kevin glanced over at Belinda and noticed that she had nodded off to sleep before they arrived at her building. The reflection of the city lights dancing off of her skin looked beautiful. He didn't want to wake her when he pulled up in front of her tower, but he did.

He offered to walk her up to her apartment door, but Belinda politely refused. Kevin leaned into the doorman and asked him to make sure she got in her unit safely. She reached into her purse to give Kevin a business card, and he dug in his wallet to give her one of his.

"Thanks for the ride."

"No...thank *you*. I enjoyed talking to you. Be safe now."

She smiled and waved goodbye to him before walking into the tower.

CHAPTER 6

The twins officially dropped out of high school during their sophomore year; they weren't going anyway. Vivica realized for the first time that she had no control over them when the school's security guards caught them with two pounds of weed sitting on the roof of their high school building in the beginning of the school year. She didn't know what to do and was tired of defending them when they defied her rules.

Elijah and Elgin were unruly, disrespectful and had even been caught twice over the past year driving stolen cars. Since Elijah and Elgin were minors, nothing ever really happened to them, except being placed on probation. Even the threat of being sent to a juvenile detention facility didn't haunt them. In fact, it seemed they'd stay in trouble just to get on Vivica's nerves.

Sometimes Vivica felt like a hostage in her own home. She was certain that they stole money from her purse a few times, but she never could prove it. She began to carry her cash on her—safety-pinned to her bras. She also put outer-entry locks on some of the bedroom doors. Vivica had no trust in them. The older they got, the more they began to remind her of their father, Eddie.

Every time they did something wrong or illegal, she made sure they knew that it reminded her of their father. The twins hated when she did that. It seemed as if they never did anything right and it only pushed them away from her more. Eventually, Elijah and Elgin did things just to see her upset. It was revenge for keeping them away from their father all those years, they reasoned.

Together the two boys terrorized Vivica's home, her other children and the neighborhood. The twins constantly created mini-wars in the house between themselves and Evan and Eric. Harassing them was their pass-time and fighting came easy to them.

Elijah and Elgin were identical twins. They, both had naturally muscular bodies like that of boxers. Vivica knew they inherited that from their father. Though Elijah was the oldest by six minutes, on the outside looking in, most people thought Elgin was the oldest because of his aggressive personality. He also edged his older brother by a couple of inches in height.

He'd always been a little larger that Elijah. Family members often joked that Elgin pushed Elijah out of Vivica's womb first, just to make sure it was safe enough for Elgin to come out. And when they were really young, Elijah would always hide and save his food whenever he was given any. It was as if, Elijah was having flashbacks of being in the womb and was afraid of not getting enough food. Though he was born healthy, Elijah was born two whole pounds lighter than his brother—and never seemed to quite catch up. In reality, that was how most people could tell them apart when they stood together.

Both teenagers wore their hair either braided in plaits or cornrows. Often time they would just let their straight hair hover over their heads wildly. Their sister, Eve, liked to tease them about how much they looked like the Treasure Troll dolls when they wore it like that. But they didn't care, nor did Vivica. About the only time they had anything kind to say to her was when they wanted her to braid their hair.

She tried to always make time for that, because she felt that was a time for them to talk, if only for an hour or so a week. She knew they didn't have a choice but to sit there and listen to her shun their nasty attitudes and uncontrollable behavior. It was the brief moment she had to offer them direction and encouragement. Vivica saw it as an even trade off.

But for the most part, Elijah and Elgin opted to leave their hair in huge wild Afros or tied up in ponytails to avoid those types of conversations. They didn't want to be coached.

Once when Vivica was at her rope's end, she tricked the twins by having them escorted to a youth mental institution. She felt that they needed help that she could not offer. The institution was the only solution she was offered after speaking to school counselors and doctors from her hospital job. Professional psychological help would provide a better assessment of their condition, she was told. Vivica needed help because she couldn't understand what was going on with them. Why couldn't they just act like normal children their ages?

The doctor she worked closest with at the hospital, recommended the place in Montgomery County. It was Vivica's last resource. She tried to get her own two brothers, Vince and Vaughn, to talk some sense into them months earlier. But after Vivica realized that the few conversations they had with the boys weren't getting through to them, she agreed to send them to the institution for help.

Elgin and Elijah never saw it coming. They were committed on a Sunday afternoon after spending the day with their uncles. Vince and Vaughn took them to play basketball that afternoon at a recreation center not too far from the institution. After shooting hoops, Vince said he needed to visit an old friend since he was in the area and they all went inside the building. It wasn't long before the twins realized their Uncle Vince didn't have a friend in the hospital, but that they were going to be committed. They became furious. Elgin cursed everyone in the room, his words sounded the way venom would if it had a sound. He and Elijah threw chairs at the security like hand grenades on the battlefield.

After ten minutes of fighting, they were restrained and placed in separate rooms to calm down. Vince and Vaughn couldn't believe the instant change in their behavior, and had no idea just how much their sister was going through with them. They never acted like that in front of them. For the first time, they realized that they really needed help. They agreed that the institution was the best place for them.

But the twins weren't in the facility for more than two weeks before Vivica agreed to let them come back home. She was never comfortable with the idea of them being there. Though she noticed a sense of peace at her house while they were gone, the stories they told Vivica about their experiences were something from a wild movie. One story they told included there being a guy who walked around all day in raggedy underwear with his hands stuffed in them, singing R. Kelly songs. Elgin told her a story about a guy who sat in a chair all day reading the newspaper in a way that blocked eye contact with everyone.

Elijah couldn't get over the girl who was in the building a few feet across from theirs. The girl would stand up in the window naked for hours on end, asking for someone to "play with her candybox," he told Vivica. They simply didn't want to be there anymore and promised to change if Vivica let them come home.

Deep down she knew they weren't mentally ill. The doctors at the facility ended up confirming that the twins' mental levels were not in the same range as the other patients. The doctors pointed out signs of depression, but nothing that couldn't be altered with further counseling. So she agreed to have them released back into her custody, but she used the facility as a threat to the twins, if they started acting up again.

When Elijah and Elgin came home, they surprised her by being respectful for a few days. But soon after they were home, the profanity and the disrespect started again. And this time, they had new ammo; they despised her for committing them to the hospital and cursed her forever even thinking of such a thing.

Vivica had given up on them, admittedly so. Her boys were too young for her to put out of her house legally. When she would call the police on them for different things that they did like fighting their younger brothers or kicking down a back door, the police always said that it wasn't anything they could do, but maybe make them spend the night in jail. And she did that once, when Elgin raised his hands at her. The police told her that there was nothing they could do unless her life felt threatened.

In an effort to maintain the slightest amount of control, Vivica put the new locks on several of the rooms in her house. Evan and Eric, who shared a room, had a lock on their door. Eve had a lock and so did Vivica. It worked for awhile, but then they would come in the rooms when they were behaving, and then refuse to leave when Eric or Evan wanted them out. It became a broken-record type of argument. Day-in and day-out...the same old song. "Get out of my room. Get out of my room!" It drove Vivica even crazier.

She was on the verge of a nervous breakdown. Between the stressful-type of job she had as being a nurse, working late and 12-hour shifts to coming home to put out even more fires, Vivica was becoming mentally and physically unstable. Everybody seemed to need her and it drained her energy and suffocated her spirit.

***

The sun was beginning to set, and some of the streetlights were starting to illuminate the dimming streets. Elijah and Elgin stood on the corner near the payphone adjacent to the corner store at the end of their block—one of their usual hangout spots. They were hanging out with a few of their neighborhood friends joking and smoking cigarettes, when one of their frequent customers, Day-Day, scurried up to them as nervous as a cat doused with water. He wore an old, shredded, Long John shirt underneath a red Champion tank-top. He also had on an army green workman's jumpsuit with the top-half of the jumpsuit folded down and tied around his waist like a belt.

"Hey y'all, what's up?" Day-Day asked bopping to a beat in his head. "Can I get a jack?"

"Man what I look like giving you one of my cigarettes? You better get out of here with that!" Elijah barked. "Don't be asking me about no bullshit!"

Elgin shook his head and blew some smoke in Day-Day's face. All of the guys started laughing at the facial expression Day-Day was making. He was middle-aged, but had the energy of a teenaged boy, bouncing around in front of them. Picking on Day-Day was one of their many pass-times. He was a hyperactive, slim guy who was strung out on the crack they sold him just about every other day.

"Come on Man, why y'all gonna do me like that?" he asked.

Elijah tapped Elgin on his arm to get his brother's attention, and said "You know you don't get nothing around here for free."

"Man, I don't have no money," Day-Day sang. He bent down a little and squeezed his legs together as if he had to use the bathroom and was trying to hold himself.

"That ain't my problem," Elijah said shaking his head and looking across the street at some girls walking by.

"OK, OK. What y'all want me to do?" he said bouncing around to each of the guys standing there. "What you want me to do, I'll do anything. Y'all know me. I'll go hard for you."

They started laughing and shaking their heads at Day-Day.

"Aiight, shorty. I got one for you. I bet you won't go lie down on the yellow line in the middle of street," said Chico, one of the guys who grew up around the neighborhood with the twins.

"Man that ain't shit, I can do that easily. Watch," he said pimping toward the busy Florida Avenue thoroughfare. The spunk in his step reeked the confidence of only a crazy person or someone addicted to drugs. Everybody doubled over laughing at Day-Day as he strutted.

The skinny man extended his arm to stop traffic as cars whizzed by blowing their horns and as drivers cursed at him to get out of the way. The guys continued to laugh and bait Day-Day as they saw him crouch down in the middle of the rush-hour traffic to lay his back on the yellow double-stripes that divided the street. Cars continued to blow their horns as a few had come pretty close to hitting him.

Then Day-Day yelled, "Is this long enough? Can I get up now?"

"Naw. Now you gotta sing the first line of the 'Thong Song'," said Elijah through hearty laughs.

Day-Day began to sing at the top of his lungs all the words he could remember:

Ooh that dress so scandalous
And you know another nigga can't handle it

All the guys on the block laughed uncontrollably at Day Day. When he got to the chorus, the group couldn't stand it any more. They were chuckling so hard that tears were coming to some of their eyes. Elgin told Day-Day to get up, then took one of his cigarettes out the pack and waved it at the eager man.

The jittering guy came rushing up to get his reward. "You're a crazy dude," Elgin said while giving him the cigarette.

"Thanks. If y'all ever want me to do anything else, just let me know. I can do it all for you. I can wash cars, polish shoes, run to the store for you, anything. Just name it," he said.

"Anything?"

"Yep, anything."

"Aiight. Go get me a six-pack of MGD real quick," Elgin said nodding towards the corner store.

"Shit, I'll do it," Day-Day said. "You gonna give me some money?"

"Naw. Handle that! You a pimp."

"That's right, I'm a pimp and I don't give a fuck! I'll steal that shit."

"Yeah, if you do that, I'll give you the rest of these," he said holding up the cigarette box.

"Yeah, I can do that. No problem. I'll be right back."

All the guys started shaking their heads at Elgin. He smiled while Day-Day turned to strut into the corner store.

"That nigga would do anything for nothing. He's so stupid," Chico said.

"I know, right? If he can steal some beer, why won't he just go ahead and steal himself some cigarettes?" Elijah asked laughing.

"Probably 'cause he gotta get that from behind the counter; he ain't really trying to go that hard. But he's still dumb as shit," Elgin said puffing on his cigarette.

But before he could even exhale, Day-Day came sprinting out of the store like Superman with two bottles of beer in his hands. He was running so fast that his Wizards' basketball cap flew off of his head and landed on the ground. They all started laughing as they saw the Korean storeowner standing in the doorway cursing Day-Day out—demanding that he come back with the beer. But he was long gone.

They all laughed.

"That nigga sprinting like shit!" Elgin said laughing.

"Hey, what's up El?" said a voice off in the distance. "Can I holla at you for a second?"

"Yeah, hold up," Elgin said walking toward the man standing in the dark crevices of the shaded oak tree. He knew who it was and shook his head. "What's up Eddie?"

"Oh, you still gonna keep calling me Eddie, huh?" his father asked.

"Psst. Hell yeah...I know you don't think I'm gonna call you dad,"

Elgin said smirking. "Just tell me how much you want, with your crack-head ass."

"Give me a twenty son."

Eddie stood impatiently before his son, with tattered clothing and matted hair. He shivered as the cool night's breeze crept over him.

"Don't call me that," Elgin said rolling his eyes. "Just give me your money."

Eddie looked at the ground and then put his hands in his pockets searching for the money.

"Give me the money, Cuz!"

"OK, here's five, ten…and another seven."

"What is that—$17? That ain't enough!" he yelled. "You better get that shit out of here."

"Come on El, hook me up."

"Hook you up? Nigga, you better go head with that bullshit," Elgin snapped.

"Aiight, aiight. What about $15 worth?"

"I only have twenties and up."

"Spot me three dollars son."

Elgin looked outraged and he squared his body up. "Spot you? What the fuck do I look like? You ain't never did shit for me and now you want me to spot you?"

"Yeah, please son…I need this."

It took Elgin one swift punch to Eddie's chin to knock his father to the concrete.

"Don't your bitch-ass ever call me son again! You ain't my fucking father."

Elgin threw the crumpled $17 on Eddie's chest, turned around and walked back toward his friends. None of them had seen what had just happened, but wouldn't have been surprised if they did.

"What's up? What's up? Did Day-Day come back yet?" he asked slapping hands with some of his friends before stuffing his throbbing hand in his coat pocket.

"Naw," some of them responded.

"That nigga ain't coming back, he probably tried to sell them joints to somebody," Elijah said.

"What y'all getting into tonight?" Elgin asked.

"Aww…nothing but the same old same old. 'Smoking that weed, feeling fine, got me a forty and a fat ass dime,' " Reggie sang the lyrics of an old school Go-Go song.

"Yeah, I hear you," said Elgin. "What about y'all?"

"I'm chillin, too. Got this girl, I'm about to break off in," said Samuel, one of the twins' best friends. Everybody called him Black, though.

"Black, you ain't got no girl," Elijah said laughing. "Nigga always faking, talking about he got a girl."

"Like shit I don't," he said cupping the crotch of his pants.

"Shiiit…whatever Cuz. Who would fuck your black ass?"

"Whatever. I'm sexy muthafucka. Y'all know dark skin is in again. Don't be jealous nigga. Bitches be loving me," he said smiling and grinding his hips.

"Who's the girl?" Elgin asked.

"You know Cat-eyed Kisha that live up the block."

"Ugh, you going to fuck her nasty ass?" Elijah asked. "That girl done been with half the damn neighborhood."

"All the more better to sleep with. The pussy ripe then," Black said chuckling. "And that means I don't have to teach her ass how to suck my dick either."

They all started laughing.

"You ain't right. Just wear a rubber nigga," Elijah said shaking his head. "I'm about to go in the house. It's cold as shit out here."

"Yeah, I'm feeling that," Reggie said. "I'm about to bounce, too."

"Wait," Black said. "I forgot to tell y'all somebody was around here the other day asking about that nigga Dante'."

"Man fuck that nigga," Elgin said.

"For real?" Elijah asked concerned.

"Yeah. Y'all might want to stay low for a minute, for real."

Elijah drew a puff from his cigarette before plucking it in the street and turning to look at his brother.

"Man forget that. This is my neighborhood," Elgin said. "Don't nobody tell me what the fuck to do. I ain't scared of no muthafuckin' police!"

"Yeah. I ain't going no where. Believe that," Elijah agreed with his brother.

"Yeah, well whatever. I'm about to go get some ass," Black said turning to go down the street. "I'll holla at y'all later."

Elijah and Elgin walked down the block towards their house. Once they turned the corner, they saw a police squad car double-parked by their mother's car. The blue and red lights were flashing and they could see two figures standing at their front door talking to her.

"Man what you want to do?" Elijah whispered.

"Shit, I don't know. Just stand right here for awhile," Elgin said turning to face Elijah. "I need to think."

"OK, think of something Man, quick," Elijah said stuffing his hands in his pocket and shifting his weight from left to right.

"I'm trying to...if you'd just shut the fuck up."

"Aiight. Calm down."

"OK. Turn around and we'll walk back around the corner," Elgin said.

"OK."

"Hey wait a minute!" one of the police officers yelled. "You two...come here!"

The twins darted down the street and back around the corner. They dipped into an alley and around another corner. Before the police officers could even get out of the front yard, the twins had already hopped on a bus.

"What we gonna do now?" Elijah asked putting a dollar and ten cents worth of change into the meter.

"I don't know, E. I don't know. I need time to think." He put his money into the machine and followed Elijah down the aisle. "You always asking me what to do. Like you can't think for your self."

They walked to the back of the bus and sat down to catch their breaths. They sat on the last row on opposite sides, staring out of the windows. Elijah rolled his eyes. He knew Elgin was right, he did always look to him for direction. But he had come to look up to his twin brother in a sense. Elgin always seemed to have the answers and he knew what was best for them in situations like this. After all the things they'd been involved in, Elgin usually had come up with the plan first. But he never looked at himself as a follower. Elijah just didn't want to make the wrong decision.

"Well, we can't ride the bus all day. And we have to go back home, eventually."

"I can't believe this shit!" Elgin yelled.

"I know. Over that dumb ass Dante'."

People on the bus stared at them because they were talking so loud.

"What the fuck you looking at?" Elgin said to a teenaged girl sitting near the back of the Metro bus.

She rolled her eyes and turned up the volume on her CD player. An older man wearing a brown Stetson hat rattled his newspaper and cleared his throat. The bus driver stared in the rearview mirror at them because of their language and their loud tone. She could sense trouble. Elijah put up his middle finger at her and turned back to his brother.

"El, I need you to come up with one of your plans, Man."

Elgin rolled his eyes and leaned his forehead up against the window. He fell into a light sleep. Elijah stared out of the window as the bus carried them further and further away from familiarity. When the bus reached the end of its route, the bus driver told them they had to get off the bus.

"Aiight," Elijah said. "When's the next bus?"

"This is the last bus for the night," said the round-faced woman. "The next one doesn't pull out of here until five in the morning."

"Oh," Elijah said shaking his head. Then he reached over to wake up his brother. "El, wake up. We gotta get off."

"Are you two boys alright?"

"Yeah," Elgin said while sitting up. He wiped his eyes then started walking towards the front of the bus. "Where are we?"

"In Hyattsville," the bus driver said curiously. She tucked a few of her gray-hair strands behind her ear and waited for the other boy to get off the bus.

"Is that Maryland or Virginia, because I know we aren't in Kansas anymore?" Elijah said laughing.

"Maryland, baby." She was confused. How could they not know where they were or where they were heading? "Do you all know where you are going? Or are you supposed to meet somebody?"

"Old lady, we are aiight, OK?"

"Old lady? I'll let that slide. It's late and I just don't want you two to be out here confused and lost. Do you want to call somebody? I can give you some change."

They both shook their heads to say no thanks and then walked off the bus.

"Look. Have you ever been to Maryland University before?"

They both shook their heads no.

"What about Prince George's Plaza?"

"Oh yeah, P.G.? I know where that is."

"Oh OK...well it's about six blocks up that street," the bus driver said pointing.

"Aiight," they both said walking down the steps.

"You are welcome," the bus driver said sarcastically.

"Oh, thanks," Elijah said.

"Some rude little boys," she mumbled to herself as she turned the bus around to go back to the station's hub. On her way, she checked to make sure she had the bottle of Hennessey for her husband, because she knew he would be mad if she'd forgotten to bring it back. It was the day before Christmas Eve, and she still had a lot of shopping to do. Thank God she had the next day off, she thought. The traffic will be horrendous, but it's the only day she can do it.

CHAPTER 7

Iralaun called Allen early in the day to say hello. And she was glad she did because they ended up spending the entire day together doing nothing but talking, drinking hot chocolate and playing board games. Brea had gone home to New Jersey for the holidays and they had the entire apartment to themselves.

Craig came by the apartment several times since Brea left, but Iralaun didn't entertain him either time. After running errands or shopping, Iralaun noticed Craig had been by because he slipped "I miss you" cards under the door, never addressing it to anyone.

Once he even had some pink roses delivered—again not having it addressed to anyone in particular. Iralaun couldn't believe Craig had the nerve to sign his name each time. His cockiness was over the top. It was obvious he didn't address it to anyone in case Brea returned early or something.

Iralaun dated Allen for a week before she decided to let him come to her apartment—a long time in her book. She called him the night after they met and Allen seemed more than happy to hear from her, especially because of the attitude she gave him.

Allen was a graduate student at Maryland University; he was working on his master's of business administration degree. He had a few more courses to take before he would graduate. Allen also worked as an assistant manager at the Foot Locker Room in P. G. Plaza. He was an only child, just like she was, and grew up in Fort Washington, Maryland.

Iralaun loved that Allen was over six feet tall, since she was 5'9. And she thought his glasses made him look adorable and professional, for some reason. She knew that he wasn't a materialistic guy, even though his car was a little flashy. She was usually attracted to men who were trendy. During the times that they hung out together, he wore long-sleeved plain t-shirts that had social slogans on them like "Love Peace Life" or "Think". Iralaun found herself intrigued by him. He was a different character for her.

Allen found the mole on Iralaun's chin to be endearingly attractive. She was graceful, yet confident. He knew she was guarded, and that attracted him. He loved the challenge of proving he wasn't the average guy. Allen knew she was bitter towards men from several of the conversations they'd had, and he wanted to be the one guy who didn't live up to her low expectations. Besides, what did he really have to lose, he thought.

Allen's aspirations of opening his own store one day, was interesting to Iralaun, although he had no idea what he wanted to sell, yet. The two of them spent most of their time talking about what they wanted to do after they finished school and she told him she wanted to become a news producer for a major broadcast network.

One of the most astonishing things Iralaun noticed about Allen up to that point was that despite the amount of time they spent together, he had yet to touch her—not even an accidental brush up or anything. The fact that they hadn't even hugged yet, was flabbergasting to her. She wasn't used to that with the men she'd previously dated. She was mildly surprised, but knew that it must've been a part of his game.

But she still found it to be both strange and unique not to know what his kisses felt like or even what it would feel like to touch his hand. She wondered what kind of hugs he liked to give—gentle and cool or strong and warm. She wondered what his skin smelled like and what texture it was.

People were always in a rush to do all of those things, and the fact that Allen hadn't even ventured there yet, left her eyes opened. She hated admitting that to herself. Deep down, she knew there was a method to the game he was playing on her. But for a change, she didn't want to dwell on it, because she liked him.

Allen made her smile and made her think about a lot of things. They could talk about anything from politics to Play Station, or from childcare issues to cartoons and never missed a beat. She was really in to him. He never tried to speak over her when she was trying to make a point and even when they disagreed about something, they could move on without arguing. She knew that she would learn a lot from him.

The night after they first went out to dinner, Iralaun woke up in a drenching sweat at three o'clock in the morning. She could still remember every scene of the dream she'd had. But instead of reaching for the phone to see if Allen wanted to come over, she closed her eyes and squeezed her pillow. She knew that as soon as she decided to be with him intimately, things would change. They always did. She would become bored—not really listening to him anymore, or anticipating seeing him.

Iralaun decided that first night, that she would take the time to get to know Allen. She wanted to be patient with him. Why not, she thought. She didn't have much to lose.

At nineteen, she had been with more than enough different men to know what she'd be missing out on. Iralaun couldn't even remember half of their names. Sex wasn't a big deal for her. It was merely an act shared between two friends. She had been having sex since she was eleven. The first time she had sex, the 16-year-old she was with, thought that she wasn't a virgin, because she responded like a veteran.

Sometimes she wanted to blame the theory that she had formed about men on her father. She compared them to animals. Not just dogs, like most women did, but specifically to the male species in general. Because of her outlook on them, she was well over the fact that men would be tempted to copulate with as many different females as possible in order to ensure the existence of their breed—an example of that would be having "one bull for two dozen cows," Iralaun reasoned.

That's part of the grounds for why Iralaun tried to avoid getting caught up emotionally with men. She accepted their role and maintained a reasonable amount of distance from them in relationships. Besides, she felt that she had the upper hand by accepting that the whole relationship factor between males and females was really just about sex for the man and how they could figure out the shortest, quickest route to reaching their orgasmic climax. Men had to be gay, she sometimes reasoned, if they just wanted to be her friend, because all straight men would sleep with their female friend if they had the opportunity.

Iralaun kept that ideology foremost when dating. The bottom line for males, she believed, was to inherently have sex—or procreate for animals. And they wanted to get it the shortest and easiest way possible, even though she did feel that men would appreciate it more if they had to work hard for it—just like with money. Sometimes she even challenged that notion.

But with Allen, his humor made her want to prolong the mating ritual. He held her attention long enough in other topics that she didn't feel the need just to pounce on him physically. While playing Jenga, a truth or dare game that involves stacking wooden blocks on top of one another, she decided to bring up the topic about her theory between the sexes.

"What?" Allen asked amused. "I can't believe you just said that."

"What? You know I'm right."

"Whatever," he said shaking his head. He was sitting on a throw pillow on the floor in front of the coffee table. "OK, there may be the slightest hint of truth there, but really?"

"Really what? Are you going to try to tell me that you don't want to sleep with me?"

"Only a fool wouldn't. But I respect you and I enjoy your company."

"Exactly. And you are willing to do whatever is necessary to sleep with me, even if it means putting in quality time, like playing these silly board games and what not."

"Listen to you," Allen said shaking his head.

"What? I'm right, right? It's the game of Trivial Pursuit sorta speak. Hanging out with me, is the trivial part of pursuing me."

Allen shook his head in disgust. "Have you ever been in a serious relationship before?"

Iralaun shook her head no. "I can't say that I have."

"I can tell."

"You have, huh? I bet you are going to tell me you never cheated, too, right?"

"Why are you so pessimistic? I'll let it go, though. You're lucky I'm interested in getting to the bottom of you."

Iralaun smirked. "The bottom of me? You act like I'm some big mystery. When's the last time you watched Animal Planet or the Discovery Channel? We are all animals, you know? It's natural instincts we're talking about."

Allen just shook his head and kept smiling. "You are a wild girl."

"What?"

"You do realize there are significant differences between those of us who walk on two legs right? They aren't our hind legs, you know?" he said laughing.

Iralaun rolled her eyes. "Whatever Allen. No single, essential difference separates human beings from other animals, you know that right?"

"Oh, so now you study science instead of communications?"

"You know I'm right. So tell me why my theory is so unbelievable?"

"OK, Iralaun. If that's how you think, then why haven't you and I had sex yet? Or better yet, how come I don't even know what your sexy body feels like in my arms? Why do you even bother to date, if you know from the beginning that sex is all a man wants?"

Iralaun didn't say anything.

"Now you are quiet. Come on answer me Dr. Fugere, surely you've studied this in your biology lab."

"I never said that women don't want or enjoy sex, too," Iralaun said getting up to take their mugs to the sink.

"Oh. Is that right?" Allen said slyly with his eyes following her to the kitchen.

"Of course they do. They have clitorises. They get aroused."

"Mmhmm," he said.

"Yep."

"But?"

"But we are emotional globs of glue. Our feelings always get attached to the men we are physically attracted to. Unfortunately, that's our nature."

"That's true," Allen said standing up and going to the kitchen. "So what's so wrong with that?"

"Every man who wants to sleep with you isn't necessarily right for you. You know what I mean?" she said putting dish soap and a little water in the mugs to soak them.

Allen nodded.

"I mean women have a tendency to think that just because a man shows them attention, and do a little bit more than the next man, that he's a standup guy."

"A standup guy?"

"Yeah. You know what I'm talking about—like he's worthy of something—extra acknowledgement or a reward of sorts."

"Mmhmmm."

"And most women have this thing—they think that because they sleep with a guy more than twice that they are in a relationship. You better believe that if she told you she likes you and ya'll are having sex frequently, you are her boyfriend or at least everything she does is to get the relationship to the point that you are considering her to be your girlfriend. I mean you are, at the very least, in a relationship."

"True. A physical one."

"Right. My point exactly. But women are the ones who are emotionally committed. Even if they try not to have an emotional attachment, they can't help it. It's just natural or at least they secretly desire to be in one. Unless there is something about the guy that completely turns them off...like the fact that he is married or has a girlfriend or is just plain uncommitted. For some reason, some women can still sleep with them, without always wanting more. Sometimes, money or attention will do. Other times, they want more, like to be in the wife's shoes, for some stupid reason."

"Hmm...you seem like you got it all down pat. Are you speaking from first hand experience?"

Iralaun shrugged and began washing out the mugs.

"At least now I know why you've never been in a relationship. You are so serious and so analytical."

Iralaun shrugged again. "I guess," she mumbled.

"I think you are making a big deal out of nothing, personally. People get their feelings hurt, get over it. You win some, you lose some. That's the game of life."

"It's that simple for you?"

"Well...not really. I've been hurt to a point that I never thought I would ever be in another relationship, but..." Allen said walking back over to the sofa, "I wiped myself off and got right back up again. No need to take it out on everyone I meet."

"Mmmm. You're a risk-taker, huh?"

"Yeah. I have to be, if I want to go into business."

"Is everything business to you?"

"No. Not really. But I think everything is about relationships, including business. I think that everything should be good for both parties involved. And sometimes relationships just don't work out, no matter how hard you try, no matter how many stock options or health care benefits you offer."

"I guess," she said turning and walking back over to the sofa.

"Can I get a hug now?" Allen asked blinking his eyes looking like a bashful teddy bear.

Iralaun smiled and said, "Nope." She stuck out her tongue and crossed her arms in front of her chest.

Allen grabbed her around her waist and started tickling her. They both laughed in each other's arms.

***

"Evan, this is Elgin. What's going on?" Elgin asked from a pay phone near the last bus stop.

"Where are y'all? The Bodines was here looking for y'all earlier." Evan was half asleep when the phone rang.

"I know. We saw them and they started chasing us. What they say?"

"They wanted to talk to y'all about some girl who said y'all gang-raped her with some other guys."

"What?!?"

"Yeah, you know Lil' Ebony that go to Shaw Junior High?"

"Rape?" Elgin asked appalled. "What the hell are they talking about? Ain't nobody rape that broad!"

"I don't know, but they're looking for y'all like I don't know what."

"Rape?" Elijah asked Elgin as he stared at his brother talking on the phone.

"Man...shit," Elgin said.

"It's been on the news and everything...talking about how young she is and all that and how six dudes raped her. They got Black, Reggie, Chico and Lil' Mike," Evan said. "What y'all gonna do?"

"I don't know I gotta think." Elgin closed his eyes for a second as he debated his options. Then just as quick, he said "We coming home and we're gonna turn ourselves in. Because I ain't rape nobody. E, ain't rape nobody either. That bitch lying like shit!"

"Man, this shit is crazy," Evan said. "Alright. Well, when y'all coming?"

"Let me speak to Ma," Elgin said.

"She sleep."

"Wake her up!" he yelled into the phone.

"OK, hold on." Evan put the phone down to get his mother.

"Elgin?" Vivica asked moments later.

"Yes."

"Where are y'all?"

"In Hyattsville."

"Hyattsville?!?"

"Yeah. We are about to come home, though. Ma," Elgin said as he stared at his shoes. "I just want you to know we ain't rape nobody."

Vivica didn't say anything. Vivica couldn't believe her sons' audacity. They were just like their father, she thought. And she hated that. But it was too early in the morning and she didn't have the strength to deal with them at that moment. She was surprised earlier by the visit from the police, and she was even more stunned when she realized they knew her by her first and last name already. That was enough for her to know her sons were neighborhood menaces.

"Ma, we ain't rape nobody. We were there, but she knew what was going on. Ain't nobody rape her."

"See, that's what I'm talking about when I say watch who you hang around with and about being places you have no business being. If your behinds was in school, instead of out on the streets, then there would be no doubt about where you been or what you been into."

Silence was the only thing between Vivica and Elgin for a minute.

"Now you don't want to say anything. So what do you want from me?"

"We want to come home and turn ourselves in."

72

"Oh, you do, do you?" Vivica asked surprised. "You must not have done it."

"We didn't."

"Hmmm…well, I'm not coming to get y'all. It's three in the morning. Get here the best way you know how and then I'll take y'all to the police when I get up."

"OK. Bye," Elgin said hanging up the phone.

"You sure we should do that Elgin?" Elijah asked. "They're already out there asking questions about Dante'."

Elgin shook his head and put on the hood of his winter coat. "I can't believe that girl lying like that."

CHAPTER 8

Y ou can spend the night here if you want," Iralaun said. "You can sleep in my bed. I'll sleep in my roommates' or you can sleep on the sofa. It doesn't matter."

"No, I think I should go home before you think I'm trying to copulate with you," Allen said laughing.

Iralaun threw a pillow from her room at him. Allen ducked and smiled.

"Just for that, you are taking the couch, and I'm not taking no for an answer. It's already three something." She handed him a sheet and an afghan blanket from the hall closet.

"Alright," Allen said spreading the blankets out to lie down.

"Alright then...see you in the morning."

"Yeah, sweet dreams sunshine."

***

"Let me get this straight," Elijah said. "We're gonna steal a car to go home, to turn ourselves in to the police? That shit don't make no damn sense Elgin."

"Well, tell me what should we do Big brother? Since you are always asking me all the damn time. Why won't you come up with something?"

Elijah rolled his eyes. "Well... I don't know but that shit don't make sense to me."

"Man fuck that," Elgin said while popping the lock of a car parked in an apartment complex a few blocks from the mall.

"It's bad enough we all the way out here and you gonna take some flashy shit with rims and tint on the window. Dumb ass, begging for us to get stopped," Elijah said.

"Man fuck you. Get your bitch ass in the car," Elgin said as he unlocked the passenger door. He hopped in the car and started up the engine. Tupac's voice blared from the speakers, and Elgin rushed to turn the volume down before he drew unwanted attention. He hurried to turn the heat on to full blast, too.

Elijah put his seatbelt on while he waited for Elgin to pull off. "Let's just hurry up."

Elgin looked at Elijah and smirked. "You look like a bitch over there with your seat belt on. Nigga, I can drive. Take that shit off."

Elijah rolled his eyes. "Man, fuck you. Let's go."

***

"Can I get some breakfast or something?" Allen joked in a jovial voice.

"You better fix you a bowl of cereal or something."

"Well good morning to you, too."

Iralaun rolled her eyes playfully and shook her head.

"But it's Sunday. Where's the pancakes, sausages and eggs?"

"Cute—this is not IHOP. There's some pop tarts in the cabinet and we might still have some frozen waffles in the freezer."

"Awww...that's messed up," Allen said going to the refrigerator. "I can't even get no home-cooked meal?"

She shook her head 'no' again.

"I'm about to get out of here. I'm going to church this morning."

"Church? You?"

"Yeah me. Want to come with me?"

Iralaun shrugged her shoulders. "Sure, why not?" She couldn't remember the last time she dated a guy who went to church.

"OK, well I'm going to go home, get dressed and come back and get you, OK?"

"Yeah, that's fine. What time should I be ready?"

"Well, I know women, so I'm going to tell you nine even though service starts at ten," Allen said folding up the blankets.

"Shut up. Go ahead, I'll do that," she said about the blankets. "You sure you don't want an Eggo?"

"No thanks," he said putting on his shoes.

Iralaun smiled.

"I'm going to stop by McDonald's on the way home."

"McDonald's? How is that better than what is in my freezer?"

"Please. You know their breakfast is hittin' " Allen said while walking toward the door. Then he walked back to give Iralaun a hug. His embrace was strong, yet, gentle, and Iralaun was glad to be in the midst of it.

"I'll see you later," he said.

"OK," she said smiling.

75

"Bye."

He closed the door and skipped down the steps to the parking lot smiling. But his smile quickly faded when he saw that his car was no where to be found.

"Damn. Somebody got me," he said shaking his head. He went back upstairs to Iralaun's apartment and knocked on the door.

She answered the door with an untoasted pop tart in her hand. "What? Don't tell me you miss me already?"

"Unless, you are going to tell me that I was towed for not having a decal or something, somebody stole my car."

"Stop playing."

"No, I'm serious."

Iralaun ran to the window and saw that his car was no where to be found. Then she turned around and looked sympathetically at Allen.

"Sorry," she offered.

"Don't worry about it. I got insurance. Just let me use the phone to call the police."

Iralaun passed him the phone and sat and listened while Allen gave them all of his information. She was surprised at how nonchalant he was about the whole situation. She found herself impressed with his level of maturity during such an unpredictable situation. He didn't complain the entire time. It was clear that Allen was a man, and not a little boy like the rest of the guys she dated.

Iralaun's attraction for him intensified. He was so in control and unfazed by the situation. She tried to hide how impressed she was and finished fixing some breakfast while Allen was on the phone. She didn't know if she wanted to continue what they were starting. Her mother told her one too many times not to fall for men, and she knew that if she stayed around him any longer that she would definitely fall from Cloud Nine. Iralaun didn't want to end up getting hurt. There was no way she would let that happen to her.

"So what did they say?" she asked him after he got off the phone.

"Well nothing really. They just wanted to make a report, and said they would send somebody out. But I want to know if you can take me home after they come. I need to get changed up. We can still go to church, can't we?"

"Sure," Iralaun said astonished that he still wanted to go. "Well, I'll start getting dressed."

"Cool," he said reaching for the plate of food she'd made him. "Do you go to church often?"

"No. Actually, I can't even remember the last time I've been."

"Really?"

"Yeah."

"Why not?"

"Well, my mother and I never went—not to my memory anyway."

"Not religious?"

"I'm not sure. Don't really think about it much. A lot of the things I've found myself praying for, I never seemed to get. And I thought the famous line was 'ask and you shall receive'...so."

Allen nodded his head. "I hear you. But I'm not going to get into that with you. Wars have been fought over the subject. I'm just glad you are open-minded enough to want to come with me now."

***

Belinda tossed and turned in her bed early Sunday morning wondering what Officer Kevin St. James had been up to. Even though he was married, she found him to be endearing and sweet. She often daydreamed about having a relationship similar to the relationship she remembered her parents having before her father's accident.

Her father, who had been a construction worker, used to remind her of Paul Bunion, big and strong. Her mother, a city bus driver, was like a flower, dainty, beautiful and the pinnacle of femininity. She loved them, because they made sacrifices to make sure she and her sister, Brandi, had whatever they needed and wanted. Even as an adult she still appreciated the values they instilled in her while growing up. They attended church regularly and made sure she and Brandi spent time helping people less fortunate than them. And her parents also taught them a lot about being responsible for their actions.

As a child, Belinda lived a fairytale life in a two-level home, with a huge yard and a swimming pool. Her parents taught them a lot about life and how working hard was essential for true happiness. Belinda learned she had to work hard for the things she valued most in life. When selling lemonade or baked cookies wasn't enough to make a dent in their little pockets for spending money, her parents would pay them to do odd chores around the house, like organizing the kitchen cabinets or cleaning out the shed in their backyard. Frank and Ingrid wanted to make sure they understood the value of money and hard work. And even though Belinda's relationship with her parents had changed over the years, she would never forget that.

The ringing telephone interrupted her thoughts. She looked over at it sitting on her nightstand and lifted it from the cradle.

"Hello?"

"Good morning sweetheart. Merry Christmas Eve," Ingrid sang to her eldest daughter.

"Hey Mama. How are you this early Sunday morning?" Belinda asked rolling her eyes and looking at the clock.

"I'm doing good. I'm glad I finally got a day off, though. My back has been starting to hurt me, but other than that I'm good. How are you?"

"I'm OK, I guess."

"You feel like going shopping with me today. There are still some things I want to get for tomorrow."

Belinda exhaled. Her mother always did this to her—waited until the last minute to do things.

"Oh, you don't feel like going? That's OK sweetie. I'll ask your sister to go with me."

"No, Mama I'll go," Belinda knew her mother loved pitting her against her sister. And she didn't want to be reminded that Brandi would drop everything for her, as if she wouldn't. Her mother acted like Brandi was perfect, she thought to herself. "How's Daddy doing?"

"Well you know your father. He's the same. There isn't anything that makes him happy anymore these days."

"Yes. I know," Belinda said staring at the ceiling.

"But he can't wait to see you girls tomorrow. Are you still going to make the desserts for Christmas dinner?"

"Yes ma'am," Belinda responded in a matter-of-fact tone. She knew her father could really care less about seeing her and her sister. He hadn't even flinched the last time she saw him, let alone said more than two words to them at Thanksgiving a month earlier. Her father had been a proud, dedicated man, who was an early riser and a workaholic. But the accident changed all of that. "Anything else you need me to do?"

"Stop talking to me like that. I don't like your tone at all. I'm the one who had a long night."

"I know, I know," Belinda said shaking her head. "How was your night Mama?"

"Well, you know…it was as usual. People busy coming and going. You know people drive like fools out there during the holidays."

"They drive like maniacs all year around Mama."

"Yeah. That's true. But anyway…on my last route, I saw the two most precious looking young men. Belinda, would you believe they were twins?"

"Oh really, mama. Wow." Belinda knew she was being sarcastic and rolled her eyes again.

"Cut that out with all that mocking. I do not approve of your attitude this morning Miss Lady."

Belinda smiled. "OK, OK. Please tell me what was so special about them."

"They were little devils."

"Hmm...what do you mean?"

"The whole ride on the bus they were just a cursing and being disrespectful to the other riders. Nearly drove me crazy the whole ride."

"Mmhhm...but you get knuckleheads on the bus all the time, don't you Mama?"

"Yeah. But it was just something about these two...they looked scared and uneasy. And can you believe it? They rode the bus to the end of the route and didn't know where the heck they were. I had to tell them."

"Uhuh?"

"I mean...like I had to tell them they were in Maryland and not in Virginia."

"That's strange, I guess. But a lot of people who live in D.C. don't know too much about the area outside of the city, especially young kids. Half of them have never even been downtown to see the monuments and museums."

"Yeah, but to not know at all—the direction you are going in when you get on a bus? Or to not care enough to pay attention where you are going at that time of night? It bothered me. They didn't even know how to get back and I was the last bus for the night. I didn't feel right about leaving them there, I really didn't."

"Mama first of all, I don't know why you still taking that graveyard shift anyway. And secondly, you don't know what those boys were into. It's good you didn't. Don't worry about it. You should be lucky nothing happened to you, because of them."

"Belinda I love working, OK? It gives me a chance to get out this house and away from your father, who stay driving me up the wall," Ingrid said breathlessly. "Anyway, I just hope they made it home safely."

Belinda frowned. "Well... is Brandi bringing one of her little boyfriends to dinner tomorrow?"

"You know Brandi ain't bringing just anybody. She's been dating Tariq for a couple of years now. Are you bringing someone?"

"Mama. I don't have a boyfriend."

"What happened to ah...what's his name?"

"James? He's engaged."

"Huh?"

"Close your mouth Mama."

"When, what, how did that happen?" she asked shocked.

"Your guess is as good as mine."

"Hmm...well find somebody to bring so you won't be by yourself."

"What's wrong with being by myself?"

"Nothing, sweetie. We just want some grandbabies from somebody. Come pick me up at ten, OK?"

"Ah..." Belinda figured her mother would come get her since Ingrid had called her. "OK. I'll be there at ten. Please be ready."

"I will be. You make sure you are here on time."

"Bye Mama."

"Bye."

Belinda hung up the phone and stared at the ceiling. She didn't feel like going shopping on the day before Christmas. Not only would the malls be packed, but so would the streets and the grocery stores. Occasions like this reminded Belinda how much she hated living in the city. Just thinking about maneuvering all the way on the other side of town to pick up her mother made her mentally exhausted.

"Darn it!" Belinda remembered that she still didn't have all the ingredients she needed for the desserts she planned to make. "I hate grocery shopping."

She thought about Christmas dinner and how it would be to see her little sister Brandi with her boyfriend who she had been with for three long years. Sometimes she envied her. They competed without trying, too. When Belinda agreed to go to Georgetown University, offering to stay near her parents to help out, she was disappointed when Brandi went to Temple in Pennsylvania two years later. Belinda wished she had gone away, too.

It was difficult for her to watch as her mother's love fell to a cold heart. Frank never responded to Ingrid the same way he used to. She became withdrawn and gained a lot of weight. And Brandi was away when the bulk of the problems peaked, leaving Belinda feeling more alone.

When the scaffolding at her father's construction site collapsed, her family never knew that they would still be feeling it's affects years later. It wasn't only her father's severe injuries, but it was the court case they lost two years later that made her father feel incompetent. His construction company refused to pay for any of his hospital bills. The company's lawyers claimed that it was because of his negligence that the accident had occurred and that the company wasn't liable for compensation.

The case went to court and dragged on for two years and when the verdict came down in the company's favor, the family's spirit shattered into a million pieces. Belinda always felt that it was because of their court-appointed attorney that her family lost the case. She thought that if they had more money to devote to getting a better attorney, then they would have received more from his settlement. The result frustrated Belinda and drove her to pursue a career in law.

Belinda didn't want to be alone at Christmas dinner, thinking about the past and watching her sister enjoy her life while everyone around her sat miserably.

She also didn't want to bring someone for the sake of not being alone either. She wondered what Kevin had planned for the holiday.

"I wonder if he wants to be with his wife," she mumbled. "It is a family holiday, even if they are separated."

Belinda reached for her wallet and pulled out Kevin's business card. She toyed with it between her fingers, staring at the phone number until she had it memorized. Belinda was disappointed when she realized that only his work number was on it. She hadn't talked to him since that night at the bar, but decided to call anyway to leave a message.

She dialed the numbers and suddenly had second thoughts. Belinda hung up the phoned and stared at the ceiling a moment longer. What would she say on the voice mail?

"OK, I'll just say, 'Hello and that I was thinking about you,'" Belinda said aloud. Then she picked up the phone again and began to dial the number. After the second ring, Kevin picked up the phone.

"Officer St. James," a huffy voice said.

She was stunned. What was he doing there on the weekend?

"Hi, Kevin?" She knew her voice sounded nervous.

"Yes, this is he. How can I help you?"

"Kevin, this is Belinda, from the bar?"

"Oh, hi Belinda," Kevin said in a way that indicated that he was smiling. She was happy to hear him delighted. "I've been meaning to call you to see if everything was OK and to see how've you been, but I've been so busy lately."

"Really?" Belinda asked. For some reason she really wanted to believe everything he said was true.

"Yeah. So how have you been?"

"I'm good. How is your Christmas Eve going so far?"

"It's going. It's going," Kevin said taking a deep breath.

"You aren't going out of town or anything?" she asked with concern in her voice. But she really just wanted to know if he had plans to be with his wife. The man still wore his wedding ring for God's sake, she thought. She was sure there was something still going on.

"No. I actually don't have any plans for the holidays. No tree. No lights. No reef and red ribbon on the front of my truck. I might just come into work tomorrow, too, actually."

"Really? No Christmas dinner or anything."

"No. I didn't have any plans."

"It's not good for people to be alone on Christmas. Why don't you come with me to my family's house for dinner."

"That's sweet. You sure they wouldn't mind?"

"No, not at all. I want you to come."

"That sounds nice."

"Well I'll call you tomorrow around four to come get you."

"OK. But wait, Belinda, what made you call me today?"

"Well I guess I was in the mood to spread some Christmas cheer," she said smiling. "I'll talk to you tomorrow. Have a good day."

"Thanks. You, too."

Belinda hung up the phone and smiled to herself. Now she just wanted to stay in bed all day savoring the conversation. She looked at the clock again and realized her mother had tricked her—it was a little after nine o'clock. She needed to hurry to meet her by ten. Belinda decided while they were out Christmas shopping that she would pick something up nice to wear to dinner the next day and maybe even give the gift she had bought for James to Kevin.

CHAPTER 9

T he twins didn't have much to say to their mother when they got home. They were just relieved that she believed them despite all the things they had done in the past. Before Vivica called the police, she called the attorney she used to get the divorce from Eddie years earlier. Even though it was a holiday, and it appeared to be a criminal case, he said that he would do his best to help her.

Elgin and Elijah told him everything about the night in question. But upon hearing the details, the lawyer said that he would have to refer her to someone else, his brother, who was a criminal defense attorney. Vivica took a sigh of relief when she heard him say that. She didn't feel like going through the motions with someone she was unfamiliar with.

When she talked to James Lomax, he told them that he was on his way to their house and that he knew exactly how to get there—that he was quite familiar with the area because he had relatives who lived near there. He also told them not to do anything until he got there. But Vivica was nervous and anxious. She was tired of hearing about the rape on the news. So many people in the city had tried and convicted the boys before they had even been arrested. Rape crisis specialists, members of the school board and even retired police officers were saturating the news with their opinions. The chaos was making her dizzy.

She did not want to deal with all of this. Reporters had been calling her house all day and she refused to comment. A Channel 4 News van was even parked across the street from their house earlier in the day. While Vivica waited for the lawyer to come, she called the local television station that had been airing the infuriated sound bytes from neighbors and other concerned citizens about the alleged gang rape. She wanted them to know her sons' side of the story. Vivica also told them that her sons were about to turn themselves in because they were innocent of the accusations and wanted them to cover it.

James Lomax was surprised to see the television news crew pulling up at the same time. He shook his head, but couldn't stop Vivica from talking to the reporters. After answering the questions James thought were reasonable,

Vivica called the police while the camera was rolling and told them the same thing she had told the reporter. Elijah and Elgin stood beside their mother firmly, and when the police read them their rights, they calmly put their hands behind their backs, awaiting the cold clasp of the steel handcuffs.

The reporter asked Elgin why they wanted to turn themselves in and he said, "Because we didn't rape that girl and the truth needs to come out. I'm not taking no charge for something I didn't do!"

"OK, that's enough," James said to Elgin and the reporters. "I'll be down there in a minute. Just be cool and keep your mouths closed."

The police escorted both twins to the car and slammed the door. Vivica looked on with sadness in her eyes as James jumped back in his car.

"I'll call you as soon as I know something," he yelled before closing his door. She nodded and watched as her other children looked on in dismay.

The police cars pulled off down the street and another chapter to her life began.

"Come on y'all, let's go on in the house," Vivica said while ushering her children toward the door.

"All this drama on Christmas Eve," Evan said shaking his head.

Vivica shook her head and led them back in the house. The police, the television crew and a few nosey neighbors left soon after the Jeffries went in the house. The chaos in front began to disappear like a parade that was on its last leg.

"Are we still going to grandma's house tomorrow?" Eve asked turning up the volume on the Rudolph the Reindeer cartoon. It came on every year and it reminded Vivica that as much as some things changed, a lot stayed the same. She knew that they had come far in life, but misery still lingered. What was she to do now she wondered? She still had to go on with her life. She still had her three other children to worry about and they all needed her.

"I don't know Evey—probably not. I have to wait to see what the lawyer says."

Eve sucked her teeth and ran to the top of the stairs. "They always mess stuff up for us around here. Now I can't have a Christmas because of them!"

"Don't be like that, Eve" Vivica said. She knew that Eve was really upset because she loved watching Rudolph the Reindeer each year. "We will still have Christmas, but we just have to make sure your brothers are OK."

"It's not like they care about us," Eve said yelling from the top of the stairs. At twelve, Vivica had already told her that she was starting to smell herself—because she was becoming more disrespectful and tried to challenge her.

"Do not talk to me like that! You watch yourself young lady and don't make me get my belt."

Eve rolled her eyes, went to her room and slammed the door. Vivica was exhausted and her chest was starting to hurt. She hadn't even told anyone beyond her immediate family any of what was going on. She didn't know what they would think or say, but she knew if they hadn't heard about it by now, they'd hear something about it on the news that night.

Celebrating Christmas was the last thing on her mind. Even though she believed her children's innocence, she just wanted to curl up in the bed and cry. Why did she have to deal with this all alone?

Hours later, James Lomax called to tell her that the twins would have to stay there until Tuesday morning, the day after Christmas. Vivica cursed and fussed because she thought the lawyer should have told her to wait until after the holidays to turn them in. But he told her, "It was always a good move to turn yourself in rather than to let the police show up at your door with handcuffs." He also told her that he admired what she did with the news media. "That was a good move," he said. "Even though, I probably would've advised you against it earlier."

"Really? Why?"

"Well, it could've worked out one of two ways—for you or against you. It could've brought too much attention to something that wasn't a big deal in the first place. The police may not have anything substantial enough to make a case. But by you letting them turn themselves in with the camera rolling," James paused, "that was an excellent public relations move. It puts a face on a story and you may get some brownie sympathy points from the public because of that, which may in turn, sway the overall perception of the case. They might get some compassion from some folks."

"Well Mr. Lomax, I'm more concerned about my children than I am about what the public thinks. I want all of them to know that they didn't do it."

"At least that's what they say."

"You don't believe my children, Mr. Lomax?"

"It doesn't matter what I believe. All I need to know is that there's enough evidence for me to prove that they didn't do it."

"It doesn't matter what you believe?" Vivica asked irritated into the phone. "It doesn't matter? It matters, because if it's between incarceration and their freedom, I'm going to need you to believe in them for me."

"You believe?"

"Yes, I do. After all they've put me through," she said rubbing her forehead and sighing. "And I know while you were down at that precinct you saw enough in their files to know that they aren't the most innocent two. But rape? No."

James was quiet.

"I need you to understand that if you are going to be their attorney that you will need to believe in them in order to defend them. If you don't, then tell me now. We can find someone else Mr. Lomax."

"Ms. Jeffries, for your information, I do believe them. But realize this...at least one of them had sex with her. And it will be a matter of not only proving which one of them did it, but also proving that it was consensual. I can help prove that, if you let me."

Vivica began sobbing into the phone. She tried to sniff back the tears, but she had no control over the stream that was eager to flow. She began to look for tissue to wipe her nose.

"Ms. Jeffries? Ms. Jeffries? I am going to do the best that I can to help you and your family. It's going to take some time, but I need you to let me do that. My brother wanted to make sure I took care of you and your family. And I will, OK?"

"Yes," Vivica managed to say through tears.

"Now try to do your best to enjoy your holiday."

"I will. You, too. Thanks again," Vivica mumbled, while wiping her nose.

"OK, I will be in touch with you tomorrow."

"Wait. Mr. Lomax...Can we go visit them tomorrow? I mean to the precinct on Christmas."

"No. Sorry you can't. It will be closed to visitors."

Vivica started sniffling again. "OK. I'll talk to you first thing Tuesday morning."

"Yes, you will. And if anything changes, I'll call you. Goodnight."

As soon as Vivica put the phone back in its cradle, she looked up and saw the news report of her and the twins on television. She cried while sitting there. Evan and Eric walked into the livingroom and watched the newscast as well. As soon as it went off, the phone rang.

"Don't answer it," Vivica said to Evan.

"But it's grandma," he said looking at the Caller ID.

"I don't feel like talking to her about it."

Evan picked up the phone anyway. "Hi Grandma. Yes, we know. No, she's right here," he said handing Vivica the phone.

"Vivica?" her mother said.

"Yes, Mama, I know, I was there," Vivica began.

***

After spending the entire day jostling her way through crowded stores and fighting over the few unbroken piecrusts in the grocery store, Belinda was happy to be home. She put the bags on the floor by the door, kicked her shoes off and threw her coat on the coat rack by the door. She started putting her groceries up except for the things she knew she would need right away to bake the German chocolate cake. Belinda saw the light on her Caller ID flashing, and saw that there was a message waiting. She picked up the telephone to call the voice mailbox.

It was Kevin saying that he didn't know whether or not he would be able to go to dinner for Christmas because something unexpected had come up.

"Darn it!" Belinda exclaimed. She was disappointed and wondered if it was because of his wife. "I wonder if I can change his mind."

She decided to call the number he left on the message. She became discouraged when she heard the sound of a woman's voice on his answering machine telling callers to leave a message for the St. Jameses.

Belinda hung up the phone rather than leave a message. She didn't know what she could've been getting Kevin into, or herself, for that matter. Suppose he and his wife had decided to get back together for the holidays. She couldn't believe how disappointed she felt.

Before she took the eggs and the butter out, Belinda poured herself a glass of wine. Then turned on the little black and white thirteen-inch television in her kitchen to see what was on. While she looked for a mixing bowl, the telephone rang.

"Hello," she said without looking at the Caller ID.

"Belinda, turn to Channel 4 right now," said Ingrid.

"Why? What's going on?"

"Just turn it on and hurry. They're going to show those two little boys I was telling you about this morning."

"They were on the news Mama?" Belinda was shocked, and started flipping the channels.

"Yeah. They showed their faces and went to a commercial. The lady said they were going to talk about it in a second."

"Really?"

"Yeah. Lord, I just hope they didn't get their selves into any trouble out there in them streets that time of night. Oh wait...turn it up."

They both listened to the newscast in silence before Ingrid spoke first.

"Wasn't that your little boyfriend I saw in the background?"

"They showed him so fast, but I think it was James."

"I just can't believe it. It's too much for me to understand all at once."

"Why not Mama? You said they were disrespectful and you also said they looked like trouble."

"Belinda, that don't mean anything. You, of all people, should know that in your position. The fear in their eyes that night nearly shook me to the core."

Belinda shook her head. "Well, it's an interesting case, I must say. I will have to follow it."

"You should call your friend, and see if there's anything you can do."

"Anything I can do?"

"Yeah. Why not?"

"What can I do Mama?"

Before Ingrid could answer, Belinda's other line clicked.

"Hold on Mama, my other line is beeping," she said before clicking over.

"Hello?"

"Belinda? This is Kevin, I just saw that you called here? I just walked in the door."

"Oh, hi Kevin. Yes, I did just call. I just wanted to know what made you change your mind?"

"It's a long story. I'd rather talk to you in person, rather than over the phone."

"Would you like to come over?" Belinda asked, being her usual persistent self.

"Ah, sure," Kevin said. "I'll be over in like thirty-forty minutes, OK?"

"Good, have you eaten dinner yet?"

"Actually I haven't, why? Would you like to go get something?"

"No, I'm actually doing a little baking right now for tomorrow's dinner. Besides I don't think anything is open since it's really a holiday. But I can whip something up real quick."

"Well, don't take this as an insult against your cooking," Kevin said laughing, "But I'll find something to bring us on the way. You already sound pretty busy."

Belinda was shocked at his courtesy.

"I hope you like Chinese. They're always open."

88

"I do," she said smiling.

"OK. Well, I'll see you in like an hour, an hour and a half."

"OK, bye." Belinda clicked back over.

"Well, G-Whiz…I thought you done fell into a coma or something the way you left me on the line," Ingrid said.

"I'm sorry Mama, a friend needs to talk to me about something and he's on his way over so I need to get off the phone."

"He? Who is he baby?"

"Just a guy I met."

"Well tell me about him, you got time to do that don't you. I mean just how long can it take?"

"There's nothing to tell Mama."

"Well how long have you known him?"

"Not long."

"And you are calling him a friend already? Belinda, you can't just be letting anybody in your house sweetie. I want grandbabies, but not that bad."

Belinda smiled. "Mama, he's a police officer and he was at my job the other day," she fudged the truth a little.

"Oh, OK. Did you ask him to Christmas dinner?"

"Yes. And, he may not be able to come depending on whatever it is he wants to talk to me about."

"Hmm…well, make sure you tell him I'm cooking my famous candied yams and fried green tomatoes."

"Yes, I will. Have you started wrapping those gifts yet?"

"No, but I will in a minute."

"OK, well. I'll be there early to help you cook in the morning."

"Don't come too early, you'll just get in my way. And plus your sister said that she was going to help me with most of it."

"Mmmhhmm." Belinda rolled her eyes. "Alright, bye Mama."

"Be careful. Bye, now."

Belinda didn't know what to do first. She was looking like a chicken with its head cut off for a minute. She ran to the livingroom to straighten up, and then to the bathroom to freshen herself up. Then she put at least one cake in the oven, so the house could smell homey. Belinda was clueless about what Kevin wanted to tell her, but it didn't matter, unless he was telling her that he was planning to spend the holiday with his wife.

She wanted to do something special to impress Kevin, so she whipped together a pound cake since she had all of the ingredients out. In the time frame it took for Kevin to come by with Chinese food, the cake was baked and cooling on the stove. After the concierge desk buzzed her to announce Kevin's arrival, she took one last glance around the apartment to make sure it was presentable and checked herself out in the mirror in the foyer.

"Hey," she said answering the door. Kevin looked sexy in his uniform, but he also looked exhausted. "You look like you had another long day."

"Yeah. I truly did. Where should I put this?" he asked with the bags of food.

"On the table is fine, but let me take your coat."

"It smells good in here. You can bake?"

She smiled and politely answered, "I try."

"That's good. My wife never could bake a lick. Let me see what you got going on in here. Oh pound cake, huh?" he said standing over the stove.

"Yeah, would you like a slice?"

"Ah, maybe later. But I thought this was for tomorrow?"

"Well, I can just slice it and lay the slices nicely. It'll be OK. It's all about presentation."

"Don't do all that for me," he said smiling. "So before I tell you about me, how was your day?"

Belinda was surprised at his politeness. He looked to be distraught, but still wanted to take the time out to find out how her boring Saturday went. She couldn't understand why a woman would opt to give that up.

"Well, it was pretty hectic with all the shopping and crowds, but it can't possibly amount to whatever it is that is making you cancel on me," she said almost purring like a cat.

"Let me go wash my hands, then we can sit down and eat," he said.

Belinda wanted to dance when he said 'wash his hands.' That was one of the small-big things that she required from men. When he came back, Kevin asked for some plates to put the food on instead of choosing to eat it out of the box. He got two more points checked on her mental list.

"Well, where do I begin? There's a lot going on right now, with this case I'm working on."

That was all Belinda needed to hear to know that he wasn't getting back with his wife just yet and she felt relief wash over her.

"I've been helping this detective who's handling a case where two of the suspects turned themselves in today—on television no less. I've always wanted to become a detective. I think I might have a break after all of this, never know. Did you see the news today?"

"Please don't tell me you are talking about the rape assault involving a bunch of juveniles?"

"Yes, that's the one. Two of the suspects also happen to be suspects to the case I'm helping the detective investigate."

"Mmmhhmm."

"They were interrogating the twins who turned themselves in this afternoon...and it's amazing how they are sticking to their stories."

"Tell me, was their lawyer present?"

"Yes."

"Do you know his name?" she asked putting plates on the table for them to eat.

"Lomax, I think."

"I thought that was him."

"You know him?"

"Yes, unfortunately," Belinda said rolling her eyes. "He was the recent relationship I was talking to you about."

Kevin shook his head. "I will say this, he's good. He was making sure the detectives were sticking by the books in the interrogation rooms."

"What's the story?"

"I don't know how much specifics I can go into... for all I know, you might end up presiding over the case," Kevin teased.

"Please don't say that," Belinda said dipping her sweet and sour chicken into some sauce. "Please don't. Besides, I don't cover criminal cases."

"Is it possible?"

"No. I work a lot with juveniles and family court issues. But that would be interesting if it was possible. Imagine it. You would be working for the prosecution and James, would be for the defense," Belinda said smiling—the thought was somewhat appealing to her.

"Who would win between he and I, do you think?" Kevin asked flirting, the first true sign to Belinda that he was interested in her romantically.

"Hmm...I think James would ask for me to be excluded from the case because of a technicality—our previous relationship," Belinda said smiling.

"Oh, you are weaseling out of the question, are you?"

Belinda blushed.

"Have you and your wife talked about spending time together for the holidays?" Belinda said changing the subject.

"No, we haven't," Kevin said looking uncomfortable. "She moved back to Georgia immediately after we separated."

Belinda raised her eyebrows. She instantly thought about the wife's voice still being on the answering machine. And then she made a mental note. "What do you two plan to do?"

"I don't know. I still love her."

Belinda felt a small pain tear through her stomach.

"We've been together for close to five years now."

"Right," Belinda said trying to catch herself from choking on her food.

"Are you OK?" he asked passing her the glass of water that sat in front of her.

Belinda nodded, and sipped some of it. She was surprised that he said he loved his wife still...so easily. That explained a lot to her.

"But we can't seem to get over this one big thing. And it's like she's just not even trying to hear anything. It seems like she has her heart and her mind set on divorcing me."

"That's interesting. You sure there isn't something else you aren't telling me? Because I can't see how that could be the only reason why she'd leave such a perfect gentleman by the wayside."

Belinda was surprised to see Kevin blush even with creamed coffee-colored cheeks.

"Well, thank you. I'm glad you appreciate me," he said.

"Have you dated since you've been separated?"

"Not really."

"Not really? What exactly does that mean?" Belinda said before putting another piece of chicken in her mouth.

"I mean, there have been friends."

"Friends?"

"You know... comfort friends."

Belinda instantly got a nasty taste in her mouth and tried to swallow the piece of chicken that suddenly felt like a rock in her throat. Comfort friends? She couldn't believe he'd let that phrase depart his lips.

"Men, want to be held, just as much women, sometimes," he said in a sly nature. "I mean, I never cheated on her, while we were together—never. But we haven't been together in nine months, Belinda. What do you expect?"

"And you still consider yourself to be in love?"

"Sex and love are two different things. I respected my wife while we were together, but once she chose to move back to Georgia, without even looking back, she basically gave me a 'Get Laid Free' license."

"Excuse me?"

"No offense. It didn't happen right away, of course," Kevin said stirring up his Won Ton soup. "I was still trying to see what we could do to make it work. But I wasn't leaving my job. I love it too much."

"More than your wife?"

"No, of course not. But equally."

"But you chose your job."

"My job is my life."

"And your wife isn't?"

"No she is too...but my job was there first. Without my job, who would I be?" he said. It seemed like he was trying to convince himself to Belinda. And then he said, "That's like taking away a singer's talent. It's like telling him to stop singing, because you don't like it. What should the singer do? Quit singing to be with his wife?"

Belinda agreed with a lot of Kevin's points but wanted to pressure him the same way she would have done a lawyer or a defendant in her court-room.

"There has to be compromise, somewhere," he said.

"And what type of compromise did you offer? I'm assuming she offered something as well?" Belinda couldn't believe she was trying to make him see that leaving his wife, may not have been the best thing.

Kevin was silent. "This is exactly where we are right now...at a fork in the road. Well actually she chose a road—which was not to be with me any-more."

"Would you say you two tried your best to compromise?"

"No, I wouldn't say that. I would say, however," he paused to play with his food, "that she gave up on us. And I'm not sure if I want to roll up my sleeves at this point."

"Would you consider counseling?"

"No, because it's not an issue of feelings, it's an issue of compromise."

"Even the best business negotiators still need mediators to help facilitate the process. Sometimes, people sitting on the outside, looking at your situation can see things from an objective point of view."

"Is that what you are doing now?"

"I guess."

"Why?"

"I don't know. I guess because you sound like it's too late for you two to fix things—almost like you're giving up or something."

"Yeah, I guess to some degree, I have." Kevin balled up his napkin and put it in his plate. "Maybe it's because I've already gone outside of the mar-riage."

"What makes you think she hasn't either?"

Kevin looked skyward and shook his head as if he didn't even want to consider that. Belinda shook her head because of the typical reaction guys made when envisioning their woman sleeping with someone other than them.

"Well. I hope I was of some help," she said pushing away from the table.

"Yeah, you gave me a lot to think about Judge Judy," he said laughing.

"Shut up," she said playfully while grabbing his plate to take to the kitchen.

"So tell me about this dinner tomorrow. Will your dad be there with his Hennessey," he said smiling.

"I'm sure," she said with a stoic look.

Kevin picked up on her lack of enthusiasm at his sense of humor and said, "Oh, he has a serious problem?"

"Yes and he doesn't want any help either. He just wants to sit and feel sorry for himself. He makes me sick."

"Why is he like that?"

"That's another long story. We'll have to talk about that another time," she said scraping the dishes in the garbage.

"I've got time."

Belinda exhaled. She wasn't really up to talking about it, but Kevin opened up to her. She told Kevin about how she grew up. How her parents were happy before his accident.

Belinda loved seeing her father surprise her mother with her favorite calla lilies when he got home from work or see her mom cook her father's favorite dessert—carrot cake. Sometimes they would all go for long drives in Virginia and have picnics on the side of the road for mini-family getaways. Belinda knew her friends were envious of the relationship she had with her parents and she had to sometimes marvel at it herself. They had a bond that most families didn't have back then.

But Belinda could still remember the day it all ended like it was yesterday. Like a snuffed candle, it all ended and things began to fall apart. She was a sophomore in high school when she was sent to the principal's office during the middle of the school day. Belinda could still remember crying in the car as she learned that her father had been severely injured. She told Kevin of the day she walked down the hospital's bright halls to the intensive care unit only to hear her mother's ear-piercing wails grow louder.

"Her voice sounded like the siren of a fire truck—filling the halls like gutters after a storm," Belinda told Kevin. "She had just learned that my dad would have to get his legs amputated."

Kevin shook his head.

"Losing his legs destroyed him," Belinda said. "And then to find out a

94

couple of years later, that the company that you loved so much turned its back on you…it destroyed whatever was left of him emotionally. My father was such a proud man. He loved that company so much. He spent a lot of time telling Brandi and I, about the quality buildings he helped to erect 'with his very own hands', he used to say. And to see them chalk it up to mere negligence devastated him."

Belinda grabbed a bottle of wine from the wine rack and offered Kevin a drink.

"No, thanks. I'm still in uniform."

She nodded and poured herself a glass.

"My father deteriorated. I watched as a once strong, robust man became addicted to a liquid that he drank like an anti-serum for his problems."

Belinda smirked at the glass in front of her and raised it to her lips. The dry bitter taste felt good sliding down her throat. Kevin looked on quietly as she soothed herself.

"He refused to let go of that bottle," Belinda said as she walked over to her off-white leather couch and sat down. Kevin left the diningroom table and sat near her. "I would come home from school when I was at Georgetown and watch him curl up on the couch with his lips still wrapped around the liquor bottle. He would be snoring and everything."

Kevin shook his head.

"My mother learned that if she didn't provide his Hennessey for him, that he wouldn't speak to her for weeks at a time. My mother hated to see him that way, so she bought it for him."

"She was just trying to make the pain easier for him to bare," Kevin said.

"I guess."

"I wish I could meet him tomorrow," Kevin said standing up and looking at some of the paintings on the walls. "Who knows I may end up having some time since the place is probably going to be quiet tomorrow since it's a holiday."

Belinda shrugged. Discussing her family made her feel nonchalant about the situation. "Well, if you can drop by, it won't be a problem. Plus, you have to taste my German Chocolate cake," she said bragging.

"Oh, can I have a slice of the pound cake now?"

"Sure, I'll cut it right now."

Belinda got up and headed toward the kitchen. Kevin followed her.

"This place looks really nice," he said admiring her all white living room. "I can tell you don't have any kids or pets."

She smiled. "I've always wanted a cat, actually," she said handing him the cake. "I've just always been too busy to care for one."

"Cats are independent. They don't need that much attention."

"Yeah, that's what I've heard."

"Well, I'm going to take this to go," Kevin said. "I want to get ready for tomorrow."

While Belinda wrapped his cake in aluminum foil, she thought about their conversation. She didn't know what to make of him yet. She was glad she told him about her family and that he decided to talk about his a little. She didn't think she'd go into so much detail about hers, but she did. In one hand she respected how he still felt about his wife and in the other, she was disappointed that he had friends that he was being pleased by on the side. But she respected his honesty.

"I'll call you tomorrow if I can stop by," he said walking to the door.

"OK, good."

"I really appreciated our conversation."

"Me, too. And thanks for bringing dinner. That was very nice of you."

"Not a problem. Talk to you soon."

"Bye," Belinda said as she shut the door and went back to her glass of wine.

CHAPTER 10

In his holding cell, Elijah laid on his back staring at the bottom of the bunk bed above him. He was frustrated about Elgin's decision to turn them selves in, but he didn't have a better solution. The thought of other criminal charges coming up while they were in jail clouded his mind. They both had been in a lot of serious trouble over the past year. Besides, he didn't have anything to do with the issue with Ebony over Reggie's house, he thought. Sure he was there, but he didn't even touch the girl.

"Your lawyer is here to see you," said a correction's officer interrupting Elijah's thoughts as he unlocked the door. "Merry Christmas, by the way."

Elijah nodded at him and waited to be escorted to the room where he could speak freely.

"Merry Christmas Elijah," said James, while standing up to greet him. "How are you doing today?"

Elijah exhaled. "I'm aiight. I thought you said you weren't coming today? Is my mother coming? And where's my brother?" he asked while the officer helped him to sit down.

"Boy don't you have a lot of questions today. Umm...your mom won't be able to visit you until tomorrow. I saw your brother earlier; he's doing OK. I just wanted to give you a chance to tell me more about what happened without him or the police in the room."

"Whatever he told you, is the same thing I'm going to say, so what difference do it make?" Elijah rubbed his forehead before looking down at his hands. He stared at the scabs that started to heal the cuts on his knuckles. They were from the fight he had with Dante'. He looked away from them and put his hands under the table.

"Look. Let me be clear with you, Elijah," James said taking a deep breath and tapping a pencil on a pad. The taps sounded like loud thumps to Elijah and mimicked his increasing heartbeat. "When the DNA tests come back, they will be able to determine who from your little group of friends actually had sexual intercourse with Ebony Jenkins. And to be honest, it could be real tricky determining which one of you participated in what is being called a rape simply based on the analysis so..."

"Look Mr. Lomax. Neither one of us raped that girl."

"Well, then be honest with me. Tell me what happened that day. I won't know unless you are honest with me, consequently I won't be able to help you until you do that either. So whenever you are ready, I'm ready to begin preparing our case."

Elijah was quiet for awhile and began to focus on the peeling mint green paint on the wall behind James' head.

"Do you want to take the fall for something your brother did?"

Elijah didn't say anything.

"Just tell me what took place that day as clear and concise as you can," James said frustrated. "And we can fix this situation."

"I already told you what happened."

"Don't be difficult Elijah. Do you know they are considering charging all of you as adults? And if that happens, that means that you each could face a maximum of twenty years in prison? This is serious. Rape is a serious offense. Are you willing to throw away the next twenty years of your life for your brother?"

Elijah was silent and continued to stare at the cracking paint that curled up in some areas of the wall. The wall looked like dessert dry skin or like the cucumber masks some women put on their faces at night. Elijah didn't want to be there and didn't want to think about that day.

"I need for you to speak up, because right now, I can't help you at all knowing what I know now. Do you understand?"

"Well, what would happen to me, if they find out I was just there."

"Are you saying that you didn't have sex with Ebony?"

Elijah nodded.

"I need for you to speak up Elijah. Did you or did you not have sexual intercourse with her?"

"No, I didn't have sex with that damn girl."

"Did Elgin?"

"I don't know."

"What happened that day?"

Elijah sucked in some air and then blew it from his lips. "All I can tell you is...nobody went to school that day. Nobody in my neighborhood really goes to school. Sometimes we go up there just to see who we might see, and to see if they want to roll with us somewhere. That day was no different, except, one of my friends said that his mother had left the country for the week...and that we all should come over there."

"Uhuh? What friend?"

"Reggie."

"OK. And then what happened?"

"Well, we went over there. It was a whole bunch of people over there already—guys and girls and it was about eleven o'clock in the morning. The music was blasting. People were smoking—me, too. And then these two guys got into a fight over some weed that one of them was smoking that the other guy didn't put money in on."

"What else?"

"So then a few people got up to break up the fight—me, my brother and Chico. There were these little girls there about 13 or 14, along with some older girls about 17 or 18. The young girls didn't belong there, at all. It was too much going on there, but they were curious.

"After a while, somebody made a run to the liquor store to buy a few bottles of Vodka, some Remy and Grey Goose. Some people were mixing it and others were drinking it straight. And then it started getting real crazy in there. Out the blue, one girl started giving head to somebody right in the livingroom, with all those people in there. She couldn't have been no more than 14 and she didn't even care. Then there were people having sex in almost every room of the house. It was ridiculous. I mean broads was pissy drunk; walking around the house with just their bras and no panties on; chilling on the sofa; talking on the phone like that and everything.

"My man Black, who never ever has a girl, even had a girl. It took Black awhile to hook up with one, though," Elijah cracked a small smile.

"At one point, I remember seeing him walk around the house with his pants dangling around his ankles and his dick in his hand, asking for somebody to suck it. It was bananas in there—a straight orgy, I'm telling you," Elijah said shaking his head. A smile spread across his face as big as the sun as he replayed that day in his mind.

"And what were you doing?" James asked while taking notes.

"Man, I'm a virgin."

James paused and gave him a 'come-on-now' look.

"I'm dead serious."

James dropped his pen and rubbed his hand over his hair. He exhaled a huge sigh.

"I've never had sex before," Elijah said assuredly. "Now I've let girls give me head, but what I look like fucking them when all of them be fucking each other all the time—sleeping with the same guys around the way. No sir, not the kid."

"You sound like you don't think you can catch a disease from receiving oral sex."

"Well...whatever. I'm not running up in these dirty broads around here."

James shook his head, because he was confused. "What's the difference between putting your penis in her mouth instead of her vagina? You can still catch a disease."

Elijah shrugged.

"So you mean to tell me you've never had sexual intercourse before?"

"I've received head a number of times, but I ain't never been inside nobody."

"Strange."

"Whatever. That's why I know I better not go down for this shit!"

"So are you telling me your brother raped her?"

"Hell no, I'm not saying that! I don't even remember seeing Elgin when all this was going on? And tell me how come this one girl, says she was raped when all these girls was in there getting fucked?"

"That's neither here nor there. If somebody says no, then that means no. It doesn't matter what everybody else was doing. Is there anything else you can tell me about that day?"

"Well, yeah, Ebony—the girl was so freaking drunk it was unbelievable. I mean she was throwing up and what not and Reggie didn't want her in there doing that. He was complaining about what his peeps were going to say if they saw how trashed the house was. He started yelling at her, because she was hurling everywhere. Reggie and a couple of us put her in the alley behind the house."

"Just like that? Ya'll picked her up and put her out."

"Yeah," Elijah said sounding somewhat ashamed as he listened to himself.

"Do you know who all had sex with her?"

"No. But I know she'd fucked that day for sure because she didn't have no clothes on...just a bra and a coat. And it was dried nut all on her thighs and stomach. We threw the rest of her clothes out there with her."

"Unbelievable," James said shaking his head in disgust. He couldn't believe the story he was hearing. What kind of person would do such a thing, he thought to himself. What was happening to the younger generation? Did they have no respect for themselves, both the men and the women in that house? The story sounded so surreal that he didn't know whether he should continue listening or if he should just stop paying attention all together.

"I know it was wrong but..." Elijah continued.

"So then what happened?" James just wanted to get to the end of this madness.

"About twenty minutes after that, some people were on the back porch smoking and saw a police cruiser creep up through the alley and stop right where we left Ebony sitting. The people who were chilling on the porch ran in the house and started screaming 'Bodines'. So everybody in the house started grabbing their clothes and knocking each other over to get out the front door. And we all ran our separate ways. I don't know who went where. I just know it was people running all over the place."

"This is unbelievable," James said shaking his head. "When did you see your brother again?"

"I saw him ride his bike up to me when I was running down the street. I got on with him and then we went home."

"Did you ever see him come from out the house?"

"No, not really."

"Hmmm…" James said pondering everything that Elijah had told him.

"So what do you think will happen to me?"

James said nothing and carefully put all the notes that he had been scribbling down into place. After he shuffled the pages together, he put them into a manila folder and slid them into his briefcase before slamming it shut.

"Mr. Lomax? What do you think will happen?" Elijah repeated staring at James with desperate eyes.

But James shook his head and started heading toward the door. He signaled the officer to let him out.

"Where are you going? What's going to happen to me?" Elijah asked confused.

"That's the same exact story your brother told me, except he was the virgin in his," said James while putting on his coat.

Elijah stared at the back of the door as it closed shut.

***

Iralaun was bored—she didn't think that she would end up spending Christmas alone. It was one of the worst feelings in the world for her. There was too much time to think about her mother and father—and the family she wished she had. Almost everything around her during this holiday reminded Iralaun in one way or another that she was all alone—from the commercials on television to the Christmas songs on the radio. There was virtually no way for her to avoid it.

Normally, Iralaun would've dipped into her stash of guys to occupy her thoughts during this season. But she was in a transition period—she and Allen were on a milder level than she would've anticipated it being at that point and she didn't want to be bothered with her roommate's boyfriend. Craig was a nut, if he actually thought he could continue to have his cake and eat it, too.

It was almost two o'clock in the afternoon, and Iralaun was surprised that Allen had yet to call her. She wanted to see him, but she reasoned that he was probably spending his day with his family. She sipped her third cup of spiked eggnog, then she got comfortable to watch another episode of 'The Martin Lawrence Show' marathon. Then she heard a knock at the door.

Iralaun sat her mug down on the coffee table and stood up to answer the door. She looked through the peephole and saw Craig with a big red and gold wrapped box in his hands. At first, Iralaun started to ignore him, but she was feeling too lonely to do that. Not to mention she was curious to know what was in the box. It was hard for her to resist gifts.

She unlocked the door and swung it open.

"Hey," she said nonchalantly.

"Is that all I get? I haven't seen you in awhile and that's all I get?"

Iralaun smirked and didn't answer him.

"Merry Christmas," he said handing her the box.

"Oh, is this for me or for Brea this time?"

"Come on now. Don't start. Of course, it's for you."

"Is my name on it this time?" Iralaun flipped the box over and over inspecting it.

Craig just smiled and shook his head. He was wearing the black leather jacket Brea brought for his birthday a couple of months ago. He took it off and hung it in the closet with familiarity. Iralaun felt a slight sense of guilt in the pit of her stomach, but plopped down on the couch anyway. She crossed her legs Indian-style and began ripping off the wrapping paper eager to see what was inside the box.

She was surprised when she saw that it was another box inside of it, also wrapped. Iralaun looked at Craig inquisitively, but proceeded opening the next box. When she got through unwrapping it, all kinds of thoughts were going through her mind when she saw another smaller box inside. She had seen something like this on television before, and began praying and hoping, she wouldn't have to embarrass Craig if he had put a ring in there.

When she opened the smallest one, she opened it slowly, and saw that there was a sliver of paper inside with some writing on it.

"What's this?" she asked irritated without even reading it.

"Read it," Craig demanded.

Iralaun looked at the paper, then looked at Craig, then looked back at the paper again.

"Anthony Fugere?" Iralaun said in a peculiar manner.

"Yep. Anthony Fugere," Craig said proudly. "That's your father's name."

Iralaun stared at Craig and then back at the piece of paper. She was confused. Could this possibly be true? How'd he get it? How does he know I had no idea about his name? Questions overwhelmed her.

Iralaun didn't know what to feel or how to express it. A mixture of joy and sadness crept over her. Her emotions were overflowing and caused tiny wells of tears to form in her eyes. She tried to blink them back, but there was no way to keep them from falling.

"But how did you..." Iralaun started to ask. She had no idea that Craig knew anything personal about her life, nor could she fathom how he found out her father's name.

"Well, Brea told me the whole story. And I did a little research. You will be amazed at what you can find with a social security number. Flip it over."

Iralaun flipped the paper over and saw that there was a telephone number and address.

"But how did you..."

"Brea got your social security number off of one of your financial aid papers and I had a good friend of mine to hack into a system or two. It didn't take long at all to find it, seeing whom my father is," Craig bragged.

"But why?" Iralaun asked wiping away tears.

"Shh..." Craig said, and leaned in to kiss her.

Iralaun didn't know how to feel about everything, but when Craig kissed her, she kissed him back with no hesitation. She even wrapped her arms around him. His warmth soothed her at the moment, and she was lost in a flurry of emotions. He had found her father for her. She didn't even realize how not knowing his name affected her so much. Her mother had made her think that she didn't need to know it. But finally learning his name made her feel alive. She finally knew the person who created her along with her mother Isabella, had a name and it was Anthony. It made a difference to her. She could feel her heart healing, as she felt less empty. Iralaun kissed Craig again.

"I thought this would definitely get your attention. Merry Christmas," he whispered.

Iralaun continued kissing Craig as if she couldn't get enough of him. She was so ecstatic and the tears continued to fall from her eyes. Craig picked Iralaun up and carried her to the bedroom, eager to be with her again. He knew he had done right.

In the middle of all the passion, Craig put Iralaun on top of him. He loved her there; it was the perfect view to see her beautiful beige body and he cherished the way she pleased him. While in the midst of riding him, Iralaun opened her eyes for the first time and stared directly at Craig. While she was in a state of utter bliss, Iralaun gazed around the room, and seemingly for the first time, realized that she was not in her bed or in her own room. Craig had brought her to Brea's room. She paused in sheer disbelief and caught her breath.

"What's wrong? What's wrong? Why are you stopping," he asked without opening his eyes.

"Did you do this on purpose?"

"What?" Craig asked confused looking at Iralaun.

"I can't believe you did this?"

"What?" he asked in a way that Iralaun couldn't tell if he was confused or not.

"I'm in Brea's room, you jerk," she said motioning to get up.

"What are you doing? Don't get up!" he said with his hands firmly on her waist.

Iralaun reached down and slapped him. "Get off of me!"

Craig reached for the spot where she had stung his face and rubbed it.

"You are totally taking advantage of this whole situation. I don't feel right anymore. I just…we just…just leave," she said flustered.

"But, it was an accident…I swear."

"Craig…I don't know what you are trying to do or why, but we have to end this."

Craig looked helpless lying in Brea's bed. His penis lied limp on his thigh.

"I feel totally disgusting right now. Do you understand?" she said. "I'm a bitch for what I've been doing. We aren't even using rubbers!"

Craig shook his head. "Look, I don't know what you want from me. You shouldn't have started this. I wasn't alone. Don't try to act like it's my entire fault. You enjoy the sneaking and you know it."

Iralaun was stunned at Craig's choice of words, but knew he was right.

"What do you want from me? You know how I feel about the whole situation now. And then you coming in here with my father's information—something that you know is very emotional for me..."

"Iralaun, what part of this don't you understand. I really like you. It's more than just the sex for me."

She gave him a bizarre facial expression, because she felt like he was losing his mind. "Are you on some sort of medication?" she asked puzzled. "How can you say such a thing?"

"It's true Iralaun. I'm not going to sit here and say that I don't feel something for Brea, of course I love her. But I just can't stop thinking about you, even when I'm with her," he said to her. His words felt like a razor slicing thin lines in her heart.

"Excuse me?"

"I do. If I could have you both I would."

Iralaun's mouth fell open. Who did this spoiled brat think he was? Just because his family had money, he thought he could have whatever he wanted. And she was giving that to him.

"OK, you know what?" Iralaun said putting her clothes back on in a hurry. "This is entirely too much for me to deal with in one day. Just too much! Craig, please leave."

"Leave?"

"Yes, please leave."

Craig looked at her and laid his arms across his chest. He wasn't moving.

"Get out Craig!"

"Naw. I'm not ready yet."

Iralaun rolled her eyes and turned to go to her bedroom. So now he was going to throw a fit because he couldn't get his way, she thought. "His ass could rot in there for all she cared," she mumbled to herself.

She locked her bedroom door and sat on her bed. She had no time to worry about Craig and his immature antics. She finally knew her father's name, she thought as she lied back on the bed.

"Are you going to call your father?" Craig asked standing behind her closed door.

Iralaun sucked her teeth. She really wished that he would leave, there was nothing Craig could say or do to change the relationship that they had. She didn't want him. And providing her father's information was simply not enough for her to continue their illicit affair.

Allen slipped the sliver of paper underneath her door. "I'm about to go Iralaun. I'll call you later."

She sucked her teeth again and yelled, "Please, lock the door behind you."

Actually having her father's phone number and name in her possession was too much for her, she thought as she picked up the paper. When she heard Craig close the door, she walked to her bedroom window to watch him get in his car. After he pulled off she walked out to the living room and picked up the cordless phone. She sat on the couch for awhile with the phone number in one hand and the cordless phone in the other, debating whether or not she should dial the number.

She didn't think having his name and number would ever mean so much to her, but the beat of her heart told her otherwise. Although she'd never even thought about her father, after the many things that her mother said about him, somewhere deep inside she did want to know more about her other half. She felt like a piece of her that was once lost, had now been found. And she was beginning to feel a small sense of healing take over her heart.

Iralaun wasn't sure what she would be unearthing if she called, but at the same time, knew it wouldn't hurt to see where this phone call could lead. After all, it was Christmas.

***

Eve begged her mother to take them over their grandmother's house for Christmas Day. She even got up early, put all of their gifts in a huge trash bag like she did every Christmas, then she went to wake up her mother. After two extra hours of prodding, Vivica finally got up to get dressed. It would be the first Christmas that the whole family didn't spend together and it didn't feel quite right to her.

They started officially celebrating Christmas together a little after they left the church. Rightway didn't believe in holidays, especially Christmas and Easter. Elder Roy preached that the holidays were too commercial and that God didn't want people to spend the day exchanging gifts, but to be in church worshipping Him on those days. And that's what they did, year after year. The children looked forward to going to her mother's because she always had presents for them. Only recently had Vivica began purchasing them all one item off of their Christmas lists.

When Vivica arrived at her mother's house in Southeast, Evan, Eric and Eve ran up the stairs eager to see what their grandmother had gotten them. All of their aunts, uncles and cousins were there already. After she made them dinner plates, the focus of the conversation shifted to what was going on with Elijah and Elgin. Vivica had tried to shy away from the topic from the moment she walked in the door. And for awhile, everyone gave her some space on it, but their patience was growing thin.

They ate her mother's famous collard green quiche, baked macaroni and cheese, juicy cornbread stuffed turkey and her sweet potato biscuits first. Everybody knew she didn't want to discuss it. But after dinner, Evan spoke up for her. Lately he had begun to act like the man of the house, since his older brothers hadn't stepped up to the plate and weren't being good role models for the rest of them. He knew that his mother had tried to do the best she could for them. He sympathized with her and tried to do the best he could to help her. He earned a lot of fights from the twins because of it, but he didn't care.

If only she could be proud of at least one of them, Evan reasoned. He knew that it wasn't her fault that things were tight for them. Evan often wondered how his father could turn his back so abruptly, but he never said much to his mother about it. When his aunt and uncles began to ask questions about the twins and he saw that his mother wasn't going to volunteer any thing, he said, "We don't know much and probably won't know until after my mother talks to the lawyer tomorrow. Can we just open our gifts now?"

"Well, wait a second," said Vivica's brother, Vincent. "Is there any truth to what's being said in the news?"

"Go ahead downstairs and play," Vivica said to her children before answering her brother. Evan glared at his mother, because he didn't know if she was going to tell them anything. But she nodded and reassured him that she would be OK. Evan gathered up Eric and Eve and the rest of his cousins and they all marched down to the basement. He could hear his mother sighing, before she said, "I don't know much Vincent. I have to talk to the lawyer."

"You can't tell us anything?" he asked perplexed.

"Nope. If ya'll would just bear with me and be there to support me and the boys, I'd appreciate it a lot," Vivica said trying to control her anger and disappointment in her family. It had grown over the past couple of years, because no one seemed to care about what she was going through, but always had a lot to say when the twins got in trouble. Everybody had some sort of remedy for their problems five minutes after the fact. None of them wanted to take on the responsibility of making sure the twins were doing the right thing before chaos erupted.

"Viv...it's not like those are some angels you got," Venice said dryly.

She was Vivica's older sister. "I mean they've been driving you crazy for the past two or three years. I say leave their behinds in there, regardless of if they did it or not. I don't know why you let them get that bad in the first place!"

"Why I let them get bad? I didn't let them do anything!" Vivica stressed.

"You never stopped them boys when they were doing stuff like messing up Mama's house when they visited or was breaking up my sons' toys when they were younger. You thought they were going to act more civilized when they got older?"

"First of all, why didn't you tell them to stop? You're their aunt. I tell your kids to act right when you aren't around. And that's what kids do Venice. They play, and if they were doing something you thought was wrong, you should have said something. I corrected your kids."

"You've never told my kids anything, because they don't act like your demons."

"I beg your pardon? How easily we forget these days? If you want to blame me for the way my kids act, then I hope you sleep better at night thinking that way, because I don't. I know the truth. Nobody in this house helped me with them—period!"

"Nobody?" asked Vivica's mother shocked.

"Mama, you helped me in other ways, but doing simple things like spending time with them, or letting them spend the weekend with y'all, no one in this room can ever say they did that."

"That's a damn lie, because the time they messed up my boys' toys, they were over my house for the night," Venice said.

"And that was the last time wasn't it? How old were they then? Seven—so get over it and grow the hell up! I'm sick of your complaining like you are so perfect!"

"Whoa, whoa! Calm down you two," said Vaughn, Vivica's youngest brother.

"Don't you tell me to calm down," Venice yelled. "She's lost her ever-loving mind talking to me like that."

"No, don't tell me to calm down, either. Where were you?" Vivica asked looking at her baby-brother. "Or you?" she asked looking at Vincent.

"What you mean?" Vincent asked. "We came over there to talk to them a couple of times."

Vivica rolled her eyes. "That was way too late then. But now you want to know what happened to them. You should have asked that years ago, when you first started noticing that they were being disrespectful and acting out of control. I asked for all of y'all's help, but everybody was too busy or too selfish to even say 'Viv, send the boys over here this weekend, so you can get a break.' Never. Nobody once said, 'I need to spend some time with them so they can feel like somebody care about them.' But that's just it. None of you care. You all act like we are extended family members who live in a different state or something. None of you cared and they feel it. And they act out because they need attention. They say all the time that nobody cares. And it's true."

"Those are your kids," Vincent said.

"And they're your nephews."

"They don't listen to me—any of us!" Vaughn fumed.

"So why do y'all think they will listen to me...if two, big, strong men can't get them to listen to them?"

"That's what you get for marrying a crackhead," Venice snickered under her breath and cut another piece of pecan pie. "Everybody knows those are crackbabies."

"You witch..." Vivica said jumping up into her sister's face. "Don't let me ever hear you..."

"Hold up!" Vincent said breaking the two of them up. "It's Christmas for God's sake! Calm down! Mama, please take Vivica in your room."

"Get off of me! I will not allow her to talk about my children that way," Vivica said pulling away from her brothers. "Especially when her ex-husband is just as bad as Eddie was. When's the last time you seen him and his other family?"

"Baby, come on," her mother said pulling her down the hall.

"Don't bring my business into this. You're just mad because you know it's true," Venice yelled at Vivica.

"I think it's so ironic, how now my life is such a concern to everybody in this house, but when I came to y'all—every single last one of y'all, when things was starting to get really bad—everybody turned a deaf ear. That's what's wrong with this family. It's everybody else's problem."

"You're right Viv. Because they don't listen, and neither do you. We were trying to tell you about Eddie a long time ago, but you just had to have him, didn't you?"

"Why don't you just shut up? What does that have to do with today? You act like ain't nobody ever tell you your ex-husband was sleeping with his coworker years ago. How long did it take you to realize that? When she had your husband's baby?" Vaughn asked.

"Shut up!" Venice yelled.

"But you want to kick everybody else's skeletons out of the closet," Vaughn said. "Can't y'all tell Vivica's stressed out over this whole situation? Two, not one, of her kids is up on some rape charges!"

"Vaughn's right," Vincent said. "Let her have a moment to calm down. Everybody needs to just calm down."

"Yes, she needs our support...not all of this. That's the least we can do after all these years of ignoring the situation."

All of the children had stopped playing X-Box games in the basement and were trying to find out what all the commotion was upstairs.

"What's going on?" Evan asked.

"Nothing, sweetheart. Go on back downstairs," said their grandmother.

"But what's wrong with my mother?" Evan asked again.

"She's in my room. You can talk to her in a little while."

Evan pushed past his grandmother to go see Vivica.

"Ma, what's going on?"

"Nothing Evan," Vivica said exhaling. "Are you enjoying your gifts?"

"Yes."

"Good. That's all that I'm worried about right now."

***

Belinda didn't know how to feel about not receiving a call from Kevin to come to Christmas dinner. Her sister's boyfriend popped the question to Brandi during dinner. Her baby sister beat her, and would be getting married before she would. And she wasn't even close to being in a relationship. Belinda couldn't wait to get back home to curl up in her bed. She felt worthless.

Though her mother was ecstatic, her father had no reaction. Ingrid couldn't convince him to come out of the bedroom the entire day. Belinda was glad Kevin didn't see all of that; she would've been embarrassed. When she went back to her condominium later that evening, the doorman told her that he had a package for her that he'd been keeping since earlier that afternoon. Belinda was surprised and couldn't wait to open it. She couldn't imagine who was thinking about her on Christmas. When the doorman picked the box up, she was surprised to see wholes punched out on the sides.

"What could this be?" she asked him baffled.

"All I know is that you might want to take it out soon, because it probably needs to have its paper changed," he said smiling.

CHAPTER 11

I just called to say thank you," Iralaun said, "For making the past nineteen years of my life difficult. I thought I'd give you a chance to say your piece, but all you got to tell me is that you tried to look for me? No, I'm sorry—that is not good enough. You can't come up with something better than that?"

"I looked for you," Anthony said again, "you and your mother."

"But?"

"But I couldn't find you."

"Is that the only pathetic answer you have for me? Nineteen years and that's all you have to say about that?"

"Iralaun, let's start over," Anthony said before taking a deep breath. "There is so much we need to talk about and over the phone is not the best way to do it."

Iralaun sucked her teeth.

"There is so much that you don't know about what happened between me and your mother and I think it's best that you know about it. Let's start over."

"Let's not!" she said pressing the 'Talk' button on the phone and throwing it across the room.

"What a waste of my time," she mumbled to herself. "I can't believe the gull of that bastard!"

Iralaun wrapped her arms across her chest, and began to talk to herself aloud.

"'Let's start over.' Just like that, huh? Let's just forget all the years you weren't there. He doesn't know a thing about me and now wants me to give him a chance? Did he give me or my mother a chance before he walked out on us? Please!" she said while straightening up the living room.

As disappointed as she was, Iralaun couldn't shake the undeniable feeling of wanting to know about her father, and his side of the family. It had always been a nagging feeling deep in her heart. It was like a tiny crack on a window shield that had begun to splinter like a spider web after time—cascading the entire glass. If only she had the pieces to fill the many tiny wholes in her heart. How could he turn his back on his own flesh and blood so easily, she wondered?

The pain in Iralaun's heart would not heal easily. Just knowing that he was alive and well and wasn't a part of her life, deflated her spirit. When she was younger, she used to dream that he had been killed or was in jail and just couldn't get to her. It was those thoughts that comforted her through the years. She felt that if he had been killed or imprisoned that it wouldn't have been his fault that he couldn't reach her. But to know that he lived in the same city she did, and that he had made no attempt to find her, only infuriated her.

Growing up without a father was a terrible and arduous thing for her. She always felt like a kid who had been adopted as a child, because she never felt complete without knowing him. To push herself ahead, she would assign characteristics to the man she didn't know. Whatever demeaning thing her mother used to say about her father, she would think the opposite.

Sometimes she felt like a traitor to her mother when she would secretly do this. But it was what helped her through it all. Iralaun couldn't accept that her father had abandoned her like that; she just couldn't comprehend the concept. Why her, she wondered. What was so wrong with her?

She used to get an effervescent feeling when daydreaming about the kind of man she hoped her father was. In her mind, he was a tall, strong, muscular man, who had a radiant smile and a thick mustache. She even dreamed that they had the same deep dimples and pudgy nose. She dreamed that he loved the same kind of animals and books as she, and that his favorite color was green like hers.

When Iralaun was in elementary school, she would tell her classmates that her father was a secret agent who worked for the CIA. She told them that he was always traveling around the world on secret missions. That fib may have worked in elementary school, but by the time she got to junior high school, she had to let that fantasy go, because no one bought it. Her new story was that her dad was killed during a recognizance mission in the Persian Gulf. Most people didn't care enough to ask any probing questions. But the lies worked as gauze for the open wounds in her heart. Her mother never knew how she felt about her father. She only listened as her mother went on various tantrums about how her father was no good or how much Iralaun reminded her of her no good father, whenever she made bad decisions on something.

Although Isabella, too, had many bad decisions in her life, she would always love her. She was the one who was there, taking care of her. She knew Iralaun's favorite animals, authors and that her favorite color was green. She knew that her favorite food was lasagna and that her favorite dessert was orange sherbet. Her mother made sure Iralaun had those things and more. She was the one who helped her late at night with homework or took her back and forth to her jazz dance lessons or to volleyball practice. Her mother was there, and the man she created in her mind, which was merely a figment of her imagination, could never replace that.

"And a partridge in a pear tree," Iralaun sang as she poured the leftover eggnog down the sink.

The phone started to ring while Iralaun bent over to pick up some of the remnants of snacks she had been gorging from off the coffee table. She stuffed the snack wrappings in the boxes Craig had brought over and put it in the garbage. The phone's excessive rings continued. Thinking it was her father trying to call her back, she started not to answer the phone, but the irritating ring was annoying her. She searched for the muffled-sounding telephone and found it under the sofa. She looked at the Caller ID, and was relieved when she saw it was Allen calling from his cell phone. She snatched it up as quickly as she could. As soon as she said, "Hello" she heard a knock at the door.

Iralaun looked out the peephole and was flabbergasted to see Allen standing there with a silver basket tied with a red ribbon in his hand. She swung the door open with a big smile on her face. Seeing Allen made her feel good again. He was right on time.

"Hey you," she said.

"Hey. I got this for you," he said handing her the basket.

"Thank you," she said taking it and placing it on the dinning room table. "How was your day?"

"It was OK. I spent all morning with my mother and visiting family. I wasn't sure if you were going to be here, but I'd just left my aunt's house around the corner and I wanted to bring this to you. Go ahead and open it," Allen said taking off his coat.

"Hmmm...Let's see. What do you have here?" she said smiling and untying the pretty red ribbon.

"How was your day?"

Iralaun heaved a sigh. "I think today is going to go down in history as one of the most bizarre of my entire young life."

"Why? What happened?"

"I don't even want to talk about it," she said pulling a box of chocolates out of the basket. "Oh you got me Mary J. Blige's new CD. Thank you. Oh, no you didn't..."

Allen started laughing as Iralaun pulled out a Discovery Animal Mating Ritual DVD. "I mean I thought we could watch that and put the debate to rest."

She started laughing. "You are silly."

"So are you going to tell me what happened today?"

"Do I have to? I'd rather not," she said opening the box of chocolates.

"OK. We don't. I'll just put this movie in," he said walking up toward the mini-entertainment center. Iralaun began reading a card that was also in the basket.

"Oh I didn't know you knew Craig," he said looking at a picture of Craig and Brea on top of the television.

Iralaun almost swallowed a chocolate whole. "Um, yeah he goes with my roommate Brea. How do you know him?"

"He's in my major. We took a couple of classes together. Been in the same circle of people you know?"

"Oh yeah?"

"Yeah, he's pretty cool. He just don't really take school that seriously. I had him in a group project once—one of those graduate/undergraduate electives I took. And he was just the worst...didn't want to do nothing. Anybody can tell that he doesn't really want to be in school."

"I guess he don't have to with all the money his parents have."

"Yeah. I guess."

The phone rang. It was sitting by Allen, so he reached over and handed it to Iralaun. She saw that it was Craig calling. He would call at that time, she thought. She didn't know if not answering it would seem weird to Allen, so she did.

"Hello."

"Hey, I left my watch over there. You mind if I come back to get it?"

Iralaun sucked her teeth. "Yes, I mind. You can get it tomorrow."

"I'm just down the street. It'll only take a second."

"No. Now is not a good time."

"You got company or something?"

"Craig, you can't go a day without your watch? Why can't you just come by to get it tomorrow?" Iralaun bit her lip as she realized what she'd just said aloud.

"That's Craig? Tell him I said what's up?" Allen said.

Iralaun started feeling nervous for some reason. She wasn't quite sure why. She and Allen weren't together, but she knew Craig was a grenade ready to explode. She had no idea how he'd react. So she just hung up the phone, hoping Craig would get the hint then turned to Allen and said, "His cell phone dropped the signal."

"Oh," Allen said snuggling closer to Iralaun.

The phone rang again, and Iralaun knew that she would have to get rid of Craig some kind of way. He could not come back over her house. The situation would've been too awkward.

"Hello?"

"What happened?"

"My friend Allen said to tell you hi. You, two, know each other from school?"

"Oh, so you do have company? Allen? Allen?" Craig said trying to recall who she was talking about. "Oh you mean Allen Richardson, he's in the 5-year MBA program?"

"Yeah."

"You messing with that bama ass nigga? I thought he was engaged or something to some white chick from Montgomery County."

Iralaun was stunned. Craig was lying and she knew it. Why was she listening to him? He had to be confusing him with someone else. Not her Allen.

"Tell him I said what's up? Can I come get my watch," she heard him say.

Iralaun just sat silent on the phone for a second. Then she turned to Allen and said, "Are you engaged?"

A smile spread across his face. "No, I'm not engaged. Is that Craig again?"

She nodded.

"Why is that man hating on me?" Allen asked.

Iralaun shook her head confused.

"Well, I could be wrong," Craig said. "But that's what I heard. Anyway, I'll just get the watch later."

"Mmmhhmm," Iralaun said before she hung up.

"What was that about?" Allen asked.

Iralaun shrugged. "You guys kill me." The thought of Allen with someone else cluttered her mind. Was that really where he was this morning? People usually spent Christmas morning with the people they love the most.

"What are you talking about?" Allen asked confused.

"I'm just tired—exhausted. I'm tired of being confused. Maybe you should leave. I had a long day and today is just not the day for more surprises."

Allen looked shocked, but could tell that Iralaun was serious about needing some space, so he got up and put his coat on. "I don't know what that was all about, but you need to have faith in somebody."

Iralaun rolled her eyes and looked for her pack of clove-flavored cigarettes. She desperately needed one. She just didn't feel like dealing with much of anything at that moment. "I just had a long day, really. And I don't know what to make of most of it."

Allen zipped up his coat, then said "Iralaun, you have a lot of issues—a lot. I know you have a hard time trusting people, and granted you may have a right to be somewhat apprehensive and cautious. We all are, to a degree. I know you don't open up to people a lot either, but I'll wait for you. I know you have a lot on your mind and even more to figure out. Just call me if you feel like talking."

"Wait Allen," Iralaun said putting her hand to her forehead and then running her fingers through her hair. There was something about his sincerity that made her want to believe him. "Please stay."

"Is it too late to say Merry Christmas?"

***

It was the day after Christmas and all of the wrapping paper from presents was in the garbage. The Christmas tree in the living room had begun to lean and stencil was all around the floor. Vivica couldn't wait to hear from James Lomax. She was anxious to learn more details about what was going on with Elijah and Elgin's case. It had been a long weekend and she decided to call him, instead of wait for him to contact her. But when James told her, how confused he was, she became just as bewildered.

"What's going to have to happen?" she asked agitated and perplexed.

"Ms. Jeffries..."James began.

"Please call me Vivica."

"Sure," he heaved a thick sigh. "Vivica, it seems that we may have a huge problem."

"Oh no...what do you mean by that?"

"We have to wait until the DNA evidence comes in–the test results may be able to totally exclude both of them—which would be great! That's what we want to hear."

"Unhuh." she said confused. She knew there was something James was trying to tell her.

"So far," he paused, then said, "the story Elijah and Elgin told me, total-

116

ly excludes both of them, as well. But it doesn't make any sense."

"What do you mean?"

James took a long deep breath, then said, "Well, you see...it's the same exact story, only told from two different people. And that's virtually impossible, unless they corroborated before they met with me."

"What do you mean?" she asked confused. James Lomax wasn't making any sense to Vivica. She heard him speaking, but nothing he was saying added up.

James took another long breath to decide what would be the best way to approach the subject.

"When Elijah and Elgin were telling me their stories...at two entirely different times—it was odd; it was like they were repeating the words to a popular song—as if what they faced was unimportant," James said shaking his head and sighing. "I was peeved. In my opinion, they are taking this case with a grain of salt. It's like a joke to them."

"Hmmm..." Vivica sighed. She was mentally spent.

"It seems I've got my hands filled with this case. Either they know something that I don't know or we may have a laborious task ahead of us."

Vivica sighed again.

"The only thing we can do now is wait for the initial DNA tests to come back. We may be good to go, if neither of their DNA samples match the semen specimens taken from the girl. But if it does...we have a huge problem."

"Why do you say that?"

"Ms. Jeffries, I mean Vivica, no two individuals have the same exact DNA fingerprints, except identical twins. If they were fraternal then that would be a different story, but identical, means just that, identical."

Vivica's mouth dropped, "You're kidding me, Mr. Lomax? Even a DNA test won't tell between the two of them?"

"Unfortunately not and please call me James."

"We'd definitely be in trouble then, right?"

"Yes. One of them would have to admit it or take the fall for the other."

"What if neither of them admits to anything? Then what would happen?"

"Then the prosecution will try to prove which one of them did it, by other evidence they may have. Whether it's first hand account from witnesses or some other evidence."

"Wow," she said shaking her head in disappointment. "This is a little too much for one person to bear."

"Believe me, I understand. I've never worked on a case like this before—not in my five years of practice. All we can do now is pray that the DNA tests will exclude both of them as participating in any sexual activity with the young lady, because after that, it's really just her word against theirs."

Vivica nodded. "Pray, I will. Will they be released soon?"

"After the preliminary hearing, they should be released in your custody. And then all we have to do is wait for the test results to come back."

Vivica groaned. She dreaded the day, but said, "OK."

"OK, well I'll call you as soon as I learn anything new."

"Thank you Mr. Lomax, I mean…James."

"You are welcome. I'll talk to you later."

***

The Christmas holiday was a complete blur for Belinda. She didn't really want to remember that her sister was getting married. When her new cat jumped up on her bed, she smiled, thinking of Kevin. His gift was sweet—a fluffy white Persian kitten. She couldn't believe that he'd brought her a gift, and a living one at that. She hadn't even given him the gift she had for James—and it felt good. It was a gift from his heart and she knew it meant a lot.

"I am so happy that you liked the cat," Kevin said a few days after the holidays. "But I'm sorry I missed dinner with your family."

"Yes, Artica, is absolutely beautiful!" Belinda said about her fluffy white cat.

"Artica, huh? I don't know about that name," he said smiling into the phone. "But I get it."

"Oh I'm funny? What did you want me to name it? Snowball?" she joked.

"When I saw her, I knew she'd be perfect for you. I mean one look at your place, with all of the white furniture and decorations and I knew that you'd love her. Plus, she's very independent, just like you. I'm sure you'll realize that she doesn't need as much attention as you think."

"Thank you Kevin," she said acknowledging his compliment. She saw it as a metaphor for herself as well. He was right. She didn't need that much attention. She was used to making things happen for herself anyway. But she wouldn't deny the fact that it felt good to be with someone. Having someone do nice and romantic things for her felt wonderful and it was done without

118

any strings attached. Kevin had a kind of chivalry that she couldn't recall seeing in years.

"So when can I make dinner up to you?" he asked.

She was surprised to hear that from him. She was disappointed that he couldn't make it to her family's Christmas dinner, but she knew it probably would've been an awkward situation for both of them—especially with the bizarre relationship she has with her family. And not to mention the fact that he was married and still wearing his wedding ring. How was she going to explain that to her family?

She still wanted to spend time with him and his offer to make up dinner would fill that void. "Um, well what about tomorrow night?"

"That sounds good. Well, I'll pick you up around seven o'clock?"

"Yes. Seven o'clock is perfect."

Belinda was too excited. She took a quick look at her docket for the afternoon, and was happy to see that she only had to attend one more hearing that day. She cleared her desk of the remnants of the turkey and Swiss on rye sandwich, and headed to the restroom. While walking down the hall, she thought she saw James heading inside one of the courtrooms. Since Belinda had another thirty minutes before her next hearing was to begin, she decided to take a peak inside the room to see if it was James.

Besides a cluster of people sitting on the rows of benches at the back of the room, the stenographer and a bailiff, the courtroom was pretty empty. She walked down the aisle and nodded at the bailiff, whom she recognized. It was James, she'd seen.

"Hello Mr. Lomax," she said. "You have a hearing here today?"

Recognizing her voice, James paced himself before looking up. "Ah...you aren't going to try to slap me or anything, are you?"

She smirked and said, "Though you certainly deserve it, I'm much more mature than that."

James smirked, too. "I know you, and if we weren't in court, you probably would've already socked me."

Belinda shook her head and smiled recalling many of the minimal physical attacks she put James through during many of their terse arguments—a plate of food here, and a glass of wine there. "I'm working on that."

"You sure you don't want to throw a chair at me or anything?"

She rolled her eyes and said "In all seriousness, you are trying to make light of this, when what you did to me was very serious and hurtful," she whispered through pursed lips.

James nodded in agreement. "You are right. But I know sorry will never suffice for you. You will never be satisfied with any apology I offer, but I will extend one any way."

Belinda rolled her eyes again and said, "Extend one? What you did to me not only hurt, but I was very humiliated that afternoon. I was humiliated throughout the whole relationship really. How any woman could continue being with you, while knowing first hand, what kind of dog you are, is beyond me."

"Look, Belinda, if you came here to argue, it's definitely not the time or the place for your usual outbursts. What you and I had was never what you thought it was. Let it go...chalk it up as a loss and move on. So if you'll now excuse me."

"Excuse me? You conceited bastard."

James sneered and asked, "Are you done, because I have work to do?"

Belinda sucked her teeth, but before leaving she said, "I hope you know Judge Malaney is planning to throw your boys the freaking book."

James huffed and Belinda turned to leave. It felt good giving him a piece of her mind and having the last word about their relationship.

***

The day of the hearing, Vivica could not get off at the hospital. Three of the other nurses were out—one was on vacation still and the other two were out sick. She kept her pager on as she waited to hear something from James. He said he would call her as soon as the hearing was over. Vivica still hadn't had an opportunity to visit them and she knew that Elijah and Elgin felt like she was turning her back on them. But that wasn't the case at all.

While she waited for word, Vivica stayed busy at work helping patients. But she was a nervous wreck. She had a hard time concentrating and her supervisor took notice of it.

"Vivica, can I see you for a minute?" she asked after Vivica assisted an elderly patient down the hall to his room.

"Yes, please give me a second."

Vivica knew immediately what it was about. After she returned from the patient's room, she walked toward the supervisor's station and sat down.

"Look Vivica, I know you are going through a lot right now. You've been calling in a lot and leaving early due to a lot of things that's been going on with you and your family. Believe me I sympathize with your situation, completely. I wish I could let you go home, but we are already down three people. I am going to need you to pull yourself together for me."

Vivica nodded in agreement. She knew her problems with her boys were starting to affect a lot of things at work. Her absenteeism rate had increased a lot over the past few months and her work ethic had begun to change as well because of all of her worries. Vivica had been on probation for three months because of the changes in her work performance. She knew that she had to improve, but she couldn't pull her mind away from her kids.

"Go take a break or a walk around the block to calm your nerves. I don't want to ask the doctor to give you some medicine while you are on duty, but I will if I have too."

"You're right. Let me just take a break. I'll be outside for a few minutes."

"Things will get better soon, I'm sure," her supervisor offered.

Vivica gave her a smug smile, turned to walk down the hall to get her coat and then walked through the hospital's main entrance. She started walking toward the back of the building, where the inoperative ambulances were parked and then around the corner. While outside, she saw several people she knew. She tried to return their smiles, but found it to be strenuous.

She felt like there wasn't much to smile about in her life anymore. Even though, she and her family had their health, sometimes she wished that she could be at total peace. Vivica felt like she was always being pulled in different directions like a child's brand new puppy. Tears rolled down her cheeks, and the cold wind quickly dried them, leaving thin white lines on her brown face.

Vivica began thinking about how much her life changed. Over the past few years, she kept a migraine headache and didn't know if she would ever totally rid them. She wasn't eating right lately or getting the rest she needed. Not having any help from her family or from her ex-husband's family was causing Vivica to feel even more alone and hopeless.

Vivica never dreamed that she would end up being a single parent— never in a million years did she think that. They were married. Wasn't that the way you were supposed to do it? Get married, have children, then live happily ever after. It wasn't like her children had a whole bunch of different fathers. They shared the same father who was once her husband and it still didn't make a difference. Eddie was worse than trifling. And here she was all alone, trying to keep their family together like glue.

So here she was a single parent, wearing twenty different hats and she wanted so much to be strong for her kids. She knew that only she could hold herself responsible for the decisions she had made in her life. It had been a long journey for her to reach the point in her life where she could even think such a thing. Yes, it was she who had to make decisions, and though some of them had been mistakes, she knew that she'd made the best decision she could at the time, with the knowledge she had. She couldn't go back and change the past; she could only redirect their future.

"Life for me ain't been no crystal stair," she mumbled to herself the opening lines to her favorite Langston Hughes poem.

Ever since she and Eddie divorced, she focused on bettering the lives of her family. Even in doing so, the twins would say that she was doing the total opposite. Elijah and Elgin never seemed to be happy with anything that she'd done. They felt that if Vivica wasn't in the house, that she wasn't making her children her top priority. It was hard for them to see or understand that many of the things she had done were only for them.

No one criticized where her shoes had been to get the things that they had in life. No one may ever know the truth about how much she struggled, going without meals, disregarding her own health, at times, to make sure they had. She never asked for a standing ovation from anyone for doing those things. She knew that it was all a part of doing what was necessary for them to survive.

No one ever told her that it would be easy, that, she knew. "Without struggle, there is no progress," she recalled an encouraging line often said by Frederick Douglass to remind herself of the even longer journey ahead. But even she needed a break from worrying. Over the years, she found small ways to find an inner-joy for herself. She started going out, to take her mind off of her home and the many uphill battles ahead.

When the twins were younger, they often complained that she had spent too much time hanging out, going to clubs and even dating. Vivica felt that she was the adult, and as long as she was the one providing for them as the head of the household, that she was entitled to do what she was pleased to do. She was entitled to be an adult, as long as she was responsible, she reasoned.

But the years began to pass by and she began to notice that her children's unruly behavior had begun to intensify the closer the week got to Friday. It was as if the children felt that they were being left behind. Vivica spent the majority of her teenaged years as a parent and in an abusive marriage. Why couldn't she do the things that people her age were doing? She continued to go out with friends and on dates. Though she never really became serious with any of the men she dated. She brought a man home only on one occasion, but because of the reaction she got from her twin sons, she stopped introducing her male friends to them.

The twins had begun hanging up on anyone who called the house whom they didn't want to speak to her—both Vivica's male and female friends. They even hung up on relatives whom they felt didn't care about them, including those who called long distance. Vivica was irate when she found out that's what they were doing. She paid the phone bill, not them. In order to alleviate the problem and to ease some of the tension in the house, Vivica got them separate lines. But the worse the children's behavior became, the less and less she went out on the town.

She relented, because she'd rather see them happy. But she felt that doing what she wanted to do showed the twins that she was still the boss in the house. They would just have to respect that. But the twins' behavior with babysitters left her without anyone wanting to care for them. They started stealing from the sitters first, and then it quickly escalated to arguments, and later threats. Once one of the sitters walked into the twins' room while Elgin was having sex with a young girl he had sneaked into the house while the sitter was in the bathroom. The babysitter was livid and embarrassed. She called Vivica immediately and told her that she was leaving because she did not want to be responsible for them anymore. "They were out of control," as she had put it. And Vivica couldn't blame her, when she found out what had happened.

Knowing that her children were having sex didn't surprise her. It was the fact they had the audacity to do it, while the sitter was in the house. They had no respect for anyone.

Over the years, the twins had been in and out of jail for a slew of misdemeanor crimes. They were no longer in school and didn't have any goals beyond making through whatever the day that it was. They stayed in the streets, and stayed involved in various illegal activities. They had begun to hang around a known neighborhood drug dealer named Osei. She despised him for the time he spent with her children. He was much older and she knew what he was involved in.

One time she saw Osei and some other neighborhood hoodlums standing in front of her fence. She knew what they were up to, and wanted to make sure they knew that they were not going to sell drugs in front of her house. With her boys begging her against it, Vivica walked right outside directly toward the crowd of young men with baggy clothes and sweat shirts on, and told them she didn't appreciate them hanging in front of her house.

She had no idea what they would say or do, but she wasn't scared of them. She had worked too hard for her house, to have them bringing attention from police and drug addicts. They stared at her and then Osei said,

"No, problem Ma'am. We'll move." Though they moved, they didn't move far enough away. She wanted them totally out of her community, not across the street at the corner store. But she was glad they weren't near her yard anymore. Later, she learned why Osei was so polite that day. He was making plans to take the twins under his wing.

Vivica felt stuck and wanted to give up. Elijah and Elgin had become so bad. They were destroying her and everything she'd tried hard to preserve. They were too young for her to put them out, yet, too old to be put into boot camp—many of which charged outlandish prices, that she couldn't afford. When the police caught them doing things, they usually let them go, because it didn't compare to the many other crimes that made the nation's capitol one of the worst places to live.

Vivica was exhausted. Her strength was waning. And though she hated to admit it, she secretly wanted something to happen to the twins. Something brash enough that would make them wake up. She hated to admit that both Elgin and Elijah were actually capable of rape. She knew they were capable of inflicting pain on people, because of fights in the streets that left one twin with a scar wound from a stabbing and the other twin with a nick on his leg, where a bullet had grazed him.

She didn't want to see her boys in jail, but they needed help before something more traumatic happened to them. No one seemed to care what happened to them, but her anyway. Vivica didn't know where to go to get help either. If the police couldn't recommend someone, then who could? When they were younger Vivica pulled out a phone book and went up and down the Yellow Pages calling places that offered the assistance she had needed. She searched every where from non-profit organizations to churches to local Boys and Girls Clubs, and as long as she didn't have control enough to make them come in to receive help, then the twins wouldn't get it. Places liked that helped at-risk children on a voluntary basis only and Vivica needed something that would be mandatory for the twins—a court order or something similar.

She even begged several judges to send them to juvenile halls or programs where they would have to be for a period of time. Once she wrote her city councilman and an editorial to the Post about her situation, to no avail. Vivica even got in the faces of several social workers. "If you won't help, then please tell me who will? Will it take for my boys to be lying in someone's gutter dead before you care that they are on their way to becoming victims of the street? It'll be far too late then," she argued.

Several times, when she was in the midst of an argument with Elijah and Elgin, they would ask her why she would even consider having "all them kids with somebody who you knew wasn't any good." Sometimes they would even argue that they acted the way they did because it was in their blood. "You're the one who keeps saying we're just like our father. How did you expect us to turn out?" they would ask.

Vivica wanted peace of mind. She couldn't take it anymore. She began walking back inside the entrance of the hospital. As soon as she took her coat off to hang up, her pager went off. She ripped it off of her waist and clutched it in her hands. She was relieved to see that it was the boys' lawyer. She raced to the nearest telephone to return his call.

"Mr. Lomax, I mean James?"

"Yes! I have news for you. Are you sitting down?"

"Oh God, what?" Vivica asked slowly sitting down.

"Ms. Jeffries…the judge announced in court this afternoon the results of the DNA tests."

"And…"

"And they're inconclusive in finding evidence for either of the twins as participants in any sexual activity."

"Oh my God…yes!" Vivica yelled. "Does that mean they're coming home?"

"Yes, it does. They are free to go!"

Vivica exhaled and put her jacket back on to leave.

"I'll be there right away," she said into the phone.

"I don't know if this is the appropriate thing to say or not, but congratulations."

"No, thank you Mr. Lomax. Thank you so much. This news has made my day! I'll be there in twenty minutes."

Vivica hung up and darted towards the hospital's entrance with the voice of her supervisor calling her name in the distance.

***

"So what's really going on up there?" Allen asked Iralaun as he tapped her head. She lied in his arms while lounging on his sofa in his apartment. "You have a lot going on up there don't you?"

She rolled her eyes. "How about you tell me what's going on with you? Why are you interested in me?"

Allen sighed. "Why are you going to ask me such an insecure question like that?" he said sitting up and shaking his head.

"What do you mean insecure?"

"It is. You should know why without a shadow of a doubt. If you knew yourself, then you wouldn't care what my particular reasons for being interested are. You would know that there are a lot reasons why any person would be interested in you."

"Who said I didn't think like that already? I just want to know why you find me interesting."

"Why don't you just tell me why you think I shouldn't be?"

Iralaun sucked her teeth and then stood up.

"Oh it's always your way or no way," Allen said. "You are something else, you know that?"

Iralaun put her shoes on and looked around the room for her purse.

"Why are you acting like that? Why are you giving up like that?" he said standing up with her.

"Excuse me," she said trying to push pass him.

"Iralaun, I'm interested in you—because you amaze me. OK? Is that enough?"

Iralaun grabbed her coat.

"Don't leave."

"Allen. Look you are a cool guy. But you yourself have said that I have a lot of issues. I want to know why you want to deal with me. That's a simple question and if you are having problems answering it, then I need to leave."

Allen shook his head. "Running. Go ahead then, run. I'm not stopping you this time. I'm not going to beg you to stay. You women are a trip."

"I beg your pardon?"

"You heard me. Always talking about you want a good man; you want this in a man; you want that in a man...and then when one is right in front of you," Allen paused then said, "But still, for some odd reason, he ain't never good enough. So leave. Because if you can't see that I'm good for you, then you don't deserve to be with me."

Iralaun looked at him with her mouth wide open. She couldn't even form her mouth to say all the things that were going through her mind.

"You're confused aren't you?" he asked. "Why don't you just go ahead and swallow your pride. Just put all those bags down that are filled with issues you keep trying to sneak into this relationship that I'm trying to build with you."

Iralaun paused and stood still with her back to him.

Allen walked up to her and said, "Iralaun, why don't you just take your coat off."

But she felt uncomfortable. His frankness shocked her. There had been something about Allen from Day One that intrigued her. As much as she wanted to curse him out and tell him how much she didn't need to be with him, she felt drawn to his wisdom. She wasn't sure if it was because of his confidence, or because she felt like he could definitely help her. All she knew was that she couldn't convince her feet to move at that moment.

"Why don't you just go ahead and accept that you met me for a reason?"

Allen leaned in and started helping Iralaun take off her coat.

"See that wasn't so hard was it?"

"I just...don't understand you," she said relenting.

"I'm not so bad am I?"

"Why don't you just give up on me? I'm such a head case?"

"Stop asking so many questions," he said and bent down to kiss her on her forehead.

"See just like that. What guy just kisses a girl on her forehead after a scene like that? You are supposed to ravish me," Iralaun said. "You're supposed to finally kiss me on my lips, then undress me and take me to your bedroom."

"Iralaun...I'm celibate. I have been for about fifteen months now."

Iralaun's mouth fell open again, and then she sat down on the couch and shook her head.

"What?" he asked. After Allen's last relationship had ended, he decided that he was in no rush to get into another intimate relationship without really knowing the woman. If he had known his ex-girlfriend was impatient, lazy and a constant complainer before they were intimate, he would've never dealt with her. So, until he felt he'd met someone worth sharing his time and himself with, he'd just take his time. He knew sex wasn't the most important part of a relationship anyway.

"I knew there had to be something. I knew it! There just had to be a catch," Iralaun said as she shook her head. She couldn't believe it, but it answered a lot of her questions. After nearly three weeks, Allen still hadn't tried to touch her more than an occasional hug every now and then. She definitely wasn't used to that.

"You be freaking, huh?" he said tickling her in her side.

Iralaun smiled. "Freaking?"

"You know what I mean?"

"No. I don't?"

127

"Whatever, you know exactly what I mean," he said smiling. " I know you have a ton of questions. What happened to your line of usual questioning?"

"Nah, not really. I don't even want to know your reasons. I wish that I was like you. Celibate," she said the word as if it were foreign. "But then again, to be honest...no, I don't."

"Oh yeah, you definitely be freaking," he nodded and laughed.

She smiled and shook her head. "Can we please change the subject?"

"Oooh, feisty again, huh? You don't want to talk about it. So are you admitting you have no self-control?"

Iralaun shook her head. "I'm with you, aren't I?"

"Oooh. Nice comeback. Here's your coat."

Iralaun's eyebrows went up. "You better stop playing with me."

"No, really," Allen said smiling. "Come with me, so I can take the rental car back. You know they found my car right?"

"For real? No. I didn't know that. Where'd they find it?"

"In D.C. somewhere. It was alright, too. I just put it in the shop the other day to double check. It should be ready by five o'clock, so if you wouldn't mind taking me to get it after we come back from Enterprise."

"Sure...so I guess, they have no clue as to who took it then, huh?"

"The police said they're still investigating, but I could care less as long as I got my baby back."

"I thought I was your baby?"

"You are...sometimes. That attitude of yours got to go though," he teased.

"You know you love it. I'm challenging."

"Please. Ain't nothing wrong with having an easy-going old-fashioned kind of romance. Why I got to feel like I'm greasing up for an after-school boxing match every time I turn around is what I want to know?"

"You like drama, I guess," Iralaun said zipping up her coat.

"Actually...no, I don't. I think somebody put some voodoo on me or something," he said grabbing his keys and walking out the door.

Iralaun got in her car, and Allen jumped in the rental. He winked at her while he started his car. She followed him out of the parking lot and out on to the street toward the main thoroughfare. Allen didn't tell Iralaun which Enterprise store they were going to, and she was trying hard to keep up with him before they became separated. There was more traffic than usual out and cars cut in between them. Allen put his hazard lights on, so other cars would go around him and to make it easier for Iralaun to catch up.

As soon as they merged onto East-West Highway, Iralaun felt someone ram into her car from behind and she jerked forward like she was being propelled out of her seat. The person hit her car with such force that Iralaun hit her head on the steering wheel. Her car spun erratically out of control into oncoming traffic and she instantly loss her steering ability. Before she knew it, her car was flipping over. Iralaun felt like she was flipping forever.

When the car stopped flipping, she closed her eyes. When she opened them again, all she could see were the paramedics and flashing red and white lights that all seemed to blur together. She could hear Allen's voice in the background telling someone that he was her boyfriend and that he wanted to ride with her to the hospital.

Boyfriend, she thought. He was her boyfriend.

Iralaun couldn't move a muscle. Her neck was locked into a neck brace strapped to the gurney. She felt herself being lifted up and pushed backwards. Iralaun assumed that she was in an ambulance. There was a lot of noise around her, but she could still hear Allen's voice even though it was beginning to trail off in the distance. She couldn't make out what he was saying. By the time she understood what he was telling her—that he was going to meet her at the hospital—all she heard was the sound of doors shutting, followed by silence. She drifted in and out of consciousness.

CHAPTER 12

Yes Kevin, I heard it on television," Belinda said applying a fresh coat of clear fingernail polish to her fingernails. "I am sorry to hear that."

"Yeah...well they aren't totally off. I just don't want them out of my sight, because I'm still working on something. I even had an informant approach me about some information he knew."

"Oh yeah? You never really went into too much detail about it. How's that case going?"

"I know, but to be honest, I don't really want to talk about it. I would love to just take a break from all of this. I've been so busy lately. I think I'm going to take a few days off and do something special for New Year's. What about you? Would you like to do something with me, like go to Atlantic City or something?"

"Ah, well...I don't..." Belinda stumbled.

"I understand. You are uncomfortable with this aren't you?"

"Ah...well, we are just really friends so..."

"Yeah, but I think we have a mutual attraction toward one another. Don't we?"

"Ah..."

"What? Cat got your tongue?"

"I mean you are..."

"Are you seeing anyone seriously?"

"Not really...but..."

"But what? You don't want to get involved with a married man?"

"Exactly," Belinda said the word like she was releasing a thirty-year-old secret. A huge weight was lifted off of her chest and she exhaled.

"Well...I can't seem to win," Kevin conceded. "I try to be honest and up front with women, and I can't win with honesty. I think most women want me to lie about it. I really do. I think they would rather hear me tell them what they want to hear, rather than what's true. They would be more willing to believe a lie than to accept the truth."

"I disagree with that," Belinda said putting the top back on her fingernail polish.

"If I had told you I was recently widowed and that's the reason why I still wore my ring, you would've felt sorry for me. We probably would've slept together the first night we met, because you would've pitied me."

"I resent that!" Belinda interjected.

"But, no, I tell you the truth," Kevin continued, "that I'm still in love with my wife, even though it's not going to work out and you don't want to even get involved. So I guess I'm stuck. I can't win."

"I understand how you feel, even though I'm slightly offended at your first impression of me. I appreciate your honesty, but being honest doesn't mean that I want to deal with it. In fact, I'll be honest. I've been trying to decide how or what I feel about the whole situation. Yes, I'm attracted to you, OK. But who knows where this will lead. I mean, I have to keep my head about this whole thing. Everything that you've said has to be taken into account for every action that you've made. Now I don't know if I want to make a risk with my heart like that. Who's to say that as soon as Mrs. St. James wants to return to your life, that you won't drop me like a hot potato? If you can't make me any promises, then I'm not sure I want to get too involved."

"You want me to make a promise to you? How can you expect me to do that, we've only just met?"

"Kevin, I don't expect you to make me promises of holy matrimony, but..."

"OK, I promise that I'll respect you—at all times."

"And whatever happen, happens, huh?"

Kevin smiled. "You can't cheat destiny."

Belinda shook her head. She thought she had begun gaining some control in the kind of men she dated. After James hurt her the way he did, Belinda wanted to demand more and set higher standards. But it seemed impossible. If she said yeah, Belinda knew that she would be opening herself up to another kind of pain, and she wasn't too sure she wanted to take that trek again. Kevin seemed genuine, but so did James in the beginning. He was only a few years older than James, but still five years younger than her. Did she really want to go there again? Why was she even thinking about all of that, the man was married? Why did she keep meeting the same kind of men? It seemed the system was flawed and stuck on screwing her.

But Belinda conceded. She didn't want to be alone, so she said, "When do you want to leave?"

***

"She appears to be going into cardiac arrest," a paramedic yelled to Vivica just as she was racing towards the door. She didn't know what to do. She wasn't running to help out; she was running to go see her boys. But the patient looked so helpless.

It was instinctive for her to commence assisting the paramedics and asking questions about the patient's status. Vivica knew she couldn't leave — not with all of this going on and the staff so shorthanded. Her boys were free. She would see them later, she resolved.

"What's the patient's name?" she asked.

"Fugere. Iralaun Fugere," someone said.

"Are any relatives with her?"

"A brother or another was at the scene. He said that he was going to meet her here," said a paramedic.

"Good."

"I am him. I mean, I'm her boyfriend. Is she going to be OK? What's happening? Please tell me something," Allen demanded.

"Sir, I'm going to have to ask you to go to the waiting room. The doctors will be with you shortly," Vivica said pointing toward the waiting area.

"Please, tell me something," he begged.

"Sir, please let the doctors assist Ms. Fugere and they will be with you as soon as they can. In the meantime, call her family and let them know what has happened?"

Allen looked at her like a boy who had lost his puppy. He felt helpless.

Vivica rushed down the hall toward the Emergency Room.

***

Two hours later, Vivica returned to speak to Allen.

"Sir, has her family arrived, yet?" Vivica asked.

"I *am* her family."

Vivica nodded, but asked "Does she have any blood relatives?"

"Her mother is dead, and I'm not sure she wants to speak to her father," Allen said.

"Sir, the doctor will only release information to her next of kin. So I suggest that you put whatever differences they may have aside and call her father."

Allen nodded. "Is she OK?"

"Sir, as soon as her family is near, the doctor will speak with them."
Vivica turned and walked away.

Allen pulled out his cell phone and began to dial Craig. He'd still had
his number from the class they had together the previous semester. Thank
God he still had it, he thought. Iralaun had told him, that Craig and her
roommate had recently found her father, but that she didn't want to be a part
of his life. He knew that it would be best for a family member to be here for
her, but wasn't sure how Iralaun would feel about it.

"Sir, you can not use your cell phone in here," Vivica announced. "You
are welcome to use one of the courtesy phones in the waiting room."

Allen nodded and stood up to leave. As soon as he got outside, he
began dialing Craig's number.

"Hey Allen, What's up? Long time no hear."

"Hey, what's up? I know, but I have a slight emergency right now. I
need you to do me a huge favor," Allen begged.

"Sure, what's up?" Craig questioned, a bit confused at Allen's urgency.

"My girl told me that you and Brea helped her find her father recently."

"Uhuh? We did," he said.

"I need you to give me his number. It's an emergency."

"Huh? What's going on?"

"Man...Iralaun's in the hospital."

"What?!? Which one?"

"District General. I need you to give me the number."

"Ah," Craig stuttered. "I can call him. And we'll both come up there."

"OK. Please, just hurry up. They won't tell me what happened to her."

"Yeah, I will. I mean... we will."

***

Elgin and Elijah waited at the courthouse with James for their mother.

"Man what's taking her so damn long," Elgin said.

"Guys, she said that she was on her way," James said. "She was at
work. Just give her some time"

"Right, she's always at work. I haven't seen her since the day we got
locked up," Elijah said.

"But she's been here every step of the way. You have to believe that.
She wanted to visit—especially on Christmas Day. She didn't want y'all to
be here without family, but the place was closed to visitors."

"Whatever. Can't we just go?" Elijah said. He was tired of being held

133

captive.

"No, you have to be released to a parent or guardian."

"Can you try to page her again? I'm ready to go, too," Elgin said. "I'm tired of this place."

"Yeah, I will." James reached over and began dialing. After he entered the number, he looked at the twins and asked them, what they planned to do after they got out. "Considering that this has been the longest time you two have spent, consecutively, in jail."

"Shoot...If I tell you that, I might get locked up again," Elgin said smiling.

"Smoke a fat one," Elijah said pounding his brother's fist.

James shook his head. "Are you two going to stop hanging out on the street? You know there was a very fine line for y'all getting let off the hook today."

"Whatever, I never touched that girl. I knew I wasn't going down for that," Elgin said.

"You were released because there was not enough evidence to link you to the crime, not because you were innocent. Remember that," James said.

"Man, fuck you," Elgin snapped.

"Fuck me? You are the one who was two minutes away from being pounded in the ass by grown men. You know that's what they like to do to people who rape little girls, right?"

"Man, whatever."

"Keep acting tough. I know you slept with that girl, Elgin," James said.

"I never denied that. I said I didn't rape her."

"You didn't rape her," James mocked the youngest brother. "But do believe that if some of your semen or DNA would've turned up on her, that you could've just as easily been accused of it. It would've e simply been your word against hers."

Elgin rolled his eyes. "That girl just lied to protect herself from getting her ass beat by her mother. That's why they couldn't find nothing on her, she had already been home for days before she called and reported it. Ebony's parents made her call us in. They were ashamed. The whole block knew that girl was sleeping with anything that had a heartbeat. Everybody knew that girl was a ho, even her parents."

Elijah looked on.

"You need to lose that attitude of yours. You two have a chance to start over—completely fresh and clean. You were given a serious wakeup call. It's up to you to take heed. Can't nobody make a change for you, but you."

"Quit talking that bull…" Elgin said while shaking his head. "Ain't nobody trying to hear all that."

The ringing phone cut through their conversation and James answered it.

"Yes, they're right here," James said before handing the phone to Elgin.

"Why you can't hurry up?" he asked his mother.

"I'll be there in twenty minutes," Vivica said.

"You are always putting other people in front of us. I can't believe this shit, man."

"You need me right now, OK? I do not need any of your attitude or your filthy language."

Vivica hung up the phone and looked at her supervisor who finally gave her the approval to take off. She grabbed her coat again, and rushed toward the lobby. She saw the young man who'd came in with the accident victim slouching in the chair half asleep. She felt sorry for him, so before leaving, she walked over and said, "I'm not supposed to tell you this, but…Iralaun has been stabilized. That means she's doing OK for now. She has a concussion, some fractured ribs, a bruised lung and a broken arm. She is very lucky to be alive."

"Can I go see her?"

"Now you know that is out of the question. Besides she is heavily sedated and being monitored. She had a very traumatic day. She needs rest."

"Thank you for your help. I appreciate it," Allen said with a worried look on his face.

Vivica gave him an assuring smile and turned to walk out of the door for the day. Her boys needed her and she was anxious to see them.

Allen felt relieved, but before he could relax, Craig and an older guy walked in behind him. He was a stocky guy with a receding hairline. Even though, Allen knew that he had been sleeping, he couldn't believe his eyes, and instantly began rubbing them. He recognized the guy that was walking in with Craig. He had seen his face before, and though it was a little rounder, Allen thought the man had died a long time ago.

CHAPTER 13

Vivica was happy to have her sons out of harm's way and back home with the rest of the family. After she signed their release papers, Elgin and Elijah went home to enjoy one of their favorite home-cooked meals: fried chicken, macaroni and cheese, mashed potatoes and green peas. She was surprised that they hadn't said much to her since she picked them up from the courthouse. And even though she hadn't had a moment to rest from her long busy day, she found energy from somewhere to help her cook dinner that evening.

"You never cook for us anymore," Elgin said. "This is so good. I was getting used to eating chips and cookies from the corner store to fill me up."

"Or Oodles of Noodles," Elijah added.

Vivica knew they were aware that she hardly ever had time to cook, but instead of pointing that out, she chose not to say anything. She didn't want to ruin the evening.

"Pass me some more rolls," said Evan while trying to help change the conversation. "So what happened to Chico and them?"

"Let's not talk about that tonight," Vivica insisted. "Your brothers don't want to think about that right now. They just got home."

"It's OK," said Elijah. "It's no big deal. They are charging Reggie, but he'll probably get off, too—especially, when that video turns up. They don't have a case and then they'll find out Ebony is lying about the whole thing. She won't be able to live with herself knowing she tried to get somebody locked up for something she knows they didn't do."

Vivica was disappointed. Knowing the entire incident had occurred at all was more than enough, but to know that some sort of video existed was too much for her to grasp. She couldn't believe what her ears were soaking in. She knew the twins were having sex a long time ago, and that's why she insisted that they used condoms. She even brought samples home from the hospital for them. One way or the other she knew they were going to have sex. She was having sex at their age, so instead of trying to fight it, she made sure they had protection.

Vivica was appalled at what they were saying in front of her, but didn't want to ruin the evening. They were facing enough drama in their lives and didn't want to add to the chaos.

"That video will tell it all," Elgin said nodding. "So what did y'all get for Christmas?"

"Oh we got an X-Box," Eric said excited. "It's alright, but I wish we had gotten the new Play Station 2 joint."

"I feel you. Pass me the hot sauce, shorty," Elijah said.

The doorbell rang, interrupting their dinner. Whomever was standing on the other side of the door was impatient because the button kept being pushed and the erratic sound was starting to annoy them. Vivica wiped her hands on her napkin and went to answer the door. When she looked out of the peephole, she saw Eddie standing on her porch looking like a decaying nomad. He stood shivering in his thin-windbreaker, bouncing around to keep warm. He appeared to be shadow boxing, he was moving around so much.

"It's y'all's father," Vivica said shaking her head. "Do you feel like seeing him?"

"No!" Elgin said. "Forget him."

"What about you, Elijah?"

"Nope. I don't know why he's coming around here. Don't nobody want to see his pipehead ass."

"Watch your mouth in my house," Vivica said before telling Eddie no one wanted to see him.

"I need to speak to Elgin, Viv," Eddie yelled through the door.

Elgin got up from the table and yanked the door open. "What your bitch ass gotta say to me?"

"Watch your mouth!" Vivica repeated.

Elgin rolled his eyes and said, "What you want?"

"Can you come out here for a second; I need to holla at you?"

Elgin stepped out of the house, assuming that his dad wanted to ask for some drugs.

"What you want?"

"I heard y'all got out today."

"Yeah, and…"

"You got anything for me?"

"Man…fuck you. Get off my porch!"

"Come on son."

"What you just call me?"

"I mean, Elgin, I need a hit bad…"

"That's not my problem," Elgin said turning to go back in the house. To think the day he gets out of jail, his own father was trying to buy some drugs from him, enraged him. He shook his head as he walked through the doorway. "Incredible," he mumbled. "This nigga is lunchin."

Eddie reached out to touch his son's shoulder to ask again, but Elgin turned back around abruptly and knocked his father flat to the ground. Eddie dropped like a ton of bricks. Elgin started kicking Eddie in his side over and over as if something had snapped inside of him. He seemed to be releasing years of aggression and frustration with every kick. Eddie yelled out, and begged Elgin to stop. He coughed up blood, but Elgin was in a zone.

"Ain't this the way you used to hit Mama?" he yelled. It took both Vivica and Elijah to make him stop.

"What is going on? Elgin get off of him?" Vivica yelled hysterically.

"Man fuck this nigga..." he yelled and continued to pummel his father.

Elijah tried to pull his brother off of Eddie. "Don't do this right here. Not right here. El?"

"Get in the house!" Vivica screamed. "Just get in the house!"

Elijah pulled his brother in the house, and Vivica closed the door. They left Eddie lying in the fetal position on the porch, whimpering. While Elijah tried to calm his brother down, Vivica frantically looked around the house for her First Aid Kit.

"Man why you let that dude get you all riled up? You know he is strung the fuck out!"

Elgin paced back and forth around the living room, trying to calm down. "I can't stand that nigga. He don't have no muthafuckin shame. He don't care about any of us. He don't even care about himself, so why should we care about his pitiful ass?"

Vivica ran pass the kids and out on to the porch. Eddie was still whimpering like a wounded animal. She began wiping Eddie's bloody nose with a washcloth to make it stop bleeding.

"Don't worry about me Viv?" Eddie said out of breath. "They're right. I am pitiful. Look at me?"

"Eddie you need to get some help," she said putting peroxide on a cut on his face.

"I deserve everything they say to me and whatever they to do me. They don't respect me. I'm as hopeless as a penny with a whole in it," he said trying to laugh. He spit out a loose tooth, and smiled at it.

Eddie stood up and wiped himself off. He started walking down the steps and turned back around and said, "I'm miserable Viv. Drugs make me feel better—it's the one thing that gives me hope." Eddie opened the gate and started limping away from the house. After taking a few steps, he sang aloud, "I can see clearly now, the rain is gone." He laughed, and then looked back at Vivica. "It's gonna be a bright, sun shiny day."

Vivica watched him until she couldn't see him anymore. That was her children's father, she thought with repulsion. She shook her head and went back into the house.

***

"Hey, how is she doing?" Craig asked. He was apprehensive towards Allen. He wasn't sure just what Iralaun had told Allen about their friendship.

"She's resting," Allen said while turning to the man that stood with Craig. "You look really familiar."

"I do?"

"Your name wouldn't happen to be Tony would it?"

"Yeah, a lot of people call me that. Do we know each other?"

"Do you remember a woman named Anita Richardson?"

"Ah…"Anthony said trying to recall the familiar name. "Vaguely, why?"

Allen twisted his face up in confusion, then said, "That's my mother."

"Oh yeah? Where's she from?"

"Fort Washington."

"Oh yeah." His face lit up. "Ni-Ni. I remember Ni-Ni. How is she?"

"Ni-Ni?" Allen asked confused, but then said, "I remember seeing pictures of you and her together when I was young. And a picture of all three of us when I was a baby."

"Oh yeah," he said with a smile spreading across his face. "I remember you. You were a little baby then, boy you've gotten big."

Allen was stunned. There was more to Tony than what he appeared to know. But Allen kept his thoughts to himself. He needed to talk to his mother first. Certainly some things weren't adding up. But Allen couldn't help himself. "After all these years. She told me you were dead."

"Did she? Why would she say that?" said Anthony shaking his head.

"That's what I want to know," Allen muttered.

"Well…" Anthony said taking a deep breath. "Anita and I were real close friends a long, long time ago."

Allen looked confused.

"Excuse me. Are either of you a relative of Iralaun Fugere?" asked a doctor, who had just walked up to the three of them.

139

"Yes, I'm her father," Anthony said with a proud tone, but a worried look on his face.

"Come with me this way, please."

Anthony followed the doctor down the hall. Craig turned to Allen and said, "Are you alright dude? You look confused as I don't know what— almost like you saw a ghost or something."

Allen sat back down in the blue chair he'd been waiting in all night and propped his arm to hold his head up. He needed to think for a second about the conversation going over and over in his mind. "I need to go home," he suddenly announced. "I'm going to leave for a little while, I'll be back."

"Are you alright? I hope everything is OK."

Allen nodded at Craig and walked out of the hospital. It had started to rain while he was inside. He couldn't pull out of the parking lot fast enough. His tires squealed when he pulled off. It was an extraordinarily long ride from D.C. to his mother's house in Fort Washington, Maryland. It seemed like hours had passed by before he reached home. Allen dreaded the conversation he needed to have, but he was so confused. All sorts of things went through his head.

When Allen got there, he unlocked the door like he usually did at the house he grew up in and walked through the foyer. He still came home a lot on the weekends to spend time with his mother. She would wash his clothes, and sometimes they'd eat dinner together. When he walked in, his mother was in the kitchen warming up a pot of soup. He threw his keys on the kitchen table and sat down.

"Hey Ma," he said in a wearied tone.

"How're you doing, Allen? You look exhausted. Want some chicken noodle soup?"

"No thanks," Allen exhaled and put his hands up to his forehead.

"What's wrong?"

Allen just shook his head. Then he stood up and walked to the mantel in the living room and took down the picture of his mother, Tony and himself as a baby. He stared at it for awhile, not sure if he wanted to ask his mother about it. Everything he knew was about to change, and he wasn't sure if he was ready for his world to change. But then Allen thought about it, he had to know, because Tony was alive and he needed answers. He walked back over to his mother with the framed picture in his hand.

"Ma, I ran into someone a little while ago."

"Oh yeah? Who baby?" she said while getting a glass out of the cabinet. She was about to pour herself a glass of orange juice. She hadn't been feeling well lately.

"Him," Allen said putting the picture in front of her.

As soon as she laid eyes on the picture, Anita dropped the glass sending it crashing to the floor. It shattered into a few dozen pieces all over the place.

"Ouch…" she squealed as a piece of glass nicked her bare foot.

Allen bent down to help her remove the sliver of glass that caused a trail of blood to trickle down to the floor.

"I'll get you a band aid," Allen said walking to the bathroom.

"I'm OK. Just hand me the broom so I can sweep this up."

Allen got the broom from out of the closet and told his mother he would sweep it up. He motioned for her to sit down.

"So tell me Ma. What's going on?"

Anita reached for her carton of cigarettes that sat on the kitchenette table. She took a moment, lit a cigarette and inhaled before she answered Allen.

"I don't know what you want me to tell you. You saw him, so you know he's not dead." She nervously took another drag of her cigarette.

"Is he my father?"

"What answer do you want?"

"What do you mean, 'what answer do I want?' I want the truth. All these years I've been thinking my father died in a car accident when I was three. But today, not only do I watch as the girl that I am falling for, gets injured in a serious car accident, but I find out her father may or may not be my father, too. All I need is the truth, right now!"

Anita became unnerved at Allen's rising voice. She inhaled her cigarette and plucked the ash in the ashtray before saying, "Sit down, Allen."

"No, I'm fine right here," he said crossing his arms in front of him. He was distressed and needed the gaps in the story to be filled.

Anita nervously took another drag of her cigarette and blew out a cloud of smoke. Silence filled the room. She took a deep breath and laid the cigarette in the ashtray on the table. She played with the lighter that was on the table, twisting it in between her fingers trying to decide which words would be best to explain to Allen. And then like the clouds had begun to roll away, it seemed all clear to her—give him the truth, she thought.

"I didn't want you to feel like you were less than a man, because your father turned his back on you. So I lied. I thought it would be easier for you to understand or accept if I told you he died."

"What are you saying?"

She exhaled again. "Tony isn't your father. He was a friend of mine.

Although we dated off and on, he and I were never serious. The man, who is your dad, was never even a boyfriend of mine."

"Huh?"

"Yes," Anita said before taking another puff of her cigarette. She looked down at the ashtray then back up at Allen. "I made decisions in the past that have affected my life, including sleeping around with men who only wanted casual sex. Things were so different back then—we didn't have as many problems as you all have nowadays with diseases you can't get rid of and what not.

"We were more carefree and we just wanted to enjoy ourselves. The sixties and seventies were something else," she said inhaling another drag of the cigarette. "I was on the pill, so I thought it didn't really matter as much. But when I got pregnant with you, I knew I had to accept responsibility for the choices I had made. I decided to have you and I raised you on my own."

Allen finally sat down. He couldn't believe what his mother was saying to him. He rested his head in his hands as he leaned forward. All of a sudden his chest began to ache.

"Allen...I don't even know who your real father is," she said shrugging solemnly.

Allen shook his head in frustration and took a deep breath. What was he to make of this information, he thought.

"I am sorry for lying to you Allen. I've always thought that it was for the best that you didn't know the truth. Look at you. You've turned out to be wonderful. You are a very respectful, caring and considerate young man. I've never had any problems with you. And you are very responsible, you have your own place, you graduated from college, you are working and even went back to school. I think I did a good job of raising you by myself.

"Nobody can ever take that away from you. I didn't want you to think that no one loved you or didn't want you, so I lied to make sure you were happy. I know I did a good job of raising you by myself."

"You did," Allen said reaching over to touch his mother's hand. "But I just wish I knew earlier. I feel empty now."

"And that's why I didn't want to tell you when you were younger. You should know that you are capable of doing anything, with or without a father."

"That's not true,"Allen said. "I did have a father. It's been you all along. You have been both parents to me and I appreciate you being there for me. As much as this news hurts, it doesn't really."

"So you aren't upset with me?" Anita asked with begging eyes.

Allen shook his head, leaned over and gave his mother a hug. "My father is dead to me."

CHAPTER 14

Belinda eagerly waited in the lobby of her building for Kevin to come pick her up. She stood with a small designer luggage bag and suitcase. She acknwoledged, that she, too, needed a break just as much as Kevin did, and couldn't wait to be on the road. Besides, she thought, the drive would give them plenty of time to talk. Belinda left her cat with her mother and agreed to pick Artica up as soon as they returned.

When she saw Kevin pull up and park on the opposite side of the street, she relished at just how handsome he was. He was clean-cut and wore a wool caramel-tone P-coat, a chocolate mock-turtleneck and chocolate-colored pants. He looked succulent with his smooth face and even complexion, Belinda thought. She stepped out of the building's lobby to meet him with a warm smile.

"Hi."

"Good morning," he said leaning in to give her a hug. "Let me take your bags."

Belinda handed it to him and walked toward his truck. "You look nice," she said.

"You always look nice," he said opening the passenger side door of his truck. "Are you ready for this long drive?"

"I guess I'm ready. It'll be worth it once we get there."

"You want to stop to get some reinforcements before we get on the highway? Snacks or drinks?"

"No. I think I'll be OK," she said smiling.

"Cool. So your mom didn't mind keeping the cat?" Kevin asked as he pulled out onto Wisconsin Avenue.

"No, she didn't. She was kind of concerned about how my father would deal with an animal in the house though."

"Really? You didn't have pets while you were growing up?"

"Mmm...I think we had a rabbit when we were younger—nothing that really got on anybody's nerves."

"Right. We had all kinds of animals when I was growing up."

"Really? Do you have any now?"

"No. I'm hardly ever home. I know I wouldn't be able to give it all of the attention it would need. It wouldn't be fair to it."

"So you should be able to understand why your wife was so disappointed, right?"

Kevin frowned and then said, "Yeah, I guess that's true. So...tell me about your dad. What's the deal with you and your dad? Do you want to repair your relationship?"

Belinda exhaled. She knew she was going to have to face this conversation eventually. "I'm not sure. He definitely needs counseling. He doesn't want it, so he drinks to run from his pain."

Kevin shook his head. "Black people have a thing with counseling, don't we? We think that it's a waste of money really."

Belinda nodded. "Most of us do."

"We'd rather listen to our friends' silly opinions, compare their problems to other people on talk shows or turn to a substance to run away from it. For some people it's drugs, for some it's sex or food, for some it's alcohol. It's sad. White people don't have that problem, they love telling those shrinks all of their business."

"Yeah. You are right," Belinda looked soberly out the window watching the trees blur together.

"Have you ever received counseling for anything?"

"No, but I've ordered a lot of counseling sessions for a number of people who've stood before me," she said facing him.

"I bet you have."

"Do you think you could use some counseling?"

"I think a lot of people could always stand to use some, whether they actually go and get help is a different story."

"But I meant specifically with you and your wife?"

Kevin took a deep breath and said "I'm not sure if we could fix our problems. She already made up her mind so..."

"I hear you," Belinda said, deciding not to probe too deep. She didn't know what would be at the bottom of the abyss.

Kevin reached down and turned on the radio. One of Belinda's favorite songs was on and she started bobbing her head.

"You want me to turn it up? I see you're jamming over there," he said smiling.

Belinda returned his smile, and started moving her mouth to the lyrics, but wasn't releasing a sound.

"Tell me how come at 38, you still aren't married and have never had any kids?" he asked.

"I don't know," she said after a long sigh. "I guess there are a lot of reasons. One of them is definitely because I made my career my number one priority."

"I can certainly relate," he said smiling.

"Another reason would have to be because…well, if you listen to this song, maybe you can see why?"

"Bag Lady, huh?" he asked raising his eyebrows as he listened to Erykah Badu wail her little heart out over his Bose speakers. "I can't see that being you."

"I think a lot of women are bag ladies to a certain degree. We can't help it."

"What do you mean?"

"Well, we try to learn from our mistakes, but old habits die hard. They are very comforting, you know? Plus we are so distrustful and nobody wants to get hurt, and especially not for a fourth or fifth time. So we latch on to what we learned from the last person, and can't help but put it foremost when we date."

"Yeah?"

"Look at us for example—from the start, I tried to impress you long before I ever really knew anything about you. Instead of learning from the many mistakes I've made in the past by doing that, I repeated them. But I couldn't help it—women by nature are competitive. I wanted you to think that I was better than the last person you were with and I wanted to show you I could do the things that the last woman wasn't doing right." Belinda gritted her teeth. "It's sad to admit that, especially because I know you are married and that you two are having problems. But still deep down, I want to make you feel appreciated and I've done things to make sure you feel that way."

"How do you mean?"

"You probably would consider it to be small, but it's really a big thing. I shouldn't care at all about whatever you and your wife are going through in your relationship. I should only focus on the fact that I've made a new friend. But…I haven't focused on just that—I've been trying to figure out how I could impress you. 'Is he interested in me?' 'Let me cook for you,' 'Let me invite Kevin to dinner'—that sort of thing."

Kevin nodded. "Funny you should point that out, because I never even paid attention to it like that. Why do you feel like you have to do those things?"

146

"I don't know. I've always been like that. Once I see somebody I want, I go after him. And plus, I guess...sometimes I see something in a person, that they don't see in themselves and I want to help them to realize it. I know it sounds strange, but that's how I feel."

"You sound like Mother Teresa or something," Kevin said smiling. "Why are you more concerned about others' well-being before you are worried about your own?"

Belinda shrugged. "Women are natural nurturers, I guess."

"Are other women in your life like that? Your mother or your sister?"

Belinda thought about it and nodded yes. "I guess they are—particularly my mother. My mother has always put my father's needs before her own, always. I guess she sees something in him, too, and is willing to do whatever she can to help him realize it, no matter the personal sacrifice."

"How so?"

"For years, I've watched her become unhappy with him. Ever since his accident, she's been unhappy. He's been depressed and despondent and she's been there all the time...trying to remind him that he's still a man. She makes excuses for him. She apologizes for him and I figure, to some degree, I do the same thing for the men I date." She could never shake the desire to want to pamper, comfort and console the men she dated, Belinda thought to her self.

"Mmhhmm," Kevin said. "But that's not fair to you, at all. What do you get in exchange for doing that?"

"Nothing. Absolutely nothing," Belinda said deflated. She stared out the window at the cars changing lanes, and getting on and off exits of the highway.

"So why do you continue to do it?"

Belinda faced Kevin and thought for awhile. Then she said, "I guess I never really noticed it as a problem before."

He shook his head. "See, that's why you need counseling."

Belinda smiled. "I've been getting counseling the low-budget way for all these years—just talking it over with girlfriends, shooting the breeze."

"And none of those women have psychology degrees, do they?" Kevin asked shaking his head.

"Nope. So I've been going in circles, I guess."

"Yep. Exactly. Somebody once told me as long as your cycle isn't complete, you will continue to go around and around, making the same mistakes, until you learn something and are ready to go to the next level."

"Interesting? Who told you that?"

"I don't know. One of my buddies on the force," Kevin said laughing.

"Mmhhmm. I guess that's why you've never gotten counseling before, either."

They both laughed.

"Police officers don't make that much. I'm on a budget."

"Right," Belinda said unconvincingly. "Your insurance probably covers all of it. Shoot, with all of the things you see on a daily basis? Please. It better be covered."

Kevin shrugged, because he knew she was probably right.

***

The doctors had finally agreed to cutback some of the medicine dosage which kept Iralaun sedated. She relied on the respirator machine to breathe for several days. The doctors wanted her to heal, and said as long as she was unconscious that she would heal faster. And she was recovering relatively fast. But having a bruised lung made it very painful for her to breathe on her own. Each day Allen, Craig, or Anthony was by her side, but Iralaun never knew it. They rotated shifts from day and night.

Initially, Craig had a problem with Allen being a part of the shift. The thought of Allen being the first person Iralaun saw when she woke up, sickened him.

"Did you tell her roommate yet?" Allen asked Craig one day when he arrived to exchange shifts.

"Yeah, I did. She's coming back to Maryland tomorrow. She was so hurt and wanted to come down right away, but I told her that Iralaun was stabilized. Plus, she wanted to be back here for New Year's Eve."

"Oh yeah? She's coming down on New Year's Eve? That's cool. She wants to get her party on, huh? Are y'all going to do anything special?"

"I haven't really been in the mood for that—not with all of this, but I don't know what Brea wants to do."

"Yeah. I understand. Well, I really appreciate you helping out," Allen said. "I didn't realize you and Iralaun were that close."

"You'd be surprised to know just how close we are," Craig said slyly but quickly added, "With Brea and Iralaun being roommates, I'm always at the crib."

"Right."

"And I know she doesn't really have any family. I didn't know you two knew each other, let alone were dating," Craig said.

"Yeah, it's pretty new. But I really care about that girl...she's special to me."

"Yeah," Craig said nodding in agreement.

"What was that engaged comment you told her about?" Allen asked.

Craig tried to laugh it off and walked toward the door. "I swear that's what I heard dog. But I wasn't trying to start nothing, for real."

"Right. That was wrong 'Cuz."

"My bad, my bad," Craig said smirking. "Well, I gotta go. I'll see you tomorrow."

Craig took one last look at Iralaun before leaving out the door and then unbeknownst to Allen, rolled his eyes at him. If they were bullets, Allen would've died in the middle of the hospital floor.

Allen hastily walked over to Iralaun's bed and frowned at all of the connections that were hooked up to her. He'd seen them every day for the last few days, but on this day, Iralaun looked a lot better than on the days before. At least, she looked well rested, he thought.

He sat in the chair nearest to the bed and flipped through one of the textbooks that he'd brought along with him. Allen had decided to get a jump on the next semester by reading early. He opened up the marketing management book and pulled out a hi-liter for his notes.

Vivica walked into the room and greeted Allen before going to check on Iralaun.

"How is she doing?" he asked her.

"She's doing a whole lot better."

"Really?"

"Yes. The doctors have actually decided to take her off of the respirator tomorrow."

"Really? That's excellent!" Allen exclaimed.

"She'll still have to wear the oxygen mask, but she will be more alert than she has been."

"She'll be able to hear me?"

"She can hear you now, she just can't respond. The sedatives are starting to taper off a lot, so her mind's in a conscious state. Think of it as if she's in a light sleep. But she can hear you."

"She can?" he asked uncertain.

"Yes. I noticed she's been crying," Vivica said while taking a wet nap to wipe her face. "Either she's been dreaming or maybe she can tell when people are here with her."

"Really? I just got here," Allen said as he thought about Craig leaving before him.

"Come here. Touch her hand. She's moving it a little."

Allen jolted up and walked over to the bed. He gently placed his hand on Iralaun's and felt her trembling slightly.

"You can talk to her. It's OK, go ahead."

Allen licked his lips nervously, shrugged and then said, "I don't know what to say to her."

"Just tell her she's doing well. She probably wants to hear a familiar voice. She'll believe you more than me," Vivica said smiling. "I'm sure she would love some attention from a loved one."

"Hi sweetie, it's me Allen."

"That's good, just keep on talking to her," Vivica said while she adjusted some of the connections on the IV device and a monitor.

"The nurse said that you are doing really well and that they're going to take you off of the respirator tomorrow."

"That's right," Vivica agreed.

"I just want you to know that I'm right here with you and I'm not going anywhere, OK? So rest and get better for me."

"How long have you two been together?" Vivica asked.

"About three weeks," Allen said rubbing Iralaun's hand.

"Oh yeah? I would've thought it's been much longer."

"I feel like I met her before...because she feels so familiar."

"Really? That's interesting. Maybe she reminds you of someone or maybe it's because you two were meant to be together," she offered. "I used to know someone like that."

Allen felt a tight grasp. "She just squeezed my hand!"

"That's because she knows I'm right," Vivica said smiling and walking out the door.

Allen was startled but said,"You *can* hear me, can't you?"

Iralaun squeezed his hand again.

"I don't know why you were crying earlier, but I'm here now. And I'm glad I'm here with you," he said rubbing her forehead. "You are a very strong person, Iralaun. I know I don't have to tell you that. You've wanted to know why I'm interested in you, and I guess it's because I know you are a fighter.

"Yeah...you are a challenge, too, but it's because you have to be. You have been taking care of yourself every since your mother became too ill to take care of you. So I know you know you are going to be alright, because you know how to survive."

A tear rolled from Iralaun's closed eyes, down her cheek.

"Baby, you know you are going to be alright. How many people you know can do that at your age? On a full scholarship, got a place of their own and all without anybody to lean on. You can lean on me Iralaun. I'm here for you."

Another tear ran down her cheek.

"Stop crying. You'll be just fine."

***

It was snowing in Atlantic City on New Year's Eve, but Belinda and Kevin enjoyed them selves despite the weather. The colored lights and the flashing signs of the casinos and hotels provided a captivating landscape for the two of them. Later that evening to celebrate the festivities, they went to a show that was held in one of the hotels on the strip. They partied and danced the whole night. Even though Kevin was married, Belinda felt a sense of pride while she was with him because he treated her in a way that she seldom was treated. This trip was a guilty pleasure that she was going to tuck inside her heart somewhere.

With Kevin, she was allowed to sit back and relax instead of feeling the need to lead everything when she was with him. And it felt good, she thought. When the countdown began, Kevin took Belinda into his arms and planted a gentle kiss on her lips.

***

Elijah and Elgin stood on their block at midnight sharing a cigar blunt-filled with marijuana. A small group had gathered to watch two pit bulls fight it out in the alley behind their house. The dogfight left the younger dog with a lacerated ear, and a bite mark on the side of his neck deep enough to see its pink flesh. The dogs belonged to Marco and Juan—two Hispanic guys from the neighborhood. Bets had been made and several people were collecting the money they'd won on the winning dog, while others stood around cracking jokes, drinking and smoking. Bringing in the New Year was no different than how'd they celebrated simply surviving another day in the streets.

Everyone was too high and too drunk to see the guy creeping through the alley, wearing a black ski mask and a black leather jacket. Both of the dogs barked out of control when they sensed him, but it was too late to warn any of the guys standing there. Everyone looked up at the same time as the slim guy started shooting towards them with a 9-millimeter. The group split up frantically and ran in different directions to avoid getting hit. Elijah and Elgin ran the same route and never turned around to see who was shooting at them or if anyone got hit.

"What the fuck man? Who was that?" Elgin yelled while running toward Georgia Avenue—a busy main street.

"I don't know!" Elijah shouted.

They ran through an alley toward an apartment complex where some of their friends lived. They started to go over Osei's apartment off of 7th Street, but they stopped running when they realized they weren't being chased anymore. They went inside one of the buildings on Rhode Island Avenue and sat on the steps in the hallway.

"Who the fuck do you think would be trying to shoot us?" Elgin asked trying to catch his breath.

"I dunno, probably somebody who's trying to scare us. You know how niggas be wildin' out on New Year's. I don't think he hit anybody," Elijah said as he tried to keep up with his brother.

"Still...people don't shoot unless, they wanna kill somebody," Elgin said. "'Cause You best believe they know if they miss their target, they're going to be getting punished."

"Man...this is some bullshit. I never been shot at before," Elijah said.

"That's the risk we take being out here on this block. This shit ain't no joke. Stop sounding like a bitch."

"Man, please. Just because you got grazed before, don't be calling me no bitch. Chico shot your bitch ass on an accident."

"Man, fuck you," he said playfully punching Elijah. They could see a lot of traffic outside from where they sat in the urine-saturated hallway. Since it was New Year's Eve, the police were on almost every corner patrolling the streets. The twins could see them driving past the glass door of the apartment building. "My thing is...I didn't even know we were beefin' with somebody like that."

"Me either," Elijah agreed. He pulled a cigar blunt out of his pocket and opened the razor blade on his keychain. He bit off the ends of the cigar and spit them out on the floor. Then Elijah sliced the cigar open and emptied out all of the tobacco. He reached into his pants pocket and pulled out a tiny Ziploc bag filled with $10 worth of marijuana.

"That's what I'm talking about," Elgin sang and clapped his hands.

Elijah smiled while pouring the contents into the cigar paper. Then he began to roll it and lick it until the blunt was properly set. He dug in his pocket for his lighter, but was irked when he realized he didn't have it. "Man, please tell me you got a lighter."

Elgin dug around in his pockets and turned up empty-handed. "Damn, I must have dropped it while I was running."

"Shit!" Elijah said.

"Damn, dog. You sound like a crackhead or something."

"Yeah, I sound like your father, bitch," he said laughing.

"The sad thing is...you do."

They both started laughing then walked out of the building. "I'm mad you beat that man like that the other day," Elijah said shaking his head. "That shit was wild!"

"Man fuck him. He deserved that shit."

"Right," Elijah agreed and stood up. "Let's go around 9th Street. Holla at them dudes for a minute."

"Aiight," Elgin said following behind him. They began walking down the block.

"Hey, Happy New Year's twin!" someone yelled to Elgin out of a car driving up the street.

Elgin nodded when he recognized the face. "Man, I wish we didn't live around here anymore."

"Why you say that?"

"Because everybody knows everybody around this muthafucka. I can't even scratch my ass without people knowing about it. For all I know, it could've been one of those dudes in that car that was just shooting at us."

"That's true...can't trust nobody."

"We've been living around here for so long and all I see is mad people struggling. You got niggas struggling on this block and you got niggas struggling on that block. Shit, we struggling on our block," Elgin said as he kicked a beer can out of his path. "People robbing each other left and right— for pennies at that. Ain't nobody around here got anything worth nothing no way, but we constantly robbing each other."

"Right," Elijah knew exactly what Elgin meant. One minute they were stealing from the same people who had robbed them weeks earlier, he thought.

"I mean look at us. We stay on the block selling fucking nickel and dime bags of weed all damn day. We might sell a couple of rocks here and there, but we ain't really making no money. Not no real money."

"True."

"What the fuck we getting for this bullshit? I'm out here running and shit in the middle of the night for somebody who is making a whole hell of a lot more than me."

"Yeah, Osei getting us like shit, for real. And it's cold as a mother out this bitch," Elijah rubbed his hands together to generate some heat. They were getting closer to the spot where some of their old high school friends hung out.

"Man you're so right? Shit, as soon as I make money off of one sell, I'm covering for the weak ass shit I did the week before. Be steadily trying to make ends meet out this muthafucka," Elgin said shaking his head. "A nigga stay robbing Peter to pay Paul."

"Ma used to say that all the time—robbing Peter to Pay Paul, remember?" Elijah said closing his eyes for a second, thinking about the past. "Shoot...Ma used to make a dollar out of fifteen cents out this mug."

Elgin laughed as he realized that they didn't see any of their friends hanging outside, so they kept walking. "Them niggas not even out here. Let's go up to U Street."

They both crossed the street walking around a homeless man who had made himself a bed out of newspapers and cardboard boxes on top of the subway ventilator. A blanket covered him, but it wasn't thick enough to really keep him warm. The ventilator added a smidgen of heat, the twins shook their heads as they noticed him suffering.

"Remember, when we were younger and we used to do that first of the month shopping?" Elijah said.

Elgin smiled and nodded.

"Ma used to call it, 'The Heavy-Duty' shopping, because we got all the stuff that was supposed to last the whole month."

"Yeah, we used to have two shopping carts," Elgin said smiling. "And they both were filled to the top. But boy did we hate giving them people food stamps. I hated that shit man."

"Yeah, me too. It was so embarrassing," Elijah said shaking his head. "Remember when it got close to the end of the month, like the third week and we were running out of food...and all we would have would be like a bottle of ketchup, a loaf of bread and maybe like some of the government cheese..."

"And we would make pizza out of it," Elgin said laughing.

"Yeah, man...that used to be a trip. We was famous for having a whole bunch of stuff in the house that didn't match up. Like peanut butter and no jelly."

"Or no bread period. Hotdog buns and no hotdogs."

"Yeah, or Kool-Aid but no sugar," Elijah said laughing. "But Ma came up with all kinds of ways to make us feel like we wasn't suffering—sometimes I hate to admit it. Remember them peanut butter cookies she used to make with all that damn thick ass government peanut butter we used to have?"

"Yeah that peanut butter used to be as thick as cement. And she used to use that thick maple molasses for sugar," Elgin said reminiscing. "Them cookies were good as I don't know what though. They were hard as shit, but shit, dip them joints in some of that WIC orange juice and it would be just right."

They both laughed again.

"She did a lot to make us feel like we had, when we knew we really didn't have anything. Remember when we used to put a piece of bread in the oven with a piece of butter and add some sugar and cinnamon. That was bangin, too. Tasted just like a cinnamon roll or something. People don't know about that kind of stuff."

Elgin nodded. "She did used to do that kind of thing for us—a whole lot more than Eddie ever did."

"Yeah, shoot...I remember when she would go to the Discount Mart and change the prices on stuff and tell the people at the register that somebody must've messed up and demand for them to give us the cheaper prices," Elijah said as he toyed with his cornrows. He had begun to unbraid them. After three weeks, the itching had intensified.

"Yeah...Then she'd come back a week later and return it, so she could get the money back for the original price and then go grocery shopping with that."

Elijah started laughing. "Yeah, Ma was a wild girl back in the day."

"But she's the one who's always told us to 'do whatever you gotta do, to get what you need to get, in order to survive.' So she can't be being so upset with us out here grinding," Elgin said as he crossed another street.

"Exactly," Elijah agreed. He had already unbraided three cornrows and was just letting his hair fly in the breeze.

"She stayed trying to cheat the system. If it wasn't with bills...choosing which was the most important and what not for the moment, she was lying, telling the government she wasn't married just to get that extra paper."

The twins were on 9th and U Street and saw that it was really busy. There were a lot of cars coming and going with their music blaring from the speakers. A lot of people were walking up and down the street, coming in and out of bars. Taxicabs were everywhere trying to catch a drunken patron or two, who may need a ride home. Elgin and Elijah walked down the street aimlessly passing time.

"Ma was trying to get us out the projects and off of welfare," Elijah said. "That's one thing I can definitely say about her—she was always trying to make ends meet—constantly juggling bills."

"No joke. Remember that time, when we were living in Border Quarters down there on K Street?" Elgin asked as he stopped to tie up his black and red Jordans.

"Yeah. I couldn't stand living in those projects. One block had four different projects on it. It was a damn battle zone and you could see the dome of the Capitol Building from my bedroom window. I swear I could reach out and touch the muthafucka. It looked damn near in 3-D, it was so close."

"Yeah, ain't that some shit?" Elgin said shaking his head. "Remember how the rental office people told us that they were about to renovate it, and asked us if we wanted to move into a new unit in the complex or move into a house somewhere else?"

"Yeah, I remember."

"Well, the only way we could get one of the newer houses, was if somebody in our family was disabled," Elgin said.

"Man, I ain't know that."

"Yeah, man. She had one of the doctors at her job say one of us was handicapped."

"That's sick!" Elijah said.

Then they both started laughing.

"But I have to admit it," Elijah said, "it was worth it."

"Shoot, it got us out of that joint—quick, fast and in a hurry. And almost everybody in that neighborhood is still living there. Most of them were born and raised around there. Hell, their parents' parents was probably living around there since they opened 'em," Elgin said as they made a left on to 14th Street heading toward Clifton Street.

"But it don't even matter, for real, if we're in the projects or not. Because even in a house, as long as we are around a whole bunch of starving ass people, people who want to come up and have a better future, then we're still basically in the fuckin' projects," Elijah said. "The projects ain't nothing but a place with a whole bunch of hungry people, who just want to better themselves. Niggas going to stay gutter, as long as this is all they know and as long as they starving—doing whatever they have to do to survive."

"Yeah, you're right. It's some ghetto ass people in those corporate boardrooms—stealing from their own companies, trying to come up on the next man," Elgin pointed out.

"Right."

They both walked quietly for awhile, each in their own thoughts. Then Elgin said, "People stay doing shit to get over. The world is fucked up in general anyway. As long as you can get away with doing it, people are going to do it. Just like us hustling, or our father turning his back on us—as long as we both can get away with it, then we're going to do it."

"Yeah it's fucked up—the whole system. Most people who ain't on welfare, ain't being raised by both of their parents, so what ends up happening, is all these damn kids out here end up raising themselves. One parent out there working two jobs or taking a whole rack of overtime just to make life livable ain't working. Kids end up learning what's right and what's wrong, on their own," Elijah said.

"On TV or in the damn streets. Sad. Just like us," Elgin said solemnly.

"I don't wanna be out here like this all my life...hustling."

"Me either."

"But the pennies I get from this, is better than working for somebody else or waiting for Ma to give it to me," Elijah said.

"Yeah. Our generation is all fucked up. Hold up I found my lighter. It seems like we're already high as a kite by the way we been talking, anyway," Elgin said handing it to his brother. They sat on a stoop of a closed store to light up the blunt Elijah had rolled earlier.

"Yeah, you are right. Life is fucked up and I don't see it getting no better either." Elijah inhaled a toke, then added, "I'll stay high 'til I die nigga."

"When I was coming up rough/that wasn't even what you called it/that's why I smoke blunts/and run with alcoholics," Elgin stood up and recited Tupac's "Fuck the World" lyrics while waiting for his brother to pass him the blunt.

CHAPTER 15

On New Year's Day, Belinda woke up under tussled sheets lying next to Kevin's warm body. She smiled as she recalled the spectacular evening they had together the night before. She had gotten to see a Moulin Rouge type of show, and could not believe how much fun she had at the party in the hotel the previous night. The whole mini-vacation was beyond what she could ever imagine it becoming. She gambled, dined and partied almost every night. Kevin treated her like a delicate flower, and she felt safe with him.

The sunlight was peaking through the curtains like a spy ready to share some of her secrets from the previous nights. Although Belinda had a couple of glasses of wine the night before, she knew that she had made a conscious decision to sleep with Kevin. And she loved every single minute of it. She didn't want to think about what the aftermath would be; she just wanted to lie in the morning-after glow.

Belinda cursed herself for not wanting to get up to take a shower. She just wanted to keep replaying their lovemaking over and over in her head. And she wasn't ready to wash his scent off of her. She felt like a young schoolgirl again.

But the sun was bothering her. It begged her to open her eyes. She raised her hand to rub them, then she pulled back the sheets and looked around the room. Kevin was on the telephone, and Belinda held her breath as she tried to listen intently to his conversation, but the whispers were too faint for her to make out what he was saying. He sat on the edge of the bed and his back was to her.

She didn't want to alert Kevin that she had awakened, first Belinda wanted to figure out whom he was talking to so early in the morning. She was unable to discern most of it, but she did catch the phrases, "I wish" and "come back home" and "I missed." Belinda was dumbfounded. She could not believe it. He had to have been talking to his wife, she thought. She popped up, got out of the bed and marched toward the bathroom. It was time for her to go; he was taking her for a fool. When Belinda turned around to close the door, she noticed Kevin flashing her one of his engaging smiles, but she did not return it.

She stared at herself in the mirror, because she felt like a dummy. "I must have a dunce cap on my head," she mumbled. She was tired of being made into a fool by the men she dated. No, she didn't just spend the night with him and he was calling his wife the very next morning begging her to come back home because he missed her, she thought.

"I am such a fool," she said to herself while turning on the water for the shower. "Who am I to decide the fate of other people's lives, if I'm such a terrible judge of character?"

Belinda undressed with the intent to leave as soon as she was done showering. First she was going to get dressed and pack all of her things, she thought. She was in the middle of plotting an escape route and thinking of calling the airport to see if she could snag a stand-by ticket when she heard the doorknob turn. She leaned up against the door, applying all of her weight to prevent Kevin from entering. She didn't know what he was thinking at the moment, but she heard his conversation and did not feel like facing him.

"Come on Belinda, open the door," Kevin said joking. "Let me see your beautiful body."

"No."

"What's wrong?" he asked with a seductive resonance. "You didn't have a problem with me licking every curve last night."

"That was before I heard your conversation with your wife!" she snapped.

"What are you talking about?" Kevin asked confused.

"I heard you, OK Kevin? And you didn't even have the decency to use the damn pay phone in the lobby," she barked while wrapping a towel around her body.

"Belinda, I am confused. Please tell me what you are talking about," Kevin said trying to maintain his composure. She turned the water off in the shower to better hear him. "If you'd open the door maybe we can talk about it."

Belinda yanked the door open and said "I just heard you telling your wife how much you missed her and how you wanted her to come back home."

"What?" Kevin asked taken aback. "You've heard no such thing. I just got finished checking my messages and my partner left a message asking for something. I was just talking to him about the information I'd forgotten to give him before I left. And for the record, your honor, I told him, that I was going to have to get it when I came back home. And that I wished I could

remember where I put it, but I'm almost certain that I missed placed it."
Belinda could feel the blood rushing to her face. She was embarrassed by her ignorance. Once again she felt like a fool for jumping to conclusions. She knew better. She would never have made such a ludicrous assumption in her courtroom. But for some reason, when it came to men, it was a totally different playing field. She felt so insecure around them, and contemplated every move they made.

"That's OK," he said smiling. "You don't have to feel bad. It was an honest mistake."

Belinda blushed and Kevin gave her a hug.

"Are we cool now?"

"I don't know. It's not like what I thought was totally impossible," Belinda said disappointed. "I know how you still feel about her and I simply just don't feel comfortable with this at all."

"I don't know what to tell you Belinda," Kevin said shaking his head in frustration. "If I tell you that what has happened between us over this break has altered my view of my separation with my wife, I would be lying to you."

Belinda grimaced because Kevin's words felt like a sword slicing her in two.

"I don't want to lie to you. I've been honest with you from the very beginning. You are special to me. I think it would be great if we got to know each other more personally," Kevin said. "What we've had these couple of days has been absolutely wonderful, but my feelings for my wife have not changed. I said that I would not disrespect you and I will try my best to live up to that."

Belinda felt uncomfortable, because she did not want feel like settling for whatever cards he dealt her. She knew once she lied down with him that she had given him a piece of her heart.

"I understand," she said. "I have a lot of thinking I need to do…"

"I know you do and I just can not make you any promises. What we have now is great. Why can't we continue to have it like this?"

Belinda shook her head; Kevin really had no clue why it wouldn't work, she thought.

"One day your wife is going to come home, Kevin. And you have already made it clear to me what your decision would be if she did. I deserve more than second place, so when we get back, we will have to part ways," Belinda said in an unconvincing tone.

"Why are you acting like you didn't know this before we came up here or before last night? I thought you were cool with it."

"Kevin, I was never cool with it."

"Then why did you let it go so far?"

"I was fooling myself. Even though you respect me enough not to lie to me, I obviously don't respect Belinda enough not to lie to her. Because that's exactly what I'd be doing—making excuses for you and your situation for my benefit."

Kevin shook his head and shrugged his shoulders. "I don't know what else to say."

"There's nothing else to say about it. I certainly am not going to try to convince you to change your mind so..."

Kevin smirked. "I may be hanging on to a dream with my wife, but I just can't give up on us—even if we have been separated for so long."

"Ten months," Belinda mumbled folding her arms across her chest.

"Yes, ten months," Kevin said smiling. "Look at it this way. If it were you, I'd do the same thing."

"I respect that. If you two are supposed to be together then it is definitely up to you two to make that happen. So I'm going to step out of the picture. That way, I won't be a problem or a distraction."

Kevin nodded. Belinda started walking back towards the bathroom. She was bowing out. Kevin would have to do what was best for him, because she had decided to do what was best for her.

"Wait," Kevin said stopping her. "How about just one more time?"

Belinda shook her head, and winked at him before continuing her path to the bathroom. She shut the door behind her, dropped her towel and stepped into the shower.

"Not this time buddy," she mumbled. "I'm not that dumb. Get off the best way you know how."

Kevin sat on the edge of the bed looking at himself in the mirror directly in front of him and shook his head. He thought to himself about the long drive back to D.C. and their awkward predicament.

"Honesty is a mother," he said while falling backwards on to the bed.

***

The $2,500 bill Vivica received in the mail was unexpected. She did not realize that the lawyer's fee would be so much for the simple services James Lomax provided. She instantly tensed up when she saw how much she owed him. It was way more than what she had anticipated and there was no way she could afford it. She never even asked about the fee, because she was so desperate at the time. Vivica wondered if it was possible for her to set up a payment plan with him. She had no idea where she would get that sort of money.

Vivica started worrying again, and decided to ask her supervisor if she could work some extra hours in order to try to make up the difference. Working overtime, alone, wouldn't do the job. She would have to come up with something else. But in the meanwhile, Vivica kept the graveyard shift and was open to anything else that would help. Once again, she returned to leaving her children home alone, but it was the only thing she could do.

She couldn't turn to her family for help because they were never really in her corner. As much as they said they were there to help her, she knew that when it really came down to it, they weren't there. She was on her own and it was times like this when she wished she wasn't.

Vivica looked over at the Bible sitting on the bookcase in her room. She walked over to it, and began thumbing through the delicate pages. The ruffled sound reminded her that the book hadn't been opened in years. She toyed with the leather covering, and ran her fingers over the embossed lettering on the front. She turned the book open to Genesis.

She had silently asked for God's help in daily matters, but she hadn't read the book or attended a church service since Rightway, years earlier. But now that she thought about it, the years felt like decades, and she wasn't sure how she felt about returning back to that way of living. She hesitantly placed the book back on the shelf and ran her finger across the spine again.

"Just where is my old prayer pillow?" she asked as she looked through her drawers. She had no idea where it was. She looked in a junk box she had in her hallway closet. When she found it, she couldn't believe how worn it looked. That pillow had helped her a lot through the years. She was surprised to find it tucked so far away from her. Vivica needed it now, because she knew she'd have to do a lot more praying these days.

***

When Iralaun finally came through, she woke up to an empty room. She was dazed and uncertain about her surroundings. The constant beeping sound forced her to open her eyes as she noticed that she was lying in a bed with tubes connected to her half-dressed body. She realized that she was in a hospital room, as she tried to blink away the harsh soft light. Her body felt swollen all over and her arm ached so bad that it felt like someone was sitting on it.

When Iralaun looked down and saw that her left arm was in a cast, she became unnerved. She immediately wanted to know what else had happened to her. With her free hand, Iralaun pushed the blanket back and pulled up her gown to look at the rest of her body. She saw gauze and tape but nothing else besides tubes. She tried to wiggle her toes and was pleased to see that everything appeared to still be intact. A deep breath of relief swelled up her chest, but she simultaneously heard the sound of a toilet flushing in her room. Iralaun waited anxiously to see who else was in the room with her.

"Good morning Pumpkin," Anthony said rushing toward the bed. "You are finally up! I've been so worried about you. You just don't know how much I've prayed that everything would be OK."

"Pumpkin? I beg your pardon?" Iralaun asked perplexed and shaking her head. Her voice was groggy from not speaking in days, but she tried to clear her throat as much as she could. "Who are you?"

"Oh...Baby Girl...I'm your Daddy."

"What?" She tried again to clear her throat. "Daddy?"

"Yeah, Baby Girl. I'm your father."

She was awe-struck. Iralaun looked Anthony over from head-to-toe, from his potbelly to his balding head; he was nothing like she had expected. She looked nothing like him, except for maybe the color of his skin and the small mole on his chin, but even that was a stretch to her. Who was this man standing in front of her declaring he was her father? She was suspicious, he didn't look like the CIA agent or the war veteran she'd imagined and was disappointed.

She sucked her teeth and asked, "What are you doing here? Who told you I was here?"

"Baby Girl, I've been here since the accident—taking care of you."

"What do you mean accident? What happened? Where is Allen?"

"He's been here every day—waiting for you to wake up, too."

Iralaun rubbed her forehead with her free hand. She didn't have the energy for this, she thought.

"Are you feeling OK?" Anthony touched her forehead to check her temperature.

"I'm fine," she said waving him off and motioning to sit up. "How did you get here? Who told you I was here? Why are you here now, after all this time?"

Anthony tried to help her sit up. "It's a long story Pumpkin. Do you remember anything about the accident?"

"No, not really," Iralaun said trying to recall her last memories. "Not much. I vaguely remember leaving Allen's apartment. We were about to take his rental car back, I think. I don't remember too much after that."

"Well, needless to say, you two never made it there. You were in a terrible car accident, Pumpkin. But thankfully they were able to save your arm— your elbow was crushed and you had to have a surgical procedure to save it. Also you had a mild heart attack, when you were being rushed to the hospital."

"What?" Iralaun asked baffled.

"Yeah, but don't worry about that. You are fine now. You had a bruised lung, but it's healing as well as a couple of fractured ribs."

"Wow," she said shaking her head. "And you have been here?"

"Yes I have and when I couldn't be here, your friend Allen was here or your other friend Craig."

"Craig?" she asked disgusted.

"I know my opinion don't count for much with you, but I really do like Allen. He's a nice young man."

Iralaun smirked, because he was right—it didn't count, she thought.

"But more than that, I am so happy that you are up. We have a lot to talk about and this may be the only time you will allow me the chance to speak to you."

Iralaun sucked her teeth and shook her head.

"A re you hungry or anything? I can get the nurse for you."

"I'm fine," Iralaun said rubbing her eyes with her hand. "Let's just get this over with, since you are so desperate to share your piece."

"Iralaun you are not giving me a fair chance, here. I think you have me totally wrong."

"If you think I am going to argue with you..."

"No, I don't want to argue about this and I don't want to stimulate unwarranted anger from you. I just want you to know that what you think you know about me is totally wrong. I didn't abandon you, Pumpkin. I swear."

"What?" Iralaun asked perturbed. "And please stop calling me Pumpkin! What in the hell are you talking about? You left us! You turned your back on your family for another woman or shall I say several women."

"No, Iralaun. That's not what happened at all!" Anthony said pausing to try and lower his voice. "I don't know how to say this...but your mom—God bless her soul—but she had an affair early in our marriage."

"What?"

164

"I walked in...on her in our bed with my brother."

"Stop lying!" Iralaun demanded. "How dare you speak like that about my mother? Who do you think you are? How dare you *lie* like that?"

"I'm not. If you just give me a moment," Anthony begged. "I can explain the whole thing."

Iralaun blew out the wind of frustration and rolled her eyes. She felt drained.

"Just hear me out. If you aren't satisfied then I'll understand."

Iralaun sucked her teeth and closed her eyes. She wished that this wasn't happening to her. Why now? Why did she have to face this after all these years? She didn't have a choice, but to listen. Anthony sat down in the chair beside the bed and took a deep breath.

"Iralaun, when I walked in on them, my first reaction was to attack my brother—which I tried unsuccessfully to do. He nearly killed me that night. After I realize that I wasn't going to beat him, I left the room and grabbed you from your crib to leave the house. Your mom was hysterical that day. She tried everything to stop me, including falling to the ground and grabbing my legs to stop me. I even dragged her a little as I tried to put you in the car seat. My brother just looked on—shaking his head. Your mother screamed and hollered and cried as I pulled off.

"I was furious. And I was so disappointed in myself for ignoring the obvious signs that were all around me. Your uncle lived with us because he had been laid off from his job. I thought we were doing him a favor by letting him stay with us for awhile. He claimed that he was always out looking for a job, but I found out that was never the case.

"Isabella was a stay-at-home mom at the time. You weren't that old, about three months, I believe. I used to work crazy hours to take care of the two of you. I didn't want your mama to ever have a reason to say she was unhappy with me. Whatever she wanted, she got. We were very young when we got married, but I loved her so much, I would've done anything to make sure she had whatever she wanted and that you had what ever you needed."

Iralaun sucked her teeth. She really didn't want to hear this from him. She knew this only made him feel better about deserting them. She imagined him having trouble sleeping at night knowing that he left his family.

"That day when I saw them together," Anthony said, "Everything in my body stopped functioning including my mind. But I never intended to hurt you."

Anthony paused for a moment as he tried to recall the events that unfolded that day. "She called the police on me and said that I had kidnapped you. She actually told them that I had abused her and snatched you from her arms."

Anthony shook his head as he replayed the day in his mind.

"While I was out driving around, trying to get my thoughts together, the police stopped me. They asked me so many questions and I was so confused. They told me to get out of the car and then...they pointed guns at me and told me to get down on my knees. I couldn't believe it. I can still remember as they took you out of your car seat. It was the last time I saw you. And I'll never forget your face that day. You had never stopped smiling."

Iralaun shook her head. "Am I supposed to believe that garbage?"

"Later," Anthony cut in, "When the police realized the story wasn't true, they released me. When I went back to our home, she was gone. The place was completely empty. There were a few of my clothes on hangers still in the closet and some other things. She didn't leave me anything. The only thing that I have that I was lucky to keep was this picture of you."

Anthony showed Iralaun the tattered photograph. "It was in my wallet when the police pulled me over."

"And you never tried to find me?" she questioned.

"I did. I found out not too soon afterwards, that my brother and your mother were living together somewhere in North Carolina. She wouldn't let me see you. My brother and I haven't gotten along since the entire incident and my family was really no help in trying to get the situation resolved. I immediately went to court to get custody of you, but back then it was hard for men to get custody of their children, especially their little girls."

"I just can't accept this," Iralaun said shaking her head indignantly.

"Iralaun, it's true. Baby, I know this is hard for you, but it's the truth," Anthony said. "Your mother and my brother didn't last long. She realized he was lazy and he didn't have any plans of being with her once the money she had ran out. Isabella was ashamed because it didn't work out and came back to D.C. looking for me. She showed up at my job one day, begging me to take her back. Of course, after I told her no and demanded that she let me be a part of your life, she said I'd never see you again if we weren't living together as a family."

"And you wrote me off just like that?" Iralaun asked angrily.

"No sweetheart, that's not what I did. Your mother cut me off. She cut me completely off from you. She took you away somewhere, and even though I tried to get custody, I could never find you again."

Iralaun rolled her eyes.

"I know it's hard for you to believe this. It's a lot of information and a bitter pill for you to swallow. I can't imagine how it feels to learn that the woman whom you've known all your life was deceitful. But it's the truth. I'm just so glad that I finally found you."

Iralaun shook her head and cried. "How am I supposed to believe that, when my mother is not allowed to defend herself? Why would she lie to me for all these years? I just don't under..."

Anthony leaned over to wipe his daughter's tears with a tissue that was beside the bed. She snatched the tissue from him. A soft tap on the door interrupted them. The door opened and Allen walked in. He was moved by what was in front of him—Iralaun finally awake and Anthony consoling her.

"Is everything OK?" he hesitantly asked.

"Allen?" Iralaun asked. She was happy to hear his comforting voice and reached her arm out toward him.

"Yes, baby, it's me," he said walking swiftly to her bedside. He kissed her as if he might not ever get a chance to do it again. "What did I tell you about crying?" he teased.

She returned his kisses. His soothing presence was what she needed.

"Hey, I'll give you two a moment. I'm gonna get something from the cafeteria. Either of you want anything?"

Allen and Iralaun continued kissing and ignored Anthony. He decided to leave the room without an answer.

"Knock, knock," said a voice interrupting the two of them.

"When I left here early this morning, you were out cold in a deep sleep," Vivica said smiling to Allen and walking over to Iralaun's bedside. "I see you are back to see your blushing girlfriend. You are a very lucky young lady, Ms. Fugere. And I don't mean because of the car accident, I mean because of this sweetheart, you got. How are you feeling?"

Iralaun managed to smile. "My arm and my chest are sore," she said gesturing to the areas that ached.

Vivica checked her bandages, and explained to her why she was still aching. "I'll have the doctor increase your pain medicine and you should feel better soon."

"Don't keep my girl too drugged up Nurse," Allen joked. "She'll stay asleep and I missed her too much for that...we got a lot to talk about."

Vivica smiled, "If she heals fast enough, she'll be out of here in no time."

"Hello, hello, hello," came a voice coming from the doorway of the room. Everyone turned to see Craig and Brea entering with a huge bouquet of flowers.

"Girl, I thought you knew how to drive," Brea kidded, leaning in to give Iralaun a hug. "I'm glad you're up. I wanted you to see these flowers Craig and I picked out before they died."

"Hey girl," Iralaun said smiling. "Thanks, they're beautiful. I'm glad you came."

"She just woke up," Vivica said enthusiastically.

"I just came back yesterday, too. So it seems I was just in time for your grand entrance. I have to leave in a second though, we were just coming to drop the flowers off first, but I have to go pay the rent, renew the lease and take care of some other things. Don't worry about anything, I can cover it…and I'll just sign the lease. I just want you to worry about getting better. I'll be back later. I gotta go pay it before the rental office closes."

"I'm glad you are doing well, Iralaun," Craig said leaning down to hug her and kiss her cheek. Iralaun grimaced as soon as he laid his hands on her.

"We'll be back later," Brea said. "Come on, Craig. Give Iralaun and her friend some space."

When they walked out of the door, Iralaun turned to Allen and said, "I have something very important to tell you."

CHAPTER 16

The ride back to D.C. was in deed a long one for Belinda, but a week after she and Kevin left New Jersey, she found herself being proud of her progress. She was happy that even though she faltered at first by accepting Kevin's situation with his wife, she was glad she told him she wasn't going to tolerate it. The strength she found to say that made her feel even stronger. Belinda knew she was entitled to change her mind about being with Kevin, but sometimes she felt like she hadn't made the right decision.

She was alone again and it was weird for her. Belinda felt like she had to start all the way over to discover herself and to believe she deserved to be with someone who treated her special. She was so used to it being the other way around. And having Sunday dinner with her mother and father reminded her of just how far she had come over the past month.

She watched her mother make her father's plate and then watched her roll him to the table, as if he couldn't do it himself. It irritated her. Even though Belinda's father was disabled, he was by no means an invalid. He could still take care of himself. He just refused to, because her mother just did it for him and he was used to it. Her father acted like a baby, and when she saw her mother wipe his mouth, she had to excuse herself from the table.

She stared at her mother in disbelief—she couldn't believe what she had seen. Instead of telling Ingrid about herself in front of him, Belinda decided to leave the room all together.

In that moment, she realized that she didn't have to tolerate what she knew she didn't want too. She did not have to be like her mother, taking care of a capable man. No longer was she going to accept less than what she deserved or make excuses for the men she dated. If they didn't approach her with at least a step above the bare minimum, then they weren't for her. And she was OK with that, even if it meant being alone.

When she went home later that evening, she was surprised by the name she saw on her Caller ID. It was as if her will was being tested. Butterflies danced in her stomach. Kevin had called her and they hadn't talked in weeks. Belinda picked up the phone to listen to the voice mail message he left.

As soon as she heard Kevin's voice, her body became weak. She debated whether or not she should return his call. Was she strong enough to deal with whatever he wanted to talk about? Belinda decided that she would call him back, because it was a courtesy. "But under no circumstances will I go out with him or let him come over," she said aloud.

"Hi Kevin," she said when he answered the phone.

"Belinda? I'm glad to hear from you," Kevin said. She could tell he was smiling and her soul felt warm all over again. "I've been thinking about you a lot."

"Really? Why?"

"I just needed someone to talk to."

"Oh really? What's going on?"

"A couple of weeks ago," Kevin said pausing, "I got a package in the mail from my wife."

"Oh yeah?" Belinda asked trying to appear nonchalant about the matter.

"It was divorce papers."

Belinda was shocked, but didn't want to be swayed by his news. "How do you feel about that?"

"I don't know...I've been thinking a lot lately and I guess the marriage was over awhile ago and I just didn't want to accept it."

Belinda was silent.

"I just don't know really. I still love her. I would have done anything for her."

"Not anything," Belinda said.

Kevin was silent and Belinda didn't know what to say to ease his pain or to end his uncertainty.

"I never thought we wouldn't be together. Even on that same day I came home and saw she was no longer there. No clothes in the closet, no pictures on the walls, no dishes in the cabinets; I still couldn't believe it. But to be honest, she wasn't mentally there for years. I guess she got tired of physically being there, too. I would've never made her happy as long as I was wearing my uniform," Kevin said sounding distraught. "I tried my best, to make her feel loved at all times. But there was nothing I could do once she realized I had made up my mind not to leave the force."

"Have you talked to her since you received the papers?" Belinda asked.

"I called her. I wanted to talk it over, just to see if she was sure that was what she wanted to do, but...I could tell that I had lost her. She didn't even sound like the same person I'd married, almost like a stranger. She was so cold to me. I could since that she despised me or something and I just couldn't understand where all the anger came from."

"Mmmm...well, I don't know what to say," Belinda said. "I know there's nothing I can possibly say that would help you make sense of this...so..."

"I just need you to be there for me. That's one thing I've always liked about you—I can talk to you. I want us to still be friends, at least."

Belinda closed her eyes, and thought to herself for a moment. Can we be friends? Am I strong enough for that?

"Of course, we can be friends," Belinda said trying to convince herself more than she tried to convince Kevin. "I'm here for you if you need to talk."

"Good," Kevin said smiling. "I wanted to tell you I've started going to counseling."

Belinda was shocked, "Really?"

"Yeah, I figured it was over due. Plus, you were right about the insurance thing. I don't have to pay a dime."

"Yeah, I told you. That's real good Kevin. How's it been going?"

"It's been helping me deal with a lot of issues I have. I mean that's what's really been keeping me stable over this divorce thing. It also has helped me realize the problem I've had with the kind of relationships I was having since my wife and I separated. It's also been helping me to understand some of my selfishness as well as some other things."

"That's great! Kevin, I'm happy for you." Belinda was impressed with his open-mindedness.

"Maybe I can get you in there one day."

"Yeah, maybe," Belinda said smiling and she relaxed because she knew that she had a good friend in Kevin, if nothing else.

***

"So how do you feel about your Dad now?" Allen asked Iralaun one night at her apartment.

"I don't know," Iralaun said shrugging. She hadn't really thought about it. With trying to get back on her feet and all. She hadn't really sat back and analyzed the whole situation. "I don't know what to believe. I figure, he knows where I am now, he has no excuse for not trying to build a relationship with me."

"So you are going to give him a chance?"

"Yeah, I guess. It's up to him to make it what he wants it to be. It's not like I have any other family. I've been without him for so long, it really doesn't matter now. Even if he's lying about the whole thing, which I don't really want to think too much about, then it's on him," Iralaun said. "How do you feel about what your mom told you about him?"

Allen shrugged. "I mean, I understand why she thought it was the best thing to do at the time, I just don't agree with her logic. I mean I would have had to find out one day. And the earlier the better I still think. But regardless I know she is both parents for me. Besides, she's only human and we all make mistakes."

"That's true. Growing up in a single parent home is something else. Unfortunately, it's the New American Family, and it happens to be the norm."

"Yeah," Allen said shaking his head. "It's unfortunate though. I mean, I just don't understand how anybody could have kids and not want them. I just don't understand that. I mean to know that there is someone out there, who looks exactly like you, and to not want to be there for them, to watch them grow and nurture them—baffles me. I can't understand how anyone would walk away from their family, or turn their backs on a life that was created because of them."

"Me either," Iralaun said shaking her head and sipping some tea. "They should be proud."

"Fifty, sixty years ago, a man would've married the woman he got pregnant regardless of whether or not, he loved her or not. And I'm not saying that I agree with that method...I mean shotgun marriages aren't the best thing, but at least men took responsibility for what happened. These kids are reminders of relationships they've previously had and the choices they've made, no matter how stupid they were when they made them. A person has to be accountable."

"You are right. They have to own up to the decisions they've made—it's not the children's fault that their parents couldn't get their act together," Iralaun said as she added more honey to her tea. "You can't take children back. Your decisions have babies, and those decisions have babies...they don't just go away. And just like the decisions, those kids grow up and they remember you."

"Yep," Allen said shaking his head and reaching for a bag of chips on Iralaun's nightstand. Since she had stopped smoking cigarettes her fetish with snack foods increased.

"I definitely think parents should be in love, because even in the womb, I think the child knows it," Allen added. "A stressed-out parent, puts stress on the development of the unborn fetus. It's enough to have to worry about bringing a child into the world. But to have to worry about if the father is going to be there to help care for it, is ludicrous."

"I agree," Iralaun said. "And even if you aren't in love with the mother, at least take care of your kids. That's the least you can do. And no, you do not deserve a pat on the back for doing it," Iralaun said shaking her head.

"Yeah."

"Imagine back during slavery how husbands and wives would get sold away from their families—sold to other states and regions of the country or world, never to see their families again. But they would never ever forget them and would still long to be with them. They would even name stars after them in their honor. Many of them would even try to escape to go find their families...after years and thousands of miles of separation."

"Not today though. Just walk right away...like the whole situation was a figment of their imaginations, or like the child evaporated into thin air," said Allen shaking his head. "I'm not bitter though. At least I know I was loved. My mother did an excellent job in making me feel that way."

"Thank God. Look how sweet you turned out," she said leaning over to kiss him.

"You feeling OK?" Allen asked while fluffing up Iralaun's pillows.

"I'm fine." Iralaun adjusted herself. "Do you remember the day I was in the hospital and I told you that I wanted to tell you something?"

"Yeah..." he asked.

"Well, it wasn't about my dad—I know that's what you thought it was about, but it was really about something else. But I just wasn't ready to share it with you back then...it was too much going on then. I've actually wanted to tell you this for awhile because I think you should know about it. I mean," Iralaun hesitated, "I know I'm putting you in an awkward situation, and it's not fair to you."

"What are you talking about?" Allen asked concerned.

Iralaun took a deep breath. "I don't even know where to start. I know you feel like you know me, but there are still a lot of things that you don't quite know, yet. And I really don't know how to tell you this—even though I know I owe you this much to tell you. Really, it's something no one else knows and what I might tell you may hurt a lot of people."

"Iralaun, just say it. I'm sure I'll understand it."

Iralaun closed her eyes and shook her head. That was easy for Allen to say at the moment, because he didn't have any idea what she was going to tell him. She exhaled and said, "Craig and I were having a secret relationship all the way up until before the car accident."

Allen blinked really quickly and then cocked his head to the side in disbelief. "What?" he asked outraged and confused.

Iralaun bit her bottom lip and looked down at her fingers, because she didn't know how to explain the relationship to him. "It has meant absolutely nothing to me. And no, Brea doesn't know anything about it. I tried to end it, but I was in a precarious situation and to some extent, I felt like I was being blackmailed."

"What?" he asked again with a puzzled look on his face.

"I don't know why? I don't. You and I weren't as serious anyway, plus I tried to get out of it. But when he showed up at my door with information about my father, I was weak. Allen, he never meant anything to me...please don't be upset."

"You're talking about the same dude that stays here—in this apartment—half the time? How could you even..."

"Please...I don't need to hear it. I know. I know. I know."

Allen stood up and paced the room.

"Allen, please don't be angry with me."

He continued to walk around the room, shaking his head. "I feel like an asshole. After all this time, that nigga been smiling in my face," Allen said trying to make sense of it all.

Allen continued to pace the room. "Craig was hoping to win you over I guess, I don't know. But whatever...how could you do that to your roommate! You don't feel uncomfortable? Y'all live together for God's sake! You had to see her every day and you continued to do it!"

"Allen...please!" Iralaun said putting up her hand. "I just wanted to tell you."

"You wanted to tell me to ease your conscious. You had to be going crazy in here. I can't see how you haven't been bouncing off the walls trying to keep your secret a secret. But it really tells me a lot about your level of self-esteem," Allen said. "Sleeping with your girl's man..."

"First of all, me and Brea aren't really the best of friends...but that's besides the point, I know...Craig and I hardly speak to each other at all, let alone have any romantic feelings towards one another," Iralaun said in an unconvincing tone.

"You mean to tell me you don't think he still wants you?"

Iralaun shook her head. "To be honest, I don't know."

Allen shook his head. Craig had spent just as much time by her hospital bedside as he had. How could she think he didn't have romantic feelings toward her? Allen couldn't believe it. He walked towards the door.

"Don't leave," Iralaun said.

"I just can't believe you. How could you not say something earlier? And how can you just smile in your roommate's face day after day? I don't know if I can ever really trust you. I just don't know if that's even remotely possible. Iralaun, you should have said something...something!"

Iralaun shook her head as tears welled-up in her eyes. She didn't want to lose Allen. She hated herself for even telling him about it—she couldn't imagine how much her life would be different without him in it. She hated lying to him, but didn't know when it would've ever been wise to tell him about Craig.

"Allen, I don't know if there's anything that I can say that'll make you change your mind about any of this," Iralaun started to say.

"You need to tell Brea," Allen interjected. "If you have any self-worth."

"No!" Iralaun yelled.

"You just got finished telling me about being accountable for your actions...and now you are contradicting yourself."

"Why should I tell her? So I can get put out? She would never forgive me."

Allen shook his head as he stood in the bedroom doorway. "That's something you will have to deal with."

"Allen, please don't go," Iralaun begged. "I need you to understand our relationship means a lot to me. I needed to tell you—not wanted to tell you. I needed to tell you. I wanted to be honest with you. I know I should have said something earlier, but I didn't. Please forgive me for that. I didn't know how to tell you or when would be the best time to tell you—I just knew that it was something that had to be done.

"My life is different now, because I've met you. You've taught me so much about myself and I know there's a lot of work that still needs to be done. Please don't abandon me because of my past mistakes. You're so much bigger than that."

Allen looked at her long and hard before looking away. He had no sympathy for Iralaun and he didn't know how much of her words he could believe, so he turned to leave.

"You're leaving?" she asked.

"I need some air," he said pausing.

"Allen...please believe me. I wasn't trying to hurt you by keeping this from you."

Allen kept walking.

CHAPTER 17

Vivica did not feel like getting out of bed the day the lawyer's first payment was due. She couldn't squeeze it; she hadn't gotten the check that would include any of the extra hours she had worked yet. Though she hated to, Vivica turned to her mother, her brothers and sister to see if they could loan her some money until she got paid. Her mother was the only one who gave her any money—a $100 check that Vivica planned to add to the extra $150 she had saved. That was still only half of the payment she had promised to pay James Lomax that day.

After the conversation she had with him about setting up the plan, Vivica didn't get the impression that he was going to be too helpful about the payments. Her stomach tied up in knots. She didn't know how she was going to get the money. Vivica was scheduled to work overtime later that evening, but felt too queasy to go. She knew it was her nerves acting up and her head throbbed.

While lying in bed, Vivica heard the twins arguing with Evan about one of the usual trivial things that they didn't agree with. Evan ran in her room and tried to hide.

"What is going on now?" she yelled, her head pounding like a racing heart beat.

"Ma, they're trying to jump me," Evan said out of breath.

"What? Jump you?"

"He got on my shirt," Elgin argued.

"And he got on my jeans!" Elijah yelled.

"What is wrong with y'all? Why you got to pick on somebody half your size—your own brother at that?" Vivica said with her agonizing headache.

"Evan, do you have on any of their stuff?"

"They've been wearing my stuff all week long! Elijah even wore my brand new shirt without asking me. I hadn't even worn it, yet."

"Arrrggghhh! Y'all are getting on my cottonpicking nerves. You two are so immature. That's what you are arguing about? Go outside or something and leave me alone," she yelled. "I have too many other things on my mind right now. Just go!"

"See...that's exactly what I mean...you don't even care. Man...I'm taking my shirt," Elgin said running up to Evan, punching him in his stomach and tearing at the shirt that was on his little brother's back.

"I'm taking my jeans," Elijah said tugging at the belt buckle Evan wore. Vivica jumped up and tried to separate the three of them, yelling for them to get off of their younger brother. Eric, the youngest son, walked in along with Eve and stared at the commotion going on in the room. When Vivica realized the twins weren't listening to her, she threw her body in between them so that the twins wouldn't pummel Evan to death. They were throwing punches that were intended for a grown man. She couldn't break them up; they were so much stronger than she was.

"Call the police!" she cried to Eric and Eve.

Eric looked like a fly stuck on glue paper, his feet firmly planted. Eve ran for the telephone and dialed the number.

"Mommy, they said 'What's the address?' " Eve yelled.

Vivica hollered out the address as she tried to protect Evan with her body. As Eve repeated the address to the police, the twins stopped throwing punches and ran out of the house.

Vivica shook her head and helped Evan to his feet. She was so tired of her life. Why couldn't she have help?

"Are you OK?" she asked Evan, her body feeling sore from some of the punches she'd taken trying to protect her middle son. It wasn't the first time she'd done that, and she was enervated.

***

Belinda was cleaning up her place when she came across a photo album she had in a box in her closet. She flipped through it, because she hadn't revisited her past in awhile. It was filled with pictures of her, her sister Brandi and their childhood. She smiled as she saw a picture of her standing on Time Square when she was in college. Belinda laughed when she turned to a picture of her at the high school Prom; her purple dress was horrendous, she thought. Looking at the pictures brought back a lot of memories. One picture of her and her father, before his accident, stuck out to her. She marveled at how happy they were in the photo. Belinda was seven, and her dad was watching her Hula-Hoop. He looked so proud of her, she thought.

She could not remember seeing her father smile since before his accident and it bothered her. It bothered her so much that she started to accept his unhappiness as a fact of life, and she tried to overlook it. Belinda couldn't understand how a once, strong and powerful man, could become so helpless and dependent on alcohol and on her mother. She knew she had given up on her father, and for some reason, she knew she could no longer do that. He deserved more than that.

She pulled the picture out of the album and toyed with the old photo. The picture was over thirty years old. Her relationship with her father had withered over the last twenty years. A relationship was actually nonexistent. Seeing the picture made her want to reach out to him to help him improve his outlook on life and maybe to help herself, as well.

Belinda grabbed her leather fitted jacket and her purse, and drove to her parents' home. She was nervous about what she was going to say, but she knew she needed to approach him. It would be the first step she'd made since she noticed his behavior change. She had virtually ignored Frank since his attitude and his behavior had made a 180-degree turn.

When she knocked on her parents' door, her mother seemed surprised, but happy to see her. Belinda smiled casually and walked in.

"How're you doing?" she asked her mother.

"I'm OK. I was just washing some dishes. How about you? I didn't know you were coming by."

"I didn't know I was coming by either."

"Everything OK with you?" she asked concerned.

"No. Everything is not OK," Belinda said distressed. "Where's Daddy?" Ingrid raised her eyebrows, because Belinda never seemed interested in her father's whereabouts. "He's in the den. Why?"

"We need to talk."

"Oh..." Ingrid said shocked. "OK."

Confused, she led Belinda toward the den.

Belinda looked around the room and noticed that things were the usual way—everything in order and neatly arranged.

"Hi Daddy," Belinda said to Frank who was eating some roasted peanuts while he watched the Wheel of Fortune.

He looked up at her and turned back toward the television and cracked open another nutshell. Frank put the nut in his mouth, before reaching for more.

"Remember this?" she asked dropping the photo of the two of them in his lap.

Frank didn't bother to look down at it. He just cracked open another nut.

"Do you remember how happy you used to be? How proud you used to be of us?"

He still didn't say anything; he continued staring at the game show.

"I used to want to be just like you when I grew up—a hard worker, a dedicated and loyal person, full of character and life. I wanted to be respected the same way you were in our community. I wanted to be responsible and sincere and caring...just like you. But not anymore...because the person I remember is no longer here.

"All I know of you now is a ghost of what used to be, what could've been and what actually is and it's a tragic reality. There's nothing left but a whole bunch of traces of memories from long ago. And it's a shame Daddy. In fact, you are disgraceful."

"That's enough!" Ingrid interrupted.

"Letting Mama take care of you like you're a baby; sitting around feeling sorry for yourself; drinking your miserable life away...being a burden to her. Because, believe it or not, what you do to yourself affects more than just yourself, you know? For years, I've tried to act the same way toward you, as you've been acting towards the rest of the family—like you didn't even exist. Have you ever wondered why nobody comes by to see you anymore? Have you ever wondered why no one even calls you?

"All of your friends have deserted you, or rather you've deserted them long ago...Just like you've done your own family. Hennessey is your only friend, your only child, your only lover."

"Stop talking to your father that way!"

"But Mama, you tolerate it," Belinda said turning to Ingrid. "You facilitate his self-hate and loathing spirit. I put half the blame of his behavior on you, because you've allowed him to believe that even if he doesn't care about himself, it doesn't matter if he ever gets better, because you'll always be there for him...wiping his mouth and probably wiping his..."

"Now you hold on a minute young lady. I will not allow you to speak to me like that—and definitely not in my house! What I do is my business. I love your father and promised to take care of him...in sickness or in health and that is what I am doing!"

"Mama, Daddy ain't sick anymore. Can't you see that? I'm tired of seeing him sitting around here feeling sorry for himself, and you acting like it's OK for him to do it. If it weren't for the alcohol, he would be healthy. He needs help Mama. Help that neither, you, nor I, nor Brandi, can give him. He needs professional help."

"No, I do not!" her father cut in. Speaking the first complete sentence Belinda heard in years. "I'm fine just the way I am. If you have a problem

179

with it, you can leave and never look back."

Belinda looked startled because her father had never spoken to her in that tone. She was surprised that he even was talking at all.

"And for the record, I do remember this picture," he said looking down at the photo that lied in his lap. "I remember it was hot outside that day and not a cloud appeared in the sky. I remember that twenty minutes before the picture was taken you and your sister was fighting over which person would show me that they knew how to use that Hula-Hoop first. I remember you allowing your baby sister to go first. You didn't even laugh when she messed up. I remember you smiling so brightly when you saw that you could do it for a long time. You see, I remember a lot Belinda. And just because I don't smile anymore doesn't mean that I'm sick."

"But Daddy, you need help. You've been reclusive and feeling sorry for yourself since the accident. You act like you are dead or dying and that is absolutely not true. You've given up on yourself! You never would've let me or Brandi give up on ourselves like that—even that very day with that Hula-Hoop. Even after Brandi dropped it and started crying, you told her not to give up and to keep on trying. You even made me show her how to do it," Belinda said. "So Daddy, I'm asking you not to give up on yourself, too. Allow me or Mama and a professional to help you make it out of this. I can't sit idly by and watch you continue to kill yourself with that bottle. I can't! I love you too much to let you do it to yourself."

Frank put his hand up to his face to hide the tears that were forming in the corners of his eyes. Belinda leaned down to hug him and her mother walked around and wrapped her arms around the two of them. They all cried together.

CHAPTER 18

It was business as usual at District General Hospital and Vivica was at work covering a shift for someone else. She was surprised to see Eddie walk through the Emergency Room sliding doors a little after nine o'clock in the evening. He was heading straight toward her. He looked frail and his skin looked ashy. She could see sores all over his face and his hands. Vivica couldn't believe how sick he appeared. She had seen him look terrible before, but nothing compared to how he looked on this day.

"Viv? I need your help. I feel like shit," he said with a forced smile.

"Ahhh..." She started to say more but didn't quite no what to say.

"I don't feel good...at all," he said to her in almost a whisper. He leaned toward her and before he could say anything else, Eddie threw up all over her. Vivica hollered as the yellow, chunky fluid landed on her chest. Another nurse ran up to Vivica to see if she could help her out.

"Sir, are you OK? I need a chair, and some help over here!" the nurse yelled to an orderly running toward her.

Vivica ran to the bathroom to clean up, but ended up changing her entire uniform. When she was done, she returned to see what happened to Eddie.

"Where is he?" she asked the nurse assisting her earlier.

"They're trying to pump his stomach. They think he may be on something and may be having a possible overdose."

"Oh, I know he's a substance abuser. They may want to run some other tests too, because he looks terrible."

"You know him?"

Vivica shook her head in disgust and shame and said, "Unfortunately I do. He's my ex-husband."

The nurse looked at Vivica with pity in her eyes. "We'll try to do the best we can for him, I'll make sure of that."

Vivica nodded and crossed her arms. She was nervous, because Eddie didn't look good at all. She walked toward the room he was being kept in and paced the hall waiting to hear something from someone. She didn't want to go in and see; she just wanted to be informed about his status. Despite all of Eddie's problems, he was once her husband and still the father of her children. She started to worry.

After twenty-minutes passed, she was hoping that there was nothing but good news to come. But after an hour with no word, she really became concerned. When she saw the doctors coming out of the room smiling, a little later, she thought they were going to tell her that everything was going to be OK. But when they walked passed her without acknowledging her, and when the nurse who was helping her earlier came out of the room with a sullen face, she was confused.

"What's going on?" Vivica demanded.

"Vivica," the nurse started. "He expired."

"What?" she asked confused.

"He OD'd. His body couldn't handle it anymore. I'm sorry."

Vivica was traumatized. "He's what?"

"I'm sorry Viv, he's no longer living."

Vivica shook her head in utter disbelief. "Noooo," she screamed. "No!"

The nurse and two orderlies took her to a room where she could calm down. The nurse gave her a sedative to relax her and Vivica fell asleep.

***

A small halogen lamp barely illuminated the hospital room where Vivica slept. When she woke up the following morning, she couldn't remember what had happened the previous night. Once she looked around the room and saw that she had been sleeping in a hospital bed, she remembered what happened and sobbed. When her eye ducts couldn't create anymore tears, she just wailed until her throat wouldn't release another sound. She stared at the wall in front of her and couldn't find the strength to lift her head. But she knew she needed to get up. She lied there for another hour before she did.

Vivica didn't know how she was going to tell her children about their father. She dreaded telling the younger two, especially, because she knew they wouldn't understand it. The twins would probably try to act like they didn't care, but she knew that they would—if not today, they would care tomorrow or the day after that.

By the time she got to her house, it was eight o'clock in the morning, and she was surprised to hear the house so quiet. It was dead silent; she wasn't used to that. Evan, Eric and Eve usually were up at that hour getting ready for school. When she climbed the stairs, Vivica was confused when she saw every bed empty and that the house was barren.

Vivica collapsed in the spot where she once stood. She had no idea where her children were and didn't have the strength to call out to them.

***

Iralaun lie in bed watching The Today Show. She had taken the spring semester off, since she'd missed so much of it because of her injuries. She was becoming a fan of morning talk shows. Brea tapped on Iralaun's bedroom door to see how she was doing before she went to class for the day. Iralaun was half-awake, but heard the soft taps on the door.

"Come in," she said.

"Hey. Feeling any better today?"

"I feel wonderful...not," Iralaun said smiling.

"Really?"

"No, really, I don't feel as bad as I used too...but still."

"Yeah I hear you. Can I get you anything before I go to class?"

"No, I'm fine. I'll get up later."

"Want me to bring something back while I'm out?"

"Yes, actually can you get me some tampons? It's getting closer to that time and I don't have anymore."

"No problem. Anything else?"

"Some Gummy Bears," Iralaun said innocently. "Please."

"I guess I can do that for you," Brea said smiling and turning to leave. "Oh yeah, I almost forgot to tell you Craig is asleep in my room, he's going to go straight to school from here. Just didn't want you to be frightened if you heard him walking around."

"Oh," Iralaun said hoping her discomfort wasn't evident. "OK, I'll see you later then. Have a good day."

"Thanks. Bye."

Iralaun was pissed, but didn't want to show it. Craig had still been making comments about them being together and how much he cared about her. He hated Allen and made sure Iralaun knew how he felt. He harassed her constantly about how much he thought Allen wasn't good enough for her. Living there could never work, and she knew she had to move out.

She felt trapped with him in the apartment alone. Iralaun knew that Craig would stop by her room at some point through out the day. Although she and Allen had been talking, it wasn't quite the same as before. She knew he probably wouldn't trust her, until she told Brea everything. Allen told her that then, and only then, would everything be out on the table. But Iralaun didn't want to risk being put out of her apartment or losing a friend. She understood Allen's point, but wasn't ready to do that.

Allen suggested that she move in with him, but that would leave Brea stuck with a huge rent she wouldn't be able to afford on her own. The lease was just renewed in Brea's name and Iralaun didn't feel good about sticking her out there like that. She was in an awkward situation and didn't know what to do. Months ago, she probably wouldn't have cared at all about what happened. She grew up in a lifestyle where it really was all about her. But since she met Allen things had changed, and she did care about how situations ended and the relationships she had with people.

Besides, Iralaun knew if she wanted to continue cultivating the relationship she had with Allen, she needed to tell Brea. She just didn't want to. If there was anyway she could get out of it, she would do it. But Allen was clearly uncomfortable with being over her house when Craig was there and she didn't like knowing she was the cause of his discomfort—so she started staying over his apartment more often. But Allen still wasn't cool with it. He knew that Craig was there on days that Iralaun was there. And there was nothing that would really stop them from continuing their relationship. It was hard for Allen to think he could trust her, after knowing what Iralaun did to her own friend.

She wanted to resolve the situation as soon as possible, but she needed more time to think.

An hour passed by before she heard Craig rummaging around in the kitchen. Before she knew it, her bedroom door was opening, and Craig walked in with waffles, bacon and orange juice on a tray. Iralaun shook her head and rolled her eyes.

"Are you ever going to give up?" she asked.

"Give up? Why?"

"Why can't you just let it go? Can't you see I'm happy with Allen?"

"Iralaun, you started this remember.?Why should I let it go? Come on...eat."

"No, thank you."

"Come on. After all this hard work I put into this meal. Girl, you are going to eat this."

"No, I'm not," she asserted. She was tired of Craig's cockiness. How dare he think that they would continue to see each other? Just how far was he trying to take it? Couldn't he see she was happy now? Why wouldn't he just leave her alone? "I'm not playing with you Craig. I don't want that."

"Why not?"

"Look, I've decided," Iralaun paused, "that I'm going to tell Brea about us."

Craig looked stunned for a second, but then he continued to place the tray beside Iralaun's bed. "No you aren't. Stop saying that."

"I've already told Allen."

Craig looked up at her in disbelief. "You are joking, right?"

Iralaun shook her head. "It's not a joke. I told him about us a while ago."

Craig began to look nervous. "Well, then he's a punk. He didn't say nothing to me. That goes to show how much he cares about you."

"Please, OK. He thought about kicking your ass, but I talked him out of it. He wants me to tell Brea about us and then move out."

"What?" he yelled. "Naw...you can't do that."

"I don't want too, and besides, I have a better idea."

Craig paced the room. "What?"

Iralaun had been tossing this idea back and forth in her mind for days. And this was the perfect opportunity to suggest it to Craig. "Why don't you break up with her? You will do both of us a huge favor."

"Hell no! That ain't even happening."

"Just for a little while or either...you can move in here with her. It's up to you?"

"Man...I'm not ready for that...that's a big step."

"If I move out, she's going to need help with the rent. If I stay and you don't tell her, I'll tell her. And then she'll put me out. But you can either break up with her and let the relationship go, or you can stay with her and move in here. You claim you love her so much, why not?"

"That's fucked up! What kind of friend are you?"

"Oh now you care?" Iralaun said dumbfounded. "You should have asked me that when you were busy fucking the shit out of me!"

"What?" Brea asked while opening Iralaun's bedroom door with her book bag in one hand, and a CVS bag in the other. "What did I hear you just say?"

Iralaun and Craig both shook their heads in disbelief.

"My fucking class was cancelled!" Brea yelled. "But I'm glad it was! All this time this shit has been going on right in my face and I trusted both of you." She threw the bag with the box of tampons and Gummy Bears at Iralaun. "I want you the fuck out of my apartment, Twat. And you..." she said turning to Craig, "You trifling no-good-sonofabitch. I can't believe you!"

Craig shook his head.

"But you..." Brea said turning to Iralaun, "to be honest, I *can* believe it! You've always been a fucking tramp. You could never keep your goddamn legs closed. They stay open more than a highway rest stop. For years I've made excuses for you about why you felt the need to do it, but now I see you are just heartless. And it has absolutely nothing to do with your relationship with your father! You are just a whore—plain and simple!"

"Brea..." Iralaun interrupted.

"Shut the fuck up! I don't want to hear it! I want you to pack your shit, so you can get the hell out of my house! You better call your little boyfriend or somebody to help you get it, before I throw it out. I want you out before five."

Brea stormed out of the apartment and slammed the door behind her. Craig ran out behind her. Iralaun shook her head and began to sob. Still with a cast on, she climbed out of her bed to go to the bathroom. Before she left the room, her phone rang. She looked at the Caller ID and saw that it was Allen. He was right on time—as always.

CHAPTER 19

I'm so glad you called," Kevin said. He looked handsome, in his mint green, brown and cream stripped button-up shirt, Belinda thought. "I really did miss your company."

"Really?" Belinda said twirling her fork in her pasta. She had invited Kevin out to dinner. She didn't feel guilty about doing it either. They were friends now.

"Yeah. I think what you did for your father is very inspirational. Are you going to get counseling, too?"

"Yeah. Well sort of... the doctor asked that we meet as a family occasionally for a few sessions."

"Well, that's a step. I'm telling you it's really been helping me to make sense of who I am."

"Is that right?"

"Yes, definitely it has. Besides this one case I've been working on, I've been taking it a whole lot easier. I haven't been in the office as much as before. I've come to realize that trying to get ahead to eventually make detective should become secondary to my happiness."

"Really? But wouldn't making detective make you happy?" Belinda wondered.

"Ahhh...without a doubt," Kevin said smiling. "But even if I don't make it, I still want to be happy. Let's just say making detective will add to my happiness."

"Oh OK." Belinda nodded. "That sounds great. I'm happy for you. You sound like you are getting there, already."

"Will you two be having dessert with us this evening?" asked the waitress.

"Yes," Kevin said, "What are your specials?"

"Well we have a Grand Marnier Soufflé that people just love or you can try our famous White Chocolate Hazelnut Cheesecake?"

"Wow, let's try the cheesecake," Belinda said smiling.

"Cheesecake it is," Kevin said.

"Great. Let me just take your plates," the waitress said.

"Well, hello, hello," James said walking up to the table with a woman on his arm.

"Hello James Lomax," Belinda said surprised to see him at her favorite restaurant. She introduced the two of them. "This is Kevin St. James."

"Hi," Kevin said nodding.

"This is…"James started, but appeared to forget the woman's name.

"Maria Cortez," said the young scantily dressed Hispanic woman in her lush accent.

"Yeah, Maria," James sang seductively.

Belinda rolled her eyes. James was nothing but a playboy. She was so lucky she wasn't with him anymore, she thought.

"How've you been?" he asked her.

"I've been wonderful and yourself?"

"OK."

Belinda nodded and gave him a dry smile—the kind where your lips disappear into a thin line. She started to ask about Cassandra, James' fiancee, but decided against it. She thought it would appear as if she really cared or like she was trying to be vindictive towards his date.

"Oh OK, well…I just wanted to say hello," James said turning to walk away.

"Goodbye," said Belinda offering the same dry smile again.

"That was your ex-boyfriend right?" Kevin asked. "I remember him at the hearing for the Jeffries boys."

Belinda rolled her eyes. "Unfortunately, yes that was the infamous Mr. Lomax. And believe it or not he's engaged and not to Maria," she said her name with her best Spanish accent.

Kevin laughed. "You aren't bitter are you?"

Belinda grimaced because she couldn't believe he thought that way. "Not hardly. I feel privileged. I could've been in his fiancee's shoes. I'm glad I found out about him before I felt like I had to tolerate it because I invested so much time or something. Good riddens."

Kevin laughed and the waitress brought them their cheesecakes.

"What's so funny?" Belinda asked.

"You. You sound like you are trying to convince yourself that you are over him."

"I am truly over that guy."

Kevin raised his eyebrows.

"What?"

"If you say so," Kevin said as he dug into the slice.

"Kevin you don't have to believe me. Why would I want to be with someone like that?"

"That's what I'm trying to figure out. Most women are attracted to the men they can't control."

Belinda shook her head and took a bite of her cake.

"You know I'm right—most women today anyway. And when they get hurt, from being with the guy that they can't control, they don't ever want to be involved again with another guy, they bail out or they take 'breaks' from dating."

"Whatever..."

"OK. If you say so, but you and I both know, what the deal is," he said smiling.

"There may be some truth to that, but I'm so over the whole relationship thing right now. I'm tired of feeling like the mad scientist trying to create the perfect man. There is no such thing as a perfect man."

"I'm glad you realize that those fairytales they read you girls when you're young were just that...there is no such thing as a Prince Charming."

Belinda grimaced. "But I still have to set standards for how I want to be treated. And a man like James Lomax is no where on my list."

Kevin raised his eyebrows. "See, why do you even have to have a list at all?"

"It's not the list, per say, for a perfect man...it's more like a list of qualities that I would want the man I'm with to have—it's my mental list with qualities that I check off," she said winking.

"Like?"

"Like being a gentleman, courteous, considerate, loyal, honest and respectful."

"I have those qualities."

Belinda smiled. "I want someone to be the way my Dad was when I was growing up—a hard worker, a loyal husband, a dedicated father."

"I'm telling you that sounds just like me," Kevin said.

Belinda shook her head at Kevin and took another bite.

"I'm serious."

"That's the scary thing," Belinda said laughing.

Kevin smiled, "So are you saying you can't see yourself being with me?"

"No, I can't see myself being with you right now," Belinda said smiling.

"Why not?"

"Because we both have too many problems that we need to work out before we hook up. Don't get me wrong you are well on your way, but until I see those papers processed, you and I will have to remain strictly friends," Belinda said winking at him again.

"Oh, so that means we can't hook up, hook up?" Kevin asked raising his eyebrows.

"Exactly—no we can't be intimate again."

Kevin nodded. "I guess I'll have to respect that."

"You have no choice."

***

Vivica woke up to the sound of knocking at her front door. When she realized that she had fallen asleep on the floor, she stood up, brushed herself off, and went downstairs to open the door.

"Yes?" she asked the older woman who stood in her doorway.

"Hello, I live across the street," the woman said pointing behind her. "I don't know if you know yet or not, but I thought I'd make sure you knew what happened last night."

"Huh?"

"They took your kids early this morning."

"Who?" Vivica demanded.

"Child Protective Services."

"Child Pro.."

"Yes. They couldn't find the two twins, but they took the younger ones with them."

Vivica started shaking her head uncontrollably and yelled "No, no, no..."

"Do you have somebody you can call?"

"I feel like these walls are suffocating me..." she hollered. She was hysterical. "Why? Why?"

The neighbor wrapped her arms around Vivica to calm her down. "There, there dear...everything will be alright. You just need to sit down for a bit."

"Why me?"

"Trust in the Lord. Just trust in him, that everything will be alright."

"What am I supposed to do? I can't do it all by myself. I can't. I tried, I tried," Vivica cried.

"No you can't. That's what God is for. There is no burden too heavy for him to carry. If you feel like you can't carry it any more let him do it for you. Just lay your burdens down, lay 'em on down Darling."

"I can't," Vivica cried.

"It's going to be OK. It's going to be OK," the woman said as she rocked.

Several minutes later, the neighbor was boiling a pot of water, fixing Vivica a cup of chamomile tea. Vivica stared off into space, sullen and weary as she sat on the couch.

"I don't even know where to start," she mumbled to herself.

"When the righteous cry for help, the Lord hears, and rescues them from all their troubles. That's from Psalms."

"Why would they take my kids from me? Everything I do is for them. I just don't understand it," Vivica sobbed.

"It's not your job to understand it. Some things aren't meant for you to understand, dear. Some things just are as they are. There is a verse in Proverbs that says 'Trust in the Lord with all your heart and lean not on your own understanding; in all your ways acknowledge him, and he will make your paths straight.' I'm telling you to let it go. Put it in the Lord's hands. Here, drink this tea, you'll feel better."

Vivica sipped the tea and closed her eyes as the hot soothing liquid filled her throat. The only person she knew she could call was James Lomax, but didn't want to increase the debt she already owed him. He might not even consider it, seeing as though she owed so much.

"My kids don't even know about their father dying last night."

"Oh," the woman gasped. "I'm sorry to hear that."

"It is going to devastate them, I know," Vivica said. "I've been thinking that it is something worth keeping to my self—at least for awhile."

The neighbor nodded her head and sipped her tea. "You have to do what you have to do sometimes. There would be absolutely no benefit in telling them about that now anyway. Just look at it as another example of crucifying Peter to redeem Paul's soul. You just want your children home with you and that's what you need to focus on doing right now."

Vivica nodded in agreement and continued sipping her tea. "Thank you. I really needed to hear that. Thank you for coming over, too. Your help has been invaluable. I really appreciate it. Besides, I could use someone to talk to."

"I've been watching you for some time, trying to make it on your own. I admire that—not too many people would do for their kids like you do. Not these days anyway," she added.

"I certainly would, without hesitation," Vivica said staring at her tea. Then she glanced at the woman and asked her which house she lived in.

"The one right across the street—the little yellow row house near the end of the corner. I saw all of the commotion last night, with the police and the social workers taking your children. It made me sick to my stomach, because I know whoever called meant well. But they didn't realize what a disservice they were doing to your family. Breaking you all up like that...you are all each other have. Family is so important."

Vivica rolled her eyes. "It's my fault. I should have been there for them. It's been so much going on and I know that at the time, it was the only option I had. It's my fault that this has happened."

"No. Don't say that. The Lord has something special in store for you," the old woman said as she reached over and touched Vivica's knee. "You watch. Patience is truly virtuous."

"I don't think it'll happen in this lifetime," Vivica said.

"God is our refuge and strength, an ever-present help in trouble, dear. You have to have faith in him. Do not give up on him, you hear?"

Vivica nodded and knew that the old woman was right. She finished her tea in silence.

"I'm going to go now—have to get to my wash and start preparing dinner for my husband. I got to clean some collards I got from the store. I got these big juicy tomatoes that are so ripe, that you'd think came straight from out of my garden in the summer. But I'll be here for you if you need me," she said standing up.

"Yes, ma'am. Thank you so much for all of your help. What is your name?"

"Mrs. Althea Lomax."

"Lomax?" Vivica asked astonished. "I know a Lomax."

"Do you really? That's not a common name."

"Yes my sons' lawyer name is James Lomax, and his brother Roger, was my divorce lawyer?"

"Why those are my grandsons. Do you know them well, darlin'?"

Vivica looked at the woman and smiled weakly. "Yes, I do. As a matter of fact, I owe James a huge sum of money for some help he did with my children a couple of months ago."

"You think he can help you with this, because I'll call him right away?"

"Ma'am I don't have any money."

"Oh, now don't you worry about that. I'll speak to him about this right away."

"Yes ma'am. I'd truly appreciate it if you did...and I'll pay him back as soon as I can," Vivica assured.

"James will do whatever I say. Don't you worry about it one bit. I know my James will do what's right."

Vivica let a smile creep on to her face. It seemed that God had already begun to put his work in motion, Vivica thought. She closed her eyes and tried to relax for awhile before she began to start making phone calls.

CHAPTER 20

I t was below freezing the day that Allen helped Iralaun move her things into his apartment. He and a couple of his buddies helped move her bed, dressers and dining room table into a storage facility. But the other things, clothes, her computer and some dishes, she'd brought into Allen's apartment.

Though it had been a few weeks that they were living together, sometimes Allen wondered if he'd made the right decision. Their relationship was moving at an unprecedented speed for either of them. And when Iralaun decided to cook dinner at the apartment for her father and Allen's mother, Allen was worried about their parents meeting.

He wasn't quite sure who he was most nervous about meeting: his mother and his girlfriend or his mother and her mother's ex-boyfriend. Anita was nervous because she had used Anthony in a lie for so many years and he still had no idea about it. At first Anita was hesitant about dinner, but she knew it meant a lot to Allen.

With one arm in a sling, Iralaun had quite some trouble cooking small Cornish hens, asparagus and rice pilaf, but she made it. Allen helped her with the salad and chilled some wine for their parents.

"You're nervous aren't you?" Iralaun asked.

Allen nodded.

"Don't worry, I won't embarrass you," she said smiling.

"I'm more worried about my mom embarrassing me," he said laughing. "She really liked your dad, you know?"

"Wouldn't it be wild if they hit it off?"

"Gross," he said laughing. "I don't even want to think about that."

"It is possible you know."

"Oh God...no."

"Don't you want your mother to be happy?"

Allen shrugged, "Of course, I do. But with my girlfriend's father? No."

"What's so bad about that?"

"It just doesn't sound right."

"My dad truly must've been a good guy, if he was special enough for your mom to say that he was your Dad for all those years," Iralaun said admittedly. "It makes me want to believe what he told me about what happened with my mother. No woman would lie on a no-good man, unless she was no-good herself. So it makes me want to question what really happened back then."

"Why not just let him prove himself wrong, instead of waiting for him to prove to you that your mother was right. It seems easier that way."

"You are right. Today's a new day. Maybe one day, you will be able to call him dad, after all," Iralaun said smiling and kissing Allen on the cheek.

There was a knock at the door, when Allen looked out the peephole he was surprised to see that both of their parents had arrived at the exact same time. He smiled and opened the door.

"Hi mom, Mr. Fugere," Allen said nodding.

"Call me Mr. Anthony or Mr. Tony, son," he said winking.

"Mr. Tony. Come on in."

"It smells good in here," Anita said. "What do you two have cooking?"

"Just a little something, something," Iralaun said walking over to greet her.

"Mom, this is Iralaun."

"Nice to finally meet you," Iralaun said hugging her. She was surprised to see how attractive his mother looked for her age. Iralaun could tell that Allen's mother was just as high-maintenance as she was. She wore nice expensive clothing and she was adorned with lots of accessories. Iralaun smiled at her.

"Nice to meet you, too. Allen talks about you quite a lot."

Iralaun blushed. "Allen, take your mom's coat for me. You can have a seat," Iralaun said pointing to the living room.

"You've made yourself pretty comfortable in here," Anita said looking around at the pictures of the two of them on walls and at some of the decorations. "Because I know my son didn't pick that out."

"Oh you mean the framed wheat stock?" Iralaun inquired. "Actually he did. I just framed it. I saw it like that in IKEA."

Anita nodded.

"Dinner is almost ready," Allen said. "Can I get anyone anything to drink? Iralaun knows she's too young for alcohol, but for the old heads...I got some Zinfandel."

"Who're you calling old?" Anita asked smiling. "I'll have whatever Iralaun's having. I'm sure it's not Kool-Aid."

"Well actually, I was going to sneak some of that," Iralaun said smiling and pointing to the wine bottle. "But since, Allen called me out...I'm going to have some lemonade."

"That sounds good to me, too."

"So how do you two feel about seeing each other after all these years?" Iralaun asked.

Anthony shrugged. "I don't know what to say. Ni-Ni still looks the same way she did twenty years ago...gorgeous."

Anita blushed. "Thank you," she said. "I do, don't I?"

"You sure do," he said smiling and shaking his head.

"This is weird," Allen said.

The evening pretty much went smoothly. Anita and Anthony casually flirted with one another throughout the night. After dessert, they all sat around and talked about the past and how things had changed over the years. Then after Allen noticed his mother yawning, and Anthony grinning, he knew the two of them would be leaving together. Anthony was a regular gigolo, Iralaun noticed. She shook her head while she and Allen walked their parents to the door to say goodbye.

Later that evening, for the first time since they had been dating, Allen picked Iralaun up and carried her to his bedroom. He was at ease with her and had a level of confidence in her that he hadn't had since she told him about Craig. He knew she was all his now. And he knew he could trust Iralaun. Allen tenderly made love to her, ending his long stint with celibacy. He was happy, and so was Iralaun, because she glowed while lying in his arms.

***

It had been days since Elijah and Elgin had seen their mother. When Child Protective Services knocked on the door early that morning, they both ran out of the back door. They hadn't been home since that day. Both of them were staying in between friends' houses. They stayed with Osei the most, he had an apartment in the projects around the corner. They looked at Osei as a big brother; he was the same person who first put them on to selling in the neighborhood when they were younger and they did most of their dealing for him.

Osei helped set them up with the deals that were going down, and if they ever needed a favor, they usually went to him. Osei also tried to keep them grounded and out of the nonsense that sometimes made how they lived more dangerous. He just wanted them to move product, and a little bit of weight. Osei didn't want them getting caught up with other day-to-day situations that led them to stealing cars, petty theft, fights and even getting the recent gang-rape charge; it drew too much attention, he had told them.

Although the twins dropped out of school, Osei made them read the newspaper whenever they came to his place. "So you can know what's going on around the way," he told them. He wanted them to read all the time. Even though they argued with him about reading books, he encouraged it.

"Besides, somebody once told me," he said, "that's the first place a narc is going to put his secrets. If you don't want a black person to know something, put it in a book, because niggas don't read."

They listened to him, even though they didn't understand him half the time. Later they realized that reading opened up a third-eye of sorts. It made them more observant and thoughtful. They started noticing things they hadn't paid attention to before and reading made them analyze situations more—all the way down to the minute details. From the people they hung out with, to the tell-tale signs of a bust about to go down. But no matter how much unnecessary trouble Osei tried to keep them out of, the twins still didn't like being told what to do. It was the one major thing they couldn't all agree on.

It was that same problem that got them caught up with Dante' months earlier. Osei told them not to trust Dante', but they trusted him anyway. Elijah fronted Dante' some cash to help him get started in the game. Dante' was going to try to flip it, but his sells kept coming up short every time he went to Osei. But as much as Osei told the twins not to trust Dante', they did what they wanted because they knew him from school—and wanted to put him on.

After weeks had gone by and Dante' was either hard to find or making excuses for why he couldn't give Elijah his money, Elgin got on his brother's back to punish him. In the end, they both taught Dante' a lesson, and Elijah took one back himself—never to trust anybody.

One day, Osei took Elijah and Elgin to the mall to pick up something new to wear. They had planned to see Rare Essence and Backyard Band—popular Go-Go bands in the area later that day. Instead of going to one of the usual local malls they went to like Pentagon City or City Place, he took them to P.G. Plaza. Osei wanted to get a pair of the new Air Jordans that had recently come out. The twins were picking up a couple of jerseys to wear to the club they were going to later on.

"Y'all see that new Ashanti video?" Osei asked lighting up a blunt.

"Naw, not yet." Elgin said.

"Why?" Elijah asked.

"She looks bangin' in it," he said smiling while making a left turn.

"For real?" Elijah asked. "Yeah, she's tight. Can't sing, but she's tight."
"She ain't gotta sing lookin' like that," Elgin said.

"No shit," Osei said passing the blunt to Elijah.

"Half them broads can't sing, but they look good than a muthafucka," Elijah said inhaling. "Who else can't sing?"

"Ah...Jennifer Lopez," Osei said laughing. "But she fine as shit."

"Yeah, ah...I can tell you who else had a top-10 song, but ain't cute, and ain't got no talent?" Elgin said reaching for the blunt.

"Who?" Osei and Elijah asked.

"Man...that girl who sings that song 'My neck, My back...'"
They both cracked up laughing.

"I know. She had her nerve talking about lick something," Osei said laughing.

"Yeah, she must've been off that 'dro when she made that song," Elijah chimed in his two cents.

***

Allen made plans to leave work early to take Iralaun to a follow-up appointment at the doctor's office. Her doctor wanted to check on her progress, and to schedule her for physical therapy for her arm. Allen asked another assistant manager working at Foot Locker Room to cover for him, before he grabbed his coat to leave.

***

"Aw shit...Five-0 trying to pull a nigga over," Osei said nervously looking in the rearview mirror at the whirling lights.

"What the fuck do they want?" Elijah asked pissed and putting the blunt in a soda can that was sitting in the cup holder.

"Man, calm down. Don't nobody say shit. If they ask y'all a question, just keep it short. I'm telling y'all now, if they try some shit, I'm ballin' the fuck out. I got all kinds of shit in this joint," Osei said as he pulled over his white Excursion sports utility vehicle.

Elgin sucked his teeth as he saw the black police officer stride up to the truck.

"Turn your car off and hand me your license and registration please," he demanded.

"Yeah," Osei said handing it to him. "Can I ask what this is about officer?"

"Turn your car off," the officer said inhaling the aroma of marijuana.
"Your plates are dead."

"Oh they are? I didn't know."

"I said turn your car off! Now step out of the vehicle, sir?"

"Why officer?"

"Please step away from the vehicle," the police officer demanded again.

***

While Allen was walking through the mall, he stopped to get a bag of
Gummy Bears from a candy shop that was in the eatery court. He knew they
were Iralaun's favorite, and wanted to give her a treat. He waited behind a
heavyset woman with two young children as they ordered chocolate-covered
pretzels and chewy worms. One of the woman's little girls wasn't sure what
she wanted and was taking a long time making a decision. The woman
smiled at Allen and apologized for his wait. He smiled back, and glanced at
his watch to see if he was running late. He thought that he might be pushing
it, but decided to wait anyway, because he loved surprising Iralaun with
sweet nothings.

***

Osei glimpsed over at Elijah who was seated in the front passenger seat
and blinked his eyes twice. Elijah was confused, but knew Osei was about to
pull a stunt, because he looked edgy. Osei looked back at the rearview mirror
and saw that the officer was alone.

"This is your last warning. Step out of the vehicle, son!" the officer
repeated with his hand on his gun holster.

Osei whipped the truck into gear and pulled off so fast that his tires
screeched. They even left black tire marks on the pavement and a cloud of
smoke in the air. He flew down East-West highway, hitting speeds as high as
ninety-miles-an-hour on the three-lane street. The officer was fast on his
trail. Osei started running red lights and making erratic turns.

"Aw shit..." Elgin yelled while looking behind him and seeing another
police car follow in quick pursuit behind the first one. Lights flashing, and
sirens blaring, a third police car tried to sideswipe the truck, but Osei dodged
it.

"It's two more coming, too," Elgin yelled.

"What you got in this joint?" Elijah asked confused.

"Don't worry about it. They ain't gonna catch me. Muthafuck this..." Osei said gunning the gas pedal.

"Man...this is some bullshit," Elgin ranted.

"Calm down...I gotta plan." Osei swerved around a corner and around a stalled car.

"What kind of plan you got? Man let me outta this joint!" Elijah fumed.

"Man, fuck that. I gotta plan," Osei repeated. "Calm the fuck down!"

Elijah shook his head and tried to hold on as tight as he could to the arm rests.

"Here, take this and as soon as I stop, start running like shit," Osei said handing Elijah a wad of cash and a sandwich bag full of crack.

"Naw, man..." Elijah said. "I don't want that!"

"Fuck that...take this too," he said handing Elijah his 9-millimeter gun.

"Are you crazy? Hell no!" Elijah yelled. "Get that shit away from me!"

"Man, you won't get no time, if you get caught. They'll send you straight to Juve. Didn't I teach y'all anything?" Osei asked.

"Man, I am not trying to go down for all this shit!" Elijah yelled shaking his head.

"Just take it! As soon as you get out, run like shit and hide this some muthafucking where. You will be aiight. This ain't no game. Do it!" Osei hollered.

Elgin shook his head and snatched the stuff from his brother and shoved it in the inside pockets of his huge parka coat. He believed in Osei and didn't want to disappoint him. In his mind, Osei had been there for him more than his own father. Osei turned to him and nodded.

"Good," he said shaking his head. "Aiight y'all put your seat belts on. It's about to be a rough ride."

Elgin and Elijah both buckled their seatbelts and pulled them tight to make sure that they were safe. And before either of them knew it, Osei drove the car up on the medium dividing the busy street on East-West Highway. The huge titanic-like truck crossed over the three lanes into oncoming traffic. Elgin looked over his shoulder and saw that they had barely lost any of the police cars.

Osei continued driving the truck up the wrong way, parting traffic like Moses and the Red Sea, before he drove into P.G. Plaza's parking lot. In an attempt to avoid a heavy-set woman crossing the street with two little children, Osei crashed the truck into two parked cars. The airbags released and the one on the driver's side exploded. Osei hurt his neck from the whiplash and couldn't move. Elijah jumped out of the front passenger seat and Elgin bolted out behind him.

They started racing toward the mall. They could hear the police yelling behind them, but neither of them turned around. They darted in and out of the rows of parked cars, trying to get away as fast as possible. At one point, they dropped to their knees to catch their breath, to hide and to think of a plan.

"We can't keep running!" Elgin said trying to catch his breath, his adrenaline pumping like a raging river just after a storm.

"I know, I know," Elijah yelled. "Look, at that lady, right there...going toward her car. Let's take her joint!'

"OK, yeah. Are you ready?" he asked tense.

"Yeah..."

"Aiight, follow my lead," Elgin said. He stood up walked toward the short Hispanic woman putting her key in the keyhole of her car. Then he put the gun in the small of her back and told her not to move. "Don't say shit! Just give me your keys."

***

Allen was walking out of the mall when he heard the shrilling sounds of police sirens coming from the left side of the parking lot. Hearing police sirens and seeing agitated police had become common sights for Allen in that area, and he wasn't surprised by their appearance. The county had been faced with a lot of complaints about their aggressive tactics and accusations of brutality over recent years. He assumed the police were arresting some shoplifters, or some other crime that had gone awry. Allen smirked, shook his head and went to his car. He was running late.

***

The short Hispanic woman, who Elgin startled, began to scream. The high-pitched loud cry got the attention of police officers that began pursuing the twins on foot. Elgin shoved the woman to the ground, then unlocked the car door. Elijah jumped in on the other side. Elgin backed the car up, and saw the police officers racing toward them. He threw the car in drive and sped through the crowded parking lot—traveling at close to sixty-five miles an hour. He tried to avoid hitting a woman who was pushing a stroller, and two men who had stepped off of the curb.

201

They were almost out of the mall's parking lot, when Elgin didn't see a car slowly pulling out of a parking space. Elgin rammed into the driver's side of the car so hard that that their car went hurling into the air. When the car landed, it landed sideways and then rolled upside down. When Elijah opened his eyes, he saw blood pouring from Elgin's head.

"Elgin!" Elijah yelled.

Elijah called his brother's name over and over again. But there was no answer. Terrified, Elijah reached over to shake his brother. There was no response. Elijah continued to shake him—hoping that what he'd feared was not true. But Elijah could tell that there was no life in him.

The police surrounded the car and demanded for Elijah to put his hands up. But the tears fell from his eyes in a steady pace. He yelled and cried out for his brother to wake up. He continued to shake him awake, but the police warned him again. The tears streamed down his face as he lifted up his hands in defeat.

CHAPTER 21

Belinda was surprised to learn that the case she had to decide upon that morning involved the parent of the twins that her mother had questioned months earlier. After reviewing the briefs for the preliminary removal hearing, where she had to determine if the children had been victims of child neglect as both Child Protective Services and Social Services had claimed, she called Kevin to say good morning. The two of them had started seeing each other regularly again. Even though Belinda had tried to push herself away from him, she couldn't help it. He was special to her.

She was still proud of herself, because she had improved a lot from her previous relationships. She knew that her road to mental recovery would be more like a yellow-bricked one, with twists and turns and adventures and new discoveries. Besides, she and Kevin weren't intimate. They had become two close friends who shared their lives with one another.

But when Belinda called Kevin, he told her that he would have to call her back because he was in the middle of a minor crisis. Belinda checked the clock on her wall, and saw that she had a couple of minutes to kill before she had to be in the courtroom. She decided to call her father to see how he was doing. Since he was receiving counseling, she wanted to do her part to make things better. They chatted for awhile and she invited him and her mother to have Sunday dinner at her house that weekend. He agreed after a bit of hesitation. Frank was taking small steps; he hadn't really been out of the house except to go to counseling.

"I'll cook your favorite Daddy," she sang. "Barbecued ribs, potato salad, and corn on the cob."

"Alright, alright," he said smiling. "We'll be there with bibs on."

After Belinda said goodbye, she put her robe on and headed out of her chambers. Inside the courtroom, she acknowledged the bailiff, and looked around the room at the defendant, who was being represented by her ex-boyfriend James. Belinda figured that since he was the same lawyer Ms. Jeffries had used earlier for her sons, that maybe she didn't feel comfortable working with another attorney more familiar with child neglect cases.

Belinda stared at the defendant. She couldn't tare her eyes away from her appearance. Vivica seemed to be exhausted—almost to the point of looking ill. There were dark circles around her eyes and her skin looked dry and gloomy. The dress she wore hadn't been ironed and her hair was a massive distraction to her overall attire. She couldn't believe James hadn't coached her to better present herself, or was that his strategy, Belinda wondered.

She continued to survey the room and she saw three children sitting with the Guardian ad Litem, who was the attorney appointed by the court to represent the Jeffries children. Then Belinda's eyes focused on the young attorney who represented Social Services. She was dressed in a chic blue skirt-suit and she wore thin frameless glasses. Belinda nodded at the bailiff to let him know she was ready to begin.

"The court is now in session," the bailiff said. "You may all be seated."

"Your honor, may I approach the bench before the prosecution begins?" James asked.

"Yes, you may," Belinda said and both attorneys walked towards her.

"Your honor, my client has been under a lot of duress. The children's father died about a week ago, one of her twin sons was killed the day after his father died and the other son is being held in jail right now, because of an incident that is currently being investigated. Is it possible that we can move the hearing to another date?" James asked.

The prosecutor protested. Belinda could sense her eagerness to prevail; it reminded her of how she used to be—with her thirst to succeed.

"Your honor," she said. "Neither issue has anything to do with this case. The defendant can no longer care for her children...plain and simple. These other factors should not even come into..."

"Your honor..." James interrupted.

"Enough," Belinda interjected. "It appears as if you do need more time. I will set an Adjudicatory Hearing in thirty days. On that day, I will listen to evidence and make my decision. Until then, the children will stay with Social Services until the hearing."

"Yes!" James mumbled while Belinda struck her gavel. The prosecutor sucked her teeth, pushed her glasses up on her nose and turned away. James walked back toward Vivica to explain the situation.

"So that means I won't be able to have my kids for at least a month?" she asked confused as she watched her children being rushed away.

"Mommy!" Eve cried.

Vivica wiped away tears that were trailing down her cheeks. She tried to smile at her children, but couldn't muster the strength to make it seem warm or convincing.

"It's the best we could do right now. You will be able to visit them during that period. But don't worry you will have your children back immediately after the hearing. I'm sure we will be able to prove the District wrong."

Vivica heaved a frustrated sigh and said, "You know to be honest…right now…I feel like giving up. What does it even matter? The way my life has been going…what does it matter if they give them back to me now or tomorrow or next week even?"

She wiped away tears. "If it ain't one thing, it's another…bills, court appearances, funerals. Everything is a mess. As hard as I try to make life better for us, something always comes by to destroy it. This madness is like a plague surviving off my family's slow destruction. I just don't get it. Why us?"

James stood motionless and shook his head. "Divide and conquer they say…if you let all of these different problems get you down, then you've proved them right and they've won the battle."

"The battle? Who cares about the battle? I'm talking about the war? Who will win the war? It's not just this situation. It's my family and my life. When you're doing things by yourself, trying to stand on your own two feet…it's hard. It's damn near impossible, as much as people want to tell you—you can do it or it's going to be OK—that's crap, when you have to do things alone. And I don't mean having a man…I mean having a family— that'll help lift you up when you can't see no light ahead of you; that'll help support you or advise you when you feel like you are swimming with a chain wrapped around you. Look at me. Not one of my family members showed up here today. So what does that say to me or to my kids? That nobody cares, not their father, their aunt or uncles and not even the system that is meant to protect them.

"For years, I've been doing things by any means necessary to take care of them, to make sure they had clothes on their backs and food in their stomachs. I even made sure they had a warm place to lay their heads at night. Sometimes, I had to do things that I never wanted to admit to doing to take care of them. Like lying down with someone who I knew could help me pay the mortgage or by bouncing checks—all of these things were temporary solutions to a greater problem. But I did what I had to do—alone and even if those temporary solutions were the recipe for making more temporary solutions.

"Yes, now I can brag about being an 'independent self-sufficient woman', but really…is this the price I have to pay to carry such a title? Why did I have to lose a son?" Vivica begged.

"To save the other one," James said taking Vivica's hands into his own. "My grandmother always used to say to me, 'Sometimes you got to crucify Peter to redeem Paul's soul'. I know it's not something you want to hear right now, but it's true. You have to save yourself and the other children. You may have had to do what you had to survive, but those were all battles that you won in life. The war isn't over yet; life isn't over yet. And I know you know this or why else are you even bothering to get your children back?"

Vivica rolled her eyes, looked down at her hands and then back up to meet James' eyes. "Because I love them. And as much as I want to give up, I can't. God won't allow me, too."

James wrapped his arms around Vivica, who was weeping. He felt sorry for her, because he knew that she had done a lot to preserve her family. He knew she loved her children and knew that she would have done anything for them. Vivica was a strong, selfless person, who didn't take life for granted as he had for years—his job, the money he made, the women he dated, his own family obligations. As James consoled Vivica, he saw himself through her struggles and wanted to become a better man. Vivica's determination, despite the adversity she faced, inspired him.

Vivica trusted in God—just like his mother and his grandmother. He decided that he would try to make sure that she got all of the help she needed and then some. James felt a since of purpose while escorting Vivica out of the courtroom. And he hadn't lost a case yet.

EPILOGUE

Weeks after Allen's death, Iralaun went to the doctor to take the follow-up exam she was scheduled to go to with him. While there, she learned that she was four weeks pregnant. Receiving that news was the brightest star in her many sleepless nights. Allen had been fatally injured in a traumatic car accident in the parking lot of P.G. Plaza mall. To know that her brief relationship with Allen had such a positive impact on her life and that he was no longer there to support her, was the hardest fact to face during her mourning.

But Iralaun knew that although their child would grow up in a family without a father, just as they both had, that she would make sure that the baby felt just as loved as she did by him. Iralaun also knew the baby would have two loving grandparents who would be there for their grandchild.

After Kevin's divorce finally came through, he and Belinda became engaged. Kevin was promoted to detective after finding Dante' Lewis' killer. A case he had been working on for months was cracked when Day-Day, an informant, gave detailed information about Dante's murder. Kevin had been determined to charge Elijah with the crime every since the analysis from a shattered beer bottle found at the crime scene, showed traces of Elijah's blood DNA and a partial fingerprint found on a broken beer bottled found at the scene. The evidence wasn't enough without Day-Day's testimony, because Elijah had the same physical characteristics as Elgin. They also found traces of Dante's blood on the pockets of Elijah's coat.

But that wasn't the only charge Elijah had to take. He was also charged with the possession of a huge amount of crack cocaine, an unregistered weapon and for having other illegal paraphernalia seized at the scene including $3,000 cash. He was also being held responsible for the death of Allen Richardson.

Osei, the driver of the vehicle, received a misdemeanor charge for the possession of marijuana. His evading police charge was dropped, because the court found that the police pulled him over illegally. His plates were current. But Osei was placed on probation. Elijah, on the other hand, was charged as an adult for his crimes and was facing a life sentence to be served at Lorton.

Belinda was ecstatic with the strides she and her family had made. They were spending more time together and opened up a lot because of the counseling they had been receiving. She was anxious to become Mrs. St. James and couldn't wait to make Kevin a happy man. She understood the nature of his job, and promised to be there to support him.

At the Adjudicatory Hearing, Vivica received permanent custody of her four children, even though Elijah was imprisoned. She was ordered to provide better supervisory care for them and to also ensure that they attended school regularly. Vivica still did whatever she had to do to make sure her children were taken cared of, but this time around she made more quality time for them. She made time for picnics, outings on the weekend and family vacations. She even put them in after-school programs that appealed to their own special interests.

James withdrew his engagement, with Cassandra, and was currently seeking counseling. He even served as a mentor to Evan in his spare time. James had his eyes on Vivica, but she paid him no attention. Dating was far from her list of priorities. She was content on taking her time and just being friends. For now, they were only going to church together and that was more than enough.

ABOUT THE AUTHOR

Kia DuPree, a native of Washington, D.C. is a public relations specialist, a college English Instructor and a freelance copy writer. She is a graduate of Hampton University and Old Dominion University. Kia is currently working on her second novel, tentatively titled "Like Holding A Butterfly."